D0030533

INTIMATE MOMENTS™

$4.50 U.S. $5.25 CAN.

Virgin Seduction

KATHLEEN CREIGHTON

ROMANCING THE CROWN

Silhouette®

Where love comes alive™

ISBN 0-373-27218-9

AVAILABLE THIS MONTH FROM SILHOUETTE INTIMATE MOMENTS®

ROMANCING THE CROWN

The crown prince of Montebello is home at last. Now the Montebellan royal family extends its hand in friendship to the Tamiri sheikdom and journeys to Tamir to celebrate a royal wedding—or is that wed*dings?*

Leila Kamal: The youngest Tamiri princess's impulsive actions have stirred up a hornets' nest. But what stings most is that her new husband has yet to make love to his wife!

Cade Gallagher: This brash Texan knows he's all wrong for a pampered princess. Still, he's never seen anyone so lovely…or wanted a woman so much.

Sheik Ahmed Kamal: This royal papa is outraged by his houseguest's seeming impertinence—and secretly impressed with his courage.

Alima Kamal: Her soothing ministrations ease her husband's anger. And the craziest suggestions suddenly seem wise when they come from Alima's lips….

Betsy and Rueben Flores: Cade's housekeeper and ranch hand aren't averse to adding a little matchmaking to their job descriptions.

Dear Reader,

Once again we invite you to enjoy six of the most exciting romances around, starting with Ruth Langan's *His Father's Son*. This is the last of THE LASSITER LAW, her miniseries about a family with a tradition of law enforcement, and it's a finale that will leave you looking forward to this bestselling author's next novel. Meanwhile, enjoy Cameron Lassiter's headlong tumble into love.

ROMANCING THE CROWN continues with *Virgin Seduction*, by award winner Kathleen Creighton. The missing prince is home at last—and just in time for the shotgun wedding between Cade Gallagher and Tamiri princess Leila Kamal. Carla Cassidy continues THE DELANEY HEIRS with Matthew's story, in *Out of Exile*, while Pamela Dalton spins a tale of a couple who are *Strategically Wed*. Sharon Mignerey returns with an emotional tale of a hero who is *Friend, Lover, Protector*, and Leann Harris wraps up the month with a match between *The Detective and the D.A.*

You won't want to miss a single one. And, of course, be sure to come back next month for more of the most exciting romances around—right here in Silhouette Intimate Moments.

Enjoy!

[signature]

Leslie J. Wainger
Executive Senior Editor

Please address questions and book requests to:
Silhouette Reader Service
U.S.: 3010 Walden Ave., P.O. Box 1325, Buffalo, NY 14269
Canadian: P.O. Box 609, Fort Erie, Ont. L2A 5X3

Virgin Seduction
KATHLEEN CREIGHTON

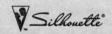

INTIMATE MOMENTS™

Published by Silhouette Books

America's Publisher of Contemporary Romance

Special thanks and acknowledgment are given to
Kathleen Creighton for her contribution to the
ROMANCING THE CROWN series.

 SILHOUETTE BOOKS

ISBN 0-373-27218-9

VIRGIN SEDUCTION

Visit Silhouette at www.eHarlequin.com

Printed in U.S.A.

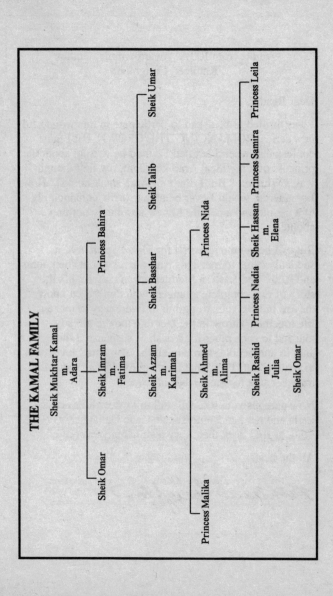

THE KAMAL FAMILY

Sheik Mukhtar Kamal
m.
Adara

- Sheik Omar
- Sheik Imram
  m.
  Fatima
  - Princess Bahira
  - Sheik Azzam
    m.
    Karimah
    - Sheik Basshar
    - Sheik Talib
    - Sheik Umar
  - Princess Nida
- Sheik Ahmed
  m.
  Alima
  - Princess Malika
  - Sheik Rashid
    m.
    Julia
    - Sheik Omar
  - Princess Nadia
  - Sheik Hassan
    m.
    Elena
  - Princess Samira
  - Princess Leila

A note from RITA® Award-winning author
Kathleen Creighton:

Dear Reader,

I was thrilled to be asked to participate in this wonderful new series, ROMANCING THE CROWN, but I must confess that when I learned I would be writing about the princess of a mythical Arab kingdom, my first thought was, "Who, *me?* But I don't *do* Arab sheik books!" How, I wondered, would I ever be able to write convincingly of a people and a culture I knew absolutely nothing about?

But as I began the research for *Virgin Seduction*, it suddenly came to me: This isn't a book about sheikdoms and Arabs and Eastern Mediterranean culture; it's the story of two complete strangers who don't even know they're in love yet, struggling to find a way to make a life together. Throw in the fact that they're already married to each other for a dash of suspense, I thought, and, lo and behold, here are all the elements I love most to write about! From that moment on, *Virgin Seduction* truly became for me a labor of love.

Now perhaps you, too, will fall in love with Princess Leila and her handsome Texan, Cade Gallagher, as I did, as they seek their very own happily-ever-after.

All the best,

Kathleen Creighton

Prologue

Sheik Ahmed Kamal, absolute ruler of the Mediterranean island kingdom of Tamir, had reason to count himself among those whom Allah has richly blessed. Indeed, he was the happiest of men as he stood in the modest but beautifully appointed mosque that was his family's traditional place of worship and prayed for divine guidance and blessings for his youngest son, Hassan, on the solemn occasion of his marriage.

Before him were the bride and groom—at this moment, at least, appropriately separated—with eyes downcast as befitted such a solemn and worshipful occasion. Today the bride—as well as many of those assembled for the *Nikah* ceremony, and Sheik Ahmed himself—was modestly veiled and dressed in the traditional costume of her husband's people. In Ahmed's opinion, it was a much more pleasing mode of dress to both the eye and the spirit than the Western styles he'd grudgingly adopted in recent years.

A fine woman, Elena Rahman, Ahmed thought to him-

self. Hassan had chosen well—or so Ahmed had been assured by Alima, his wife, whose judgment in such matters
he had learned to trust. To be honest, he'd had reservations
about the girl at first—she was, after all, an American. And
the daughter of a terrorist! But as Alima had pointed out,
she was at least a true believer by blood and birth. And it
must not be forgotten that Elena Rahman was CEO of one
of the most prosperous oil refining companies in the American state of Texas. Yes, thought Ahmed, who had ambitious plans for his country's own oil resources…Hassan had
made a very good choice, indeed.

As he began the first of the required Quranic verses,
Ahmed's gaze expanded to include the two people standing
with the bride and groom as witnesses, and his heart grew
near to bursting with pride and thanksgiving. His eldest son,
Sheik Rashid, and Rashid's wife, Princess Julia of Montebello, were only recently wed themselves, and parents of
Sheik Ahmed's first grandchild, Omar—already the apple
of his grandmother's eye, and, it must be confessed, of his
grandfather's as well.

As serene and happy as the couple appeared today, the
truth was that Rashid and Julia's union had come about
only after much intrigue and extreme peril. In the end, it
had brought about the reconciliation of a century-old feud
between their respective countries, and as a result, prospects
for a future of prosperity and mutual cooperation between
Tamir and Montebello had never been more promising.

It was time now to conclude the ceremony with the traditional prayers for the bride and groom, for their families
and friends and for the community at large. As he intoned
the beautiful and time-honored words, Ahmed raised his
head and his arms to encompass them all: his two sons and
their wives; his own beloved Alima, still as lovely as the
day of their own *Nikah* ceremony; their three daughters,

Nadia, the eldest; gentle Samira; and Leila, the youngest and secretly his favorite—and most vexing—child.

The ceremony was almost concluded. Quickly, Ahmed's eyes continued their sweep of those assembled inside the mosque—a small, select group, for the most part close family and friends, according to the traditions of his people. There in the back, he caught sight of Butrus Dabir, his trusted advisor and—who knows?—perhaps soon-to-be son-in-law, if only Nadia—stubborn daughter!—would see fit to accept him.

But that small cloud over the sheik's happiness passed quickly.

Also among the guests assembled in the mosque were the bride's two guests, from Texas—that rather outspoken woman who was Elena's friend—what was her name? Oh yes, Kitty. And the tall and somewhat mysterious man who had come as the bride's guardian and protector. According to Elena, the man was her adopted brother and only family, although, since there was no actual blood tie between Cade Gallagher and Elena Rahman, and Ahmed being a suspicious and extremely traditional man by nature, he thought it a strange relationship.

Near the front of the assembly, dressed in well-tailored Western-style suits, was the contingent from Montebello. Several, including Ahmed's new ally and in-law King Marcus Sebastiani and his firstborn son, Prince Lucas, stood with heads respectfully bowed. The day after tomorrow, to conclude the weekend's festivities, there would be a state dinner and reception to celebrate the joyous occasion of the prince's miraculous return from the dead as well as the new alliance between the two countries as personified by the marriage of Rashid and Julia.

But first…tomorrow would be the *Walima,* the feast given by Hassan to celebrate the consummation of his marriage to Elena Rahman. The palace would be ablaze with flowers and light and alive with laughter and music. There would be an abundance of good food, good friends and good conversation, all of which Ahmed most especially enjoyed. It would be a joyous occasion. On this day, all was well with the Kamal family. Tamir was at peace, and prospects for its future prosperity were bright.

Yes, thought Sheik Ahmed as he uttered the final words of the *Khutba-tun-Nikah,* life is indeed good.

Allah be praised.

Chapter 1

From a balcony overlooking the palace gardens, Leila watched the man in the dove-gray cowboy hat stroll unhurried along tiled pathways. She'd watched many people traverse the garden that morning, but she particularly liked the way this man moved—confidently but without arrogance. The way he seemed to study everything around him—the flowers, the fountains, the colorful mosaics at his feet—with unselfconscious interest reminded her of a child at the zoo.

She laughed out loud as a brightly colored bird flitted across the man's path, startling him. He lifted his head to follow the bird's flight, revealing a deeply tanned, hard-boned face, cheeks creased, teeth bared in a smile. For several seconds he seemed to look right at Leila, and her breath caught, stifling the laughter. Oh, she knew he couldn't really see her. She was well concealed behind the balcony's intricately carved screen. It was just that he had such a *nice* smile.

"That one," she said in a conspirator's whisper to the woman beside her. "Who *is* he—the one in the hat? I saw him yesterday at the wedding. He *must* be an American."

"Oh yes, Princess, he is—and not only that, but from *Texas*." The servant Nargis threw a guilty glance toward the divan where her mistress, Leila's sister Nadia, had her nose—and her attention—safely buried in her sketchbook. She lowered her voice anyway. "His name is Cade Gallagher. The princess—er...Mrs. Elena invited him. Salma heard her tell Madam Alima that he is her guardian."

Leila made a derisive sound, forgetting to whisper. "Do not be silly. Elena is an American. In America women don't have guardians." She couldn't keep a note of envy out of her voice. Her new sister-in-law was only four years older than Leila, but so smart and sophisticated, and the head of her own company! And still she had managed to attract and win the love of a handsome and powerful man like Hassan.

Nargis shrugged. "It is what I heard."

"Perhaps Elena only wished to honor the customs of our country," said Leila's sister Samira in an appeasing tone, laying aside the needlepoint she'd been working on and coming to join them. "You know that since the death of her father, she has no family of her own. This man may be a distant relative, perhaps a friend or even a business associate. Anyway," she added, gently chastising, "if Hassan has agreed to have him here as a guest, there can be nothing improper about it. You should not gossip, Leila."

Leila hooked her arm through her sister's, not in the least chastened. "Oh, but look at him, Sammi—do you not think he is handsome?" But at the same time she was thinking that the word "handsome" really did not suit the tall man in the gray suit and cowboy hat. It seemed too pale and feminine a word, somehow.

"He seems very...rugged," said Samira after a moment's consideration, voicing Leila's very thoughts. "Quite imposing, really." She tilted her head sideways as she thought about it. "It would be difficult not to be intimidated by such a man."

"Oh, I know," Leila teased, rolling her eyes, "you'd prefer someone more suave...someone smooth, someone sophisticated—" she pointed "—like that one there—the dark, beautiful one with the impossibly gorgeous eyes." And much too aware of how gorgeous they are, she thought with disdain. She didn't know quite why, but she found something about the man vaguely unpleasant. Rather like food that had been cooked in too much grease. "And...is he not the one I saw talking with you yesterday?"

"That is Desmond Caruso, Princess," Nargis interrupted eagerly, pleased to be the bearer of information that would make her once more the center of attention. "He is one of the Sebastianis—you see, that is Duke Lorenzo with him. And the woman with the red hair is Duke Lorenzo's new wife, Eliza. She is an American, too, you know." Her voice dropped to a gleeful whisper. "A *newspaper* reporter."

"Really?" As always, Leila's interest perked up at the mention of America, and she did not stop then to wonder why Samira had suddenly gone so pale and silent.

"*Really*—you three are the worst gossips," said Nadia, making a tsk-tsking sound. But she said it good-naturedly as she, too, came to join them at the screen.

There was a little silence while the four women watched the shifting patterns below in the gardens...people gathering, greeting, moving on. Sounds drifted up to them on the balcony...the tinkle of water in the fountains, snatches of laughter and the murmur of conversation.

"Well," Leila said flatly, "I do not trust a man who is that handsome." A small, involuntary shiver surprised her. Funny—the same thing had happened to her when she had seen him talking with Samira yesterday in the corridor near the great hall. Something about the man was definitely off, but Leila did not mention it. No one would take her seriously anyway. She smiled with lowered lashes and added in a voice like a purr, "I much prefer the tall American. Do you not think he looks like a cowboy? Even dressed in a business suit?"

Samira smiled indulgently. "Oh, Leila, you just like Americans. You have a fascination with that country."

"Why not?" said Leila, tossing back her long, black hair. "America *is* fascinating."

"How do you know?" Samira asked with a trill of laughter.

Leila could feel her cheeks growing warm. "Hassan evidently thinks so. And Elena has told me about America—especially Texas. Since Elena is from there, it must be a very wonderful place, must it not? She is so smart, so..." She caught herself before she could say the word in her mind—*free!*—and instead turned her back on Samira and addressed the sister on her other side. "Nadia? Wouldn't you like to visit America?"

Nadia gave an indifferent shrug. "What is so special about America? It is just...very, very *big*."

"But," said Leila eagerly, "that is what makes it special." She threw her arms wide. "It *is* so big. And Tamir—" she brought her hands almost together "—is so small." She finished with a sigh. "It is hard to imagine a place so enormous."

Oh, but Leila could imagine it. If she closed her eyes she could see herself mounted on one of her brother Rashid's polo ponies, riding like the wind across the green-gold fields of his farm on the outer island of Siraj, with the wind blowing back her hair and the sky cloudless and blue above and all around her and the land seeming to go on and on forever.

Only it did not go on forever, of course—how could it,

on Siraj or even Tamir? Very quickly the land ended and there were the cliffs, and below them the white sand beaches and blue-green water. Someday, she thought with a sudden and intense yearning, I want to go to a place where the land does not stop.

"Where would you like to go in America, little sister? What would you want to do there?" Nadia was looking at her, smiling in that tolerant, affectionate way she had, as if Leila were a particularly appealing, perhaps even moderately amusing child. "Shopping, I'm sure. Perhaps...New York City?"

Leila had shopped in London boutiques and Paris salons; her shoes were custom-made in Italy. What, she thought, would New York City have to offer her that those fashion centers did not? But she only said with a shrug and a superior smile, "I was thinking more of Hollywood. Maybe...Rodeo Drive?" But images of endless desert vistas and ranges of snowcapped mountains remained wistful and golden in her mind. Like memories, except—how could she have memories of places she had never seen?

Nadia laughed. "Hollywood? Oh, Leila, you are a dreamer."

Stung, Leila said, "Why is it so impossible to think of going to America?"

"You have no reason to go," Samira answered in her matter-of-fact way. "Father would never allow you to make such a trip just for fun, and what other reason would you have, when Europe is so much closer?"

Leila had to bite her lip to keep from mentioning the fact that Hassan had attended college in America. Her own education had been restricted to an all-female boarding school in Switzerland, capped off by a year in England, and her brother's engineering degree from M.I.T. was a source of envy to her.

"What about business?" she said after a moment. "Now

that Hassan has married Elena, and she is head of an oil company—''

"But that is Hassan's business. It has nothing to do with you. No, Leila, dear—'' Samira gave her arm a not unsympathetic squeeze as she turned away from the screen ''—I am afraid the only hope you would have of visiting America is if, like Hassan, you were to marry an American.'' She and Nadia exchanged laughing glances. "And for that, you must first wait until Nadia and I have found husbands.''

"I will be old and ugly before that happens,'' Leila grumbled.

Never one to entertain a dark mood for long, she straightened, dimpling wickedly as she peered through the screen. "Speaking of prospective husbands—guess who has just arrived. Look, Nadia, it is Butrus Dabir.'' She slid her eyes toward her oldest sister, lips curving in an innocent smile. "Is it true he has asked Father if he may marry you?''

Her teasing was rewarded by a most satisfactory gasp of dismay from Nadia. "Where did you hear that?'' Hands on her hips, she rounded on her servant. "*Nargis?* How many times—''

Nargis was already making a hasty retreat, after sneaking Leila a delighted wink. "Yes, Princess—I am going to prepare your bath now. Did you wish the jasmine scent, or the rose? Or perhaps that new one from Paris...'' She ducked through the draperies and disappeared into the princesses' sitting room.

"She is *such* a terrible gossip,'' Nadia said crossly, snatching up her sketchbook from the settee and preparing to follow. In the doorway she paused to give her sisters a piercing glance. "I have *not* said I will marry Butrus.''

"She will, though,'' said Samira with a shrug when Nadia had gone. "I am almost sure of it.''

Still gazing intently into the garden, Leila could not repress a shiver. "I wish she would not. Even if it means we both must wait longer before we can marry."

"You do not like Butrus?" Samira looked at her in surprise. "He is very handsome, in his way. And he has been almost a member of the family for so many years. Father trusts him."

"It is just that...he seems so cold. I do not see how Nadia can possibly love him."

"Perhaps," said Samira thoughtfully, "there are other reasons to marry besides love. Not," she hastened to add, "that I would ever do such a thing. But...who knows what is in another person's heart? Nadia's, after all, has been broken once already. Perhaps she does not wish to risk such pain again. And I suppose if the other reasons were important enough..."

Leila said nothing. Once again she was watching the man in the dove-gray suit and cowboy hat stroll along the tiled pathways. This time she did not take her eyes off of him until he had disappeared from view beyond a stone archway thickly entwined with climbing roses.

In the shaded promenade beyond a rose-covered archway, Cade Gallagher paused to light a cheroot—a small sin, and one of the few vices he allowed himself. He was alone, for the moment, in this secluded part of the palace grounds, and he relished the solitude and the quiet, pulled it into himself along with the honey-sweet smoke of the cigar. As he exhaled, the chatter of strangers' conversation receded to background noise. Nearby he could hear the twitter of birdsong, and the musical ripple of water. The air was cool and fragrant, misty with breeze-blown spray from distant fountains.

Not quite the juniper and live oak-covered vistas of his Hill Country ranch retreat back home in Texas, he thought, but not at all bad.

Admittedly, he hadn't seen much of Tamir so far, save for the mosque and the royal palace and gardens. Thanks to the usual flight delays, he'd arrived late yesterday afternoon, just barely in time for the marriage ceremony. He found it all interesting, though frankly he was already beginning to feel cooped up and restless. He was more than ready for all this partying and celebrating to be over with so he could get on to his real reason for flying halfway around the world to this remote little island kingdom— business.

More specifically, oil business. In the beginning he'd resisted Elena's invitation to attend the wedding as her honored guest, and to stand up for her as her guardian—ridiculous idea, he knew of no one on earth less in need of guardianship than Elena Rahman—in place of nonexistent family. At first. Until she'd mentioned that Sheik Ahmed Kamal, her father-in-law to be, was interested in refitting his country's oil refineries, perhaps even building new ones. Cade was in the business of building and refitting oil refineries. The opportunities had seemed too promising to pass up.

There was very little in this world that impressed him, certainly nothing having to do with wealth or title or positions of power. But the old sheik—Sheik Ahmed—he'd made one hell of an impression on Cade, even after only one brief meeting. He was sharp, that one. Silver-haired and carrying the weight of a little too much good living, but still crafty as they come. Surprisingly unpretentious, too. The man was the absolute monarch of his country, yet he'd elected to use the title of sheik—a general all-purpose title of respect, was the way Cade understood it—rather than king. Cade liked that.

He liked the sheik's son, Hassan, too, though he wasn't ready to admit as much to Elena. Cade was beginning to think Elena hadn't completely lost her mind after all, marrying into a Middle Eastern royal family. Hassan seemed westernized enough, and Elena was just hardheaded enough, as he well knew from personal experience, that they might actually make a go of it.

All at once he was remembering the unheralded softness in Elena's voice on the telephone when she'd called to tell him of her plans to marry Hassan. He was remembering last night, and the way her eyes had shone when she'd lifted them to her new husband's face as he'd drawn aside her veils... Twinges of unfamiliar emotions stirred in his chest—envy and longing were the only two he recognized. Annoyed, he drew deeply on the cheroot, his motions momentarily jerky and disconcerted.

It was at that moment when a low murmur of voices reached him from beyond the rose-covered archway. Glad of the distraction, he hurriedly composed himself, preparing to make polite small talk with intruders on his private corner of Eden. Instead, the newcomers—two of them, from their conversation—halted just on the other side of the arch. About to step through and join them, Cade hesitated. Something—the sneering quality of the speaker, perhaps—made him go still and alert and stay right where he was, hidden from view by a lush bank of hibiscus.

"...*joyous* occasion!" Suddenly raised, the voice was sharp, sarcastic and clear. That was followed by a distinct snort.

"You seem less than pleased, Desmond," the second voice remarked in a mildly surprised tone. "Lucas is our cousin. Even if he were not family, I would have thought King Marcus's joy would be reason enough for us to celebrate. After all, he had all but given his son up—"

"Now, don't get me wrong," the first speaker broke in hastily, his voice now smooth as oil. "I'm as thankful as anyone that Prince Lucas has turned up alive and...*apparently* none the worse for wear." There was a

pause, and then in a decidedly unctuous voice, "I'm thinking of *you*, Lorenzo."

"What do you mean?" The question was curt, a little
wary.

"Oh, come now—don't pretend you don't know that in
the crown prince's absence, King Marcus had been groom-
ing you as his heir. Now that Lucas is back in the picture,
your position in the royal court can hardly be the same."

There was an ambiguous sound that could have been
amusement or reproof. "It's never been my ambition to
govern a country, Desmond. I'm happy with the position I
have, thank you." And after a pause... "In any case, I
really don't think it's *my* position you're concerned about."

The reply was blustering. "Look, I'm thinking of my
own future, too—sure I am. I'm not going to deny having
ambitions."

"My God, Desmond, are you that mercenary? That
you'd wish Lucas had *not* returned, for the sake of your
own—"

"How can you think such a thing of me, your own
brother?" Whoever he was, Cade thought, this Desmond
had apparently really stepped in it, and was now backped-
aling so fast he was almost sputtering. "I only meant—I
was referring to our future in service to King Marcus. My
only ambition is to serve His Highness, in any way I can,
as he sees fit..."

As the voice babbled on, Cade almost snorted out loud.
This Desmond guy was slippery as a snake oil salesman.

Apparently his companion was starting to have some
doubts about the man's character, too, brother or not. There
was a formidable chill in his voice when, after a marked
silence, he suddenly said, "I see my wife is looking for
me. Excuse me."

Footsteps quickly retreated. A moment later Cade heard
the hiss of an exhalation followed by some mutterings that

sounded mostly like swearing, and then a second set of footsteps moved off aimlessly along a tiled path, fading finally into the general noise of mingling guests and whispering water.

Cade released a breath he'd not been aware of holding, then took a quick drag on the cheroot he'd all but forgotten. Cautiously, casually, he stepped around the clump of hibiscus. Interesting, he thought as he watched two men in white dinner jackets move off in different directions. Apparently all was not entirely rosy after all in this Garden of Eden.

Back in the crowded main courtyard, he snagged a waiter, resplendent in white brocade and saffron yellow turban.

"Excuse me—uh, do you speak English?"

Balancing a tray of fruits carved to look like flowers, the waiter dipped his head respectfully. "Of course. How may I help you, sir?"

Cade smiled in mild chagrin. The man sounded as if he'd stepped right off the campus at Oxford—or wherever it was those British lords went to school.

"Uh...yeah, I was wondering if you could tell me who that gentleman is—the one with the lady with red hair. I was just talking with him, and didn't catch his name."

"That would be his lordship, Duke Lorenzo Sebastiani of Montebello, sir. The lady is his wife—an American. I believe her name is Eliza."

"Ah—of course. And that gentleman over there—the dark one? I think he said his name was Desmond...."

"Yes sir—that is Duke Lorenzo's brother, Desmond Caruso, an advisor to King Marcus."

"Ah," said Cade. "Yes...thank you."

"I am happy to be of service, sir." The waiter bowed and went on his way.

Interesting, Cade thought again. But, since it didn't have

anything to do with Tamir or Elena or her new in-laws, it didn't concern him, either.

He winced as a piercing "Yoo-hoo!" rose above the pleasant chuckle of a nearby fountain. "Cade—oh, Cade!"

He groaned and glanced around in hope of finding cover. Seeing none, he rolled his eyes and fixed what he hoped was a welcoming smile on his face as, with one last fortifying puff of his cigar, he went forth to greet Elena's other guest, her loud and annoying friend, Kitty.

Leila was bored. The wedding banquet had been going on for more than three hours, and showed no signs of concluding any time soon. The parade of waiters bearing trays laden with an incredible variety of delicacies seemed endless, even though Leila—and, she was sure, most of the other guests—had already eaten as much as they could possibly hold. The food had been wonderful, of course, befitting a royal *Walima*—chicken simmered in pomegranate juice and rolled in grape leaves, veal sauteed with eggplant and onions and delicately spiced with tumeric and cardamoms. And for the main course, Leila's favorite—whole lamb stuffed with dried fruits, almonds, pine nuts, cracked wheat and onions, seasoned with ginger and coriander and then baked in hot ashes until it was tender enough to be eaten with the fingers. Leila had eaten until she felt stuffed herself—which was, she supposed, one advantage in being forced to wear the gracefully draped but all-concealing gown that was Tamir's traditional female costume. At least she didn't have to hold her stomach in.

The trays now were offering a variety of fruits, as well as an amazing assortment of sweets—cakes, pastries and candies, even tiny baskets made of chocolate and filled with sugar-glazed flower petals. Ordinarily Leila had an insatiable sweet tooth, but tonight she was too full to do more than nibble at a chocolate-covered strawberry.

She had also drunk much more of her country's traditional mildly fermented wine than she was accustomed to, and as a result was becoming both sleepy and cross. Not to mention frustrated. It was such a beautiful evening— stars were bright in the cloudless spring sky that canopied the palace's Great Courtyard. The *Walima* was being held outdoors in order to accommodate the great number of guests, as, according to tradition, everyone in the immediate vicinity was invited to a marriage feast, rich and poor alike. Tiled in intricate geometric patterns and flanked on both sides by stone colonnades, the Great Courtyard was a formal rectangle that extended from the palace to the cliffs, where arched portals framed a spectacular view of the sea. Tables draped in linen and set with fine china and crystal had been set up on both sides of a chain of fountains and narrow pools that divided the courtyard down the middle and reflected the stars and hundreds of flickering torches. A light breeze blowing in from the sea was heavy with the scent of night-blooming jasmine and moonflowers. It was a beautiful night. It might also have been—*should* have been—a very romantic night.

Except that Leila had been trying all evening without success to catch the eye of the man she would very much have liked to share such an evening with—the man she had noticed that morning in the garden, the Texan in the dove-gray suit and cowboy hat. As luck would have it, he was sitting at a table almost directly across the reflecting pool from hers. Tonight the hat was absent, and, like many of the other male guests present, particularly those from Montebello and America, he wore a white dinner jacket. Though in Leila's opinion, none of the other guests looked so lean and fit and dangerous in theirs, or boasted such broad and powerful shoulders. She could see now that his hair was thick and wavy, a rich dark blond. It gleamed like gold in the flickering light of the torches. She would like to know

what color his eyes were, but they were set deep in his
rugged face, and masked in shadows.

If only we could dance like Americans do, she thought
wistfully as she watched a line of professional performers
of the traditional Tamari dances, faces veiled and torsos
cleverly concealed, undulating their way down the length
of the courtyard, weaving in and out among the tables to
the rhythmic keening of native flutes and sitars. Jewels
flashed from their ankles, wrists and hair as they performed
the intricate hand movements and kept time to the music
with tiny finger cymbals. Like most girls in her country,
Leila had learned secretly as a child how to dance the traditional dances, though of course it would not have been
proper for a princess to actually perform for anyone—except, perhaps, for her husband, in the privacy of their marriage chambers. If I ever *have* a husband, she thought
moodily, as without her realizing it, her body began to
move and sway in time to the music.

On her right, Samira nudged her and hissed, "Leila—
stop that. Someone will see you."

Leila rolled her eyes. *So what?* she wanted to say. It
would not be the first time. Many people had seen her
dance in Switzerland and England, and the world had not
come to an end. When she was in boarding school she had
learned to dance the western way, to rock and roll music,
and in England she had even—and she was sure her father
would have a heart attack if he knew—danced with boys
the way westerners did. *Touching* one another. And nothing
terrible had happened then, either. She was still, alas, very
much a virgin. And likely to remain one for the foreseeable
future.

"I am *bored*," she whispered back. "I have eaten too
much and I want to lie down. When is this going to be
over?"

"Hush," Samira scolded. "This is Hassan and Elena's night. Remember your manners."

"I wish we could at least mingle with the guests—talk to them," Leila said, wistfully eyeing the golden-haired man across the reflecting pool. But his head was bowed as he listened, apparently with close attention, to the frizzy-haired woman seated next to him. Leila sighed. And before she could stop it, her mouth opened wide in a blatant, jaw-popping yawn.

"I'm sorry?" Cade politely lowered his head in order to hear what the woman at his side was saying above the discordant wailing these people called music.

Kitty repeated it in a loud, hoarse whisper. "I said, that girl across the way over there has been tryin' her darndest all evenin' long to catch your eye. I believe she'd like to flirt with you."

Cade's glance flicked upward reflexively. "Oh yeah? Which one?" Anything, he thought, to relieve the tedium. He wasn't accustomed to spending three hours over dinner.

"That one—the real pretty one in the aqua blue dress…long black hair with gold thingies in it…looks like something out of *The Arabian Nights.* See her?"

Cade looked. He'd already noticed the girl, since she was drop-dead gorgeous and he was a man and only human. Now, though, he felt a shiver of silent laughter ripple through him. "You mean, the one who looks like she's about to swallow herself?"

His amusement blossomed into an unabashed grin as the girl's bright and restless glance collided suddenly with his. Her eyes went wide with horror and she slapped a long, graceful hand over her mouth in a belated and futile attempt to cover up the yawn. Next, he watched, fascinated, as a parade of expressions danced across her face like characters in a play: dismay, chagrin, vexation, arrogance, pride, irony...and finally, to his delight, a dimpled and utterly winsome smile.

Kitty gave a little crow of triumph. "There, you see? I told you she was flirtin' with you."

"Kind of young, don't you think?" Cade drawled. "Not to mention," he added, as the significance of that circlet of gold medallions on the girl's head sank in, "if I'm not mistaken, she's a princess."

"*Really?*" Kitty gasped before she caught herself, then added with a lofty sniff, "Well, so what if she is? Hassan's a prince. That didn't stop Elena." She gave an excited little squeal. "Oh—I just realized—that would make her Elena's sister-in-law, wouldn't it? I'll bet she could introduce us— uh, you."

"I wouldn't count on it," Cade said dryly. "Looks to me like they keep those princesses pretty tightly under wraps."

Pretending disinterest, he watched out of the corner of his eye as an older woman flanked by a cadre of female servants suddenly appeared beside the princesses' table across the way. This woman he knew. He'd been presented to Tamir's first lady—Elena's new mother-in-law—along with her husband, Sheik Ahmed, following the wedding ceremony last night. Alima Kamal—who, he'd been told, preferred not to use a royal title—was dressed in the same gracefully draped style of gown as were her daughters, this one deep royal blue liberally trimmed with gold. Like her daughters, she wore a circlet of gold medallions in her still-raven black hair. They glinted in the torchlight as she grace-fully inclined her head. Without a word, all the occupants of the princesses' table rose and were swallowed up by the royal entourage, which then moved away in the direction of the palace, veils fluttering, like a dense flock of brightly plumed birds.

"Wow," breathed Kitty. "It really *is* like something out

of *The Arabian Nights*. Do you think they keep them in a harem?''

Cade gave a snort of laughter. ''I'm sure they don't. For starters, the sheik only has one wife. And, if Hassan is any indication, they're pretty westernized here. All this native costume stuff tonight—the turbans and veils—I'm sure is just for this occasion. Some kind of wedding tradition, probably.''

''Umm-hmm…'' Kitty was thoughtfully chewing her lip. ''Well, I'll still bet Elena could introduce you to that cute little sister-in-law of hers, if you asked her to.''

''No, thanks.''

''Why not? She's *very* pretty, and she was definitely interested in *you,* Cade.''

''Not on your life.'' Cade's grin tilted with grim irony. A knockout she might be, but not really his type and way too young for him, anyway. Not to mention that the very last thing he needed was to get tangled up with some royal pain-in-the-ass princess, when what he was really hoping for was to close a nice, lucrative business deal with her father, the sheik.

Chapter 2

Eight horses thundered in close formation down a grassy plain on what appeared to be a collision course with disaster. Long-handled mallets flashed and winked in the bright morning sunlight to the accompaniment of guttural cries, grunts of effort, and shrill and imperious whistles, while on a sideline shaded by olive trees that looked as though they might easily have dated from biblical times, Cade watched the proceedings with an interest that could best be described as ambiguous.

He wasn't a polo fan—in fact, he knew next to nothing about the game. He considered it a rich man's sport. And while there were some who'd place Cade in that category, *he* certainly never thought of himself in those terms. As far as he was concerned he was just a hardworking businessman who happened to have made a lot of money, which put him in an altogether different class than those who had nothing better to do with their time than gallop around a field on horseback jostling one another for the chance to whack a little ball with a big mallet.

"Snob," said Elena teasingly when he voiced that opinion to her. "I knew it. You, Cade, are a working-class snob. Come on—polo is the sport of kings."

"I rest my case," Cade said around the stem of his cheroot.

"*And,* it's one of the oldest sports, maybe the first ever invented." She shot him a mock-piercing look. "What's this prejudice you have against royals? Seeing as how I'm now one."

"Prejudiced? *Me?*" he countered in mock outrage. "I don't even know any royals—except Hassan, I guess."

"That's what prejudice is," Elena said smugly. "Forming an opinion without personal knowledge." Her eyes went to the riders on the field, seeking and fastening on one in particular. "Anyway, you've met a few more in the past couple of days. Hassan's parents... What did you think of them, by the way?" Her tone was carefully casual, but Cade heard the question she was really asking: *Do you like him...my husband, Hassan? Please like him.*

He glanced down at the woman he'd thought of as a sister for most of his life, arguably the only family he had left. He said gruffly, "I had my doubts about your husband for a while. You know that." His voice softened. "But as long as he does right by you, that makes him okay in my book." He paused. "So...are you? Happy?"

She drew in a deep breath and let it out slowly, then smiled up at him, and he read her answer in her shining eyes before she spoke. "Yeah, Cade...I am."

Cade took a quick sip of his cheroot, surprised again by that sudden fierce ache of envy. "Then that's what counts."

Elena shot him a searching look. "So...what *did* you think of them—Hassan's family? The old sheik?"

He took a moment to consider, though he didn't need to. "Ahmed's a sharp old fox," he said finally. "Knows what he wants for his country, and won't give an inch until he gets it. He'll drive a hard bargain, but he'll be fair." He gave a dry chuckle. "I'm looking forward to doing business with him."

"What about his wife—Alima?" Elena smiled ruefully. "My mother-in-law." She paused, shaking her head. "Boy, I never thought I'd say *those* words."

"She seems very nice—warm." He didn't tell her that for some reason the sheik's wife had reminded him, in ways that had nothing to do with physical resemblance, of his own mother. What he remembered of her, anyway.

"And Rashid?" Elena's eyes were once more on the field of play, watching the swirling mélange of men and horses. Sunlight glinted off helmets and goggles and sweat-damp horsehide, while brightly colored jerseys tangled together like ribbons. Eyes sparkling, she answered herself before he could. "He does raise some fine ponies, you've gotta admit."

Cade grinned. "He does that." He'd been admiring Rashid's own mount in particular, a dapple gray stallion with the Arabian's classic dish face and high-arched neck, graceful, delicate lines and, it appeared, the courage of a lion. He was hoping to find an opportunity to talk horse breeding with the prince...maybe discuss an exchange of bloodlines—

His thoughts scattered like dry leaves as several ponies thundered down the field in tight formation, close to the sideline and only a few yards from where he and Elena were standing, shaking the ground beneath their feet. A gasp went up from the spectators, followed by shouts— mostly of triumph, intermingled with a few moans of dismay. Apparently the Tamiri team, jubilant and easily distinguishable in bright gold and black, had just scored on the scarlet-clad Montebellans.

Distracted by the celebration on the playing field, it was a few seconds before Cade noticed the woman running—

no, dancing—along the sideline, keeping pace with the ponies galloping barely an arm's length away beyond the low board barrier. He had an impression of slenderness and grace as unselfconscious as a child's, of vitality as voluptuous and lush as Mother Earth herself. The unlikely combination tugged at his senses—and something else, some cache of emotions hidden away, until that moment, deep inside him. His breath caught. Protective instincts produced electrical impulses in all his muscles.

She's too close. She'll be trampled!

The alarm flashed across his consciousness, there one second, gone the next. Cynically, he thought, *She's a grown woman, she's got sense enough to stay out of harm's way.* His heart was beating fast as he settled back to watch her. He realized that, incongruously, he was smiling.

She was dressed all in earth tones—shiny brown leather boots to the knee, a divided skirt in soft-colored camel suede that hugged her rounded hips like kid gloves, and a cream-colored blouse made of something that looked like—and undoubtedly was—silk, with long flowing sleeves cuffed tightly at the wrist. The skirt was belted at her waist with a silk scarf patterned in the Tamari team colors—yellow and black. She wore a hat to shade her face from the blistering Mediterranean sun, the same soft suede as her skirt with a wide brim and flat crown, like those Cade associated with Argentinean cowboys. A hatstring hung loosely under her delicate chin to keep the hat from blowing off in the unpredictable sea breeze. Beneath the hat, raven-black hair swept cleanly back from a high-cheekboned face to a casually wound coil at the nape of a long, graceful neck.

Entranced, Cade thought, *I wonder who she is.* And following that, clearly, distinctly, *I want her.*

He acknowledged the thought unashamedly but with a wry inner smile. He was fully grown-up, no longer a child, and years ago had learned that *wanting* did not necessarily mean *having*.

Shouts of outrage and a shrill whistle interrupted his appraisal of the woman. He almost chuckled aloud as he watched her express her own dissatisfaction with what was happening on the field, whirling in fury and stamping her foot like an angry child. Moments later she was in motion again as the horses and riders careened back down the field, once more dancing along the sideline, completely caught up in the action, her body bobbing, jerking and weaving in unconscious imitation of the players. As if, Cade thought, she longed to be one of them, rather than just a spectator.

And then...he caught his breath. As she moved directly in front of him, a gust of wind caught her hat from behind and tipped it neatly forward off her head. She gave a little shriek of dismay and grabbed for it, but it was already tumbling across the trampled grass, directly into the path of the oncoming horses. Cade felt his body lurch involuntarily, before the thought had even formed in his mind. *She's so damned impulsive! My God, is she crazy enough to go for it?*

As if she'd heard his thought or maybe sensed his forward lunge, she stopped herself abruptly and spun toward him, delightfully abashed, like a little girl teetering on the edge of the curb, preparing to earnestly swear, "I wasn't really going to run out in the street, *honest.*"

Perhaps loosened by that movement, her hair came out of its sedate coil, unwinding like a living creature, something sleek and sinuous awakening to vibrant life. As it tumbled down her back in a glorious black cascade, at that precise moment she locked eyes with Cade. Catching her lower lip between white teeth, she gave him a winsomely dimpled smile.

Recognition exploded in his brain even as desire thumped him in the groin. The double whammy caught him off guard. Breath gusted from his lungs as if he'd taken an actual blow.

"Don't even think about it."

Cade jerked toward the quiet voice, mouth open in automatic denial. One look at Elena's face told him protest was pointless, so instead he laughed and wryly shook his head. "Let me guess—one of the princesses, right?"

She nodded. She was smiling, but her eyes were grave. "Leila—the youngest. I'm serious, Cade. If the sheik catches you laying so much as a finger on that girl, all bets are off. He watches her like a hawk."

"Evidently not today," he murmured out the side of his mouth as the princess approached them, stepping gracefully up the slight incline into the shade of the ancient olive trees.

Holding out her hand to Elena and, for the moment, ignoring Cade completely, she cried out in obvious delight, "Elena—hello!" And then, her expressive face scrunching with chagrin, "You saw what happened?" She had a charming accent, more pronounced than Hassan's—the result, Cade surmised, of having had much less contact with westerners. The quality of her voice was low and musical but with a huskiness that caressed his auditory nerves like coarse-textured fur.

"Oh, I did," Elena said with a moan of feminine commiseration. "I'm so sorry. It was such a beautiful hat."

The princess pursed her lips in a brief but charming pout, then smiled and gave a little shrug. *C'est la vie.*

She turned to Cade, finally, her eyes emerging from under thick sooty lashes like mischievous children peeking out from behind a curtain. "Hello. I am Leila Kamal." The way she held her hand out made him wonder if she expected him to kiss it.

Which was probably why, out of pure contrariness, he did nothing of the sort, but instead took her hand in a good old Texas American-style handshake. A moment later he wondered if that had been a mistake as well. Her hand was smaller and at the same time firmer than he'd expected. It left an impression on his senses of both strength and vulnerability, and he found himself holding on to it for a lot longer than was probably sane, while his mind filled with images and urges that had nothing whatsoever to do with sanity.

"This is Cade," said Elena. "Cade Gallagher—my friend and, uh, guardian."

"Of course." Lashes lifted; eyes gazed at him, somehow both dark and bright, mysterious as moonlit pools. He had a sudden sensation of leaning slightly off balance, as if his internal gyrocompass had been knocked out of kilter. "And also your brother—but not *really*." The dimples flashed. "For that I am glad, because if you were truly Elena's brother, and she is now my sister, then you would be *my* brother, as well." Her laugh was low, a delightful ripple, like water tumbling over pebbles. "And I most certainly do *not* need any more brothers. Two is quite enough!"

Cade found himself floundering in unfamiliar territory, at least when dealing with a beautiful woman. Not that he considered himself suave—far from it—but he'd never found himself utterly at a loss for words before, either. At least, not since about seventh grade. He was muttering something unintelligible when a discreet cough from Elena reminded him that he was still holding the princess's hand. He released it…laughed…and felt as awkward and abashed as the twelve-year-old Cade he painfully remembered.

"Are you enjoying the game, Mr. Gallagher? Exciting, is it not? Especially since Tamir is winning." Her eyes held a gleeful sparkle.

He wondered suddenly if the reason he felt so young was simply because *she* was, and the thought helped restore him to sanity. That, and a calming sip of his cheroot. "I am, very much," he drawled, gazing over her head to where the action was taking place now, at the far end of the field. "Especially the horses. That gray stallion of Rashid's—"

"Oh, but they are all Rashid's ponies. He raises them, you know, on one of the other islands. Siraj—it is just south of Tamir. Perhaps you would like—"

"Cade raises horses, too," Elena interrupted. "Arabians."

"Really? But that is wonderful!" In her eagerness and enthusiasm she seemed almost weightless, like a bird, he thought—a blackbird one sudden motion away from taking flight. "How I wish that I could see *your* horses, Mr. Gallagher."

"Maybe someday you will," Cade murmured, and felt a strange little shiver go through him—some sort of primitive warning. He coughed, glanced at Elena and gruffly added, "When you come to Texas to visit your brother."

And he watched the light go out of the girl's eyes as if someone had thrown a switch, shutting off all circuits. Her lashes came down and her smile faded. Her body grew still.

"Yes," she said softly. "Perhaps..." She turned away, one hand going to her forehead. "Oh—I see the play has been stopped. Someone has fallen off. I think now it is safe to get my hat. Please, excuse me—"

Maybe it was because she'd looked so sad—Cade had no other rational explanation for doing what he did. He shot out a hand and caught her by the arm. The feel of her flesh beneath the silk fabric of her blouse sent impulses tingling along the nerves in his fingers as he gruffly said, "Here— I'll get it."

With that, he strode past her down the slope, stepped over the low barrier and scooped what was left of the hat out of the trampled grass. Grimly ignoring the smattering of applause from nearby spectators, he whacked the hat once against his thigh, then retraced his steps to where Elena and the princess were waiting for him under the trees.

"There you go," he said as he handed the hat over to its owner. "For what it's worth. Looks in pretty bad shape."

"It is only a hat," Leila said, smiling but without a trace of the sparkle that had lit her eyes before. Cade was conscious of a vague disappointment. It was like watching the sun set without colors. "It is not important. But it was very kind of you to retrieve it for me. Thank you.

"Well—" She looked quickly, almost guiltily, around. "I must go now. Someone will be looking for me. Elena, I am so glad to have had a chance to see and talk to you. And Mr. Gallagher, it was very nice meeting you. Thank you…goodbye…." Cade watched her disappear into the crowd like a doe in dense forest.

"Cade," Elena said in a warning tone, "I mean it—she's absolutely off-limits."

He pulled his gaze back to her, covering the effort it cost him with a snort and a wry smile. "Hey, she's too young for me. Besides," he added after a moment's contemplation of the end of his cigar, "she's not really my type."

Elena gave a derisive hoot—not very ladylike, but pure Texas. "Oh, yeah, I know all about your 'type.' Whatever happened to that Dallas Cowboys cheerleader, by the way?"

"She was a nice girl," Cade said with a small, reminiscent smile. "We…wanted different things, is all. She was thinkin' in terms of wedding bells and baby carriages, while I—"

"I *know* what you were thinkin' about," Elena said dryly. "The same thing you're thinking right now, which is absolutely out of the question. You promise me, Cade—"

Laughing, he held up both hands in a gesture of surrender. "Hey—you've got nothing to worry about. Like I said earlier, and like I told your friend Kitty last night—where

is she, by the way? Haven't seen her around this morning."
He looked around furtively, half expecting to see a fuzzy
brown head bobbing through the crowd, to hear that gawd-
awful, *"Yoo-hoo!"*

Elena grinned. "I think maybe she overdid a bit on the
rich food last night. She was planning on taking it easy this
morning, getting all rested up for this evening's festivities."

Cade made a sound somewhere between a groan and a
sigh.

Leila ran across the courtyard, the patterned tiles smooth
and warm under her bare feet. She had taken her boots off
in her chambers, but had found it impossible to stay there.
She felt too stirred, too restless to stay indoors—which admittedly was not an uncommon way for Leila to feel.

But this was different. Today the pounding of her heartbeat was only an echo of the thunder of horses' hoofbeats.
The breeze from the sea tugged gently at her hair, but she
longed to feel it whipping in the wind as she raced wild
and abandoned across fields without boundaries. Today,
every flower and tree and shrub in the gardens, every fountain and vine-draped arch and pillar, seemed like the bars
of a prison to her. A very beautiful prison, it was true, but
a prison nonetheless.

And something else. Today as she ran, she thought of
the way a garden feels when it rains—a contradiction of
freshness and excitement and anticipation, but also a bit of
gloom and sadness, a yearning for the sun's familiar
warmth. And all of her insides seemed to quiver like the
leaves of flowers and shrubs and trees when the raindrops
hit them.

The palace gardens were vast, and Leila knew every inch
of them, including hidden nooks and bowers where she
occasionally sought refuge from turbulent thoughts like
these. Today, though, it wasn't refuge she wanted. After

this morning, she very much needed to confront those disturbing thoughts, face them head-on, and then, if at all possible, decide what she was going to do about them. For this she had chosen a spot she was almost certain would be empty at that hour—the private terrace adjacent to the family's quarters where she sometimes took breakfast with her sisters, or her mother and her mother's faithful servant, Salma, who had once been Leila's nanny. The terrace faced northeast and overlooked the sea. Now, approaching midday, it would be shaded, with a nice breeze from the sea to cool her burning cheeks while the gentle trickle of the fountain and the heady scent of roses would, she desperately hoped, help to calm her fevered thoughts.

Never had Leila so desired to be alone with those thoughts! Oh, such humiliating, embarrassing thoughts. And so she was dismayed to find, as she plunged headlong through the arched portal that was the garden entrance to her retreat, that someone was there before her.

Worse, a stranger. A woman with drab brown hair—rather frizzy—was sitting in a chair beside the fountain, reading a paperback book.

Leila's headlong plunge had already taken her several steps onto the terrace before she realized it was already occupied. She lurched to a halt, arms flung wide, body tilted forward, and uttered a soft, disappointed, "Oh!"

The woman quickly set aside her book, a romantic novel, by the looks of the cover. She smiled, and Leila recognized her then—the woman who had been talking with Cade Gallagher during the banquet the night before. She felt a jolt of excitement, then an alarming twinge of jealousy. But it was fleeting. The woman wasn't very pretty, and besides, Leila told herself with a mental sniff, she's old. At least forty.

"I'm sorry," the woman said, and Leila noticed that she had an accent just like Elena's. "Gee, I hope I'm not where

I shouldn't be. I was looking for someplace cool and quiet, and...well, the roses just smelled so good...."

"No, no, it is quite all right." Leila had been raised to be polite to her elders. She advanced, hand outstretched. "I am Leila Kamal. Please—do not get up."

In spite of Leila's assurance, the woman half rose and at the same time managed to execute an awkward sort of curtsey. "I'm Kitty." And oddly, it was she who sounded out of breath, though it was Leila who had been running. "Elena's friend."

"Yes, I saw you last night at the banquet. You were talking with Mr. Gallagher." Leila spoke slowly, absently. An idea was beginning to take shape in her head.

"That's right!" Kitty looked pleased, perhaps flattered that Leila had noticed her. Then her pleasure changed to concern. "My, but you look warm. Would you like something cold to drink? There's a lot more here than I'll ever need." She indicated a water-beaded pitcher and several glasses sitting on a tray on the glass-topped table an arm's length away. "It's some kind of fruit juice, I think—got a little bit of a bite to it. It's not quite up to sweet tea, but it's pretty good."

"Thank you," Leila said with an absent sigh, then gave the plain woman a friendly smile. "I have been watching the polo match. You do not care for polo?"

She sat down in a chair beside the table and only then realized she was still holding what was left of her hat. She glanced at it, frowning.

"Well, you know, it's not really my sport. I'm more a Dallas Cowboys fan," Kitty began apologetically, then gave a gasp of dismay as she, too, noticed Leila's hat. "Oh, my goodness, what in the world happened? That's a real shame."

Leila shrugged and placed it on the tabletop. "The wind blew it onto the field and the horses trampled it," she explained matter-of-factly as she poured herself a glass of the blend of pomegranate and grape juices. She sipped, and found it nicely chilled and just slightly fermented. She lowered her lashes, veiling her eyes, and casually added, "Elena's friend—Mr. Gallagher—got it back for me."

Kitty chuckled and rolled her eyes. "Oh yeah, that sounds like something Cade would do."

Leila flashed her a look of what she hoped was only polite interest. "You know this Mr. Gallagher—Cade—very well?"

"Not *real* well, no—mostly through Elena." But then Kitty gave a little smile and sort of waggled her shoulders as she settled back in her chair, reminding Leila so much of her favorite source of gossip, Nargis, that she almost laughed out loud. "He is a good-lookin' man, though, isn't he?"

"He is handsome," Leila said in a considering tone, then made a brushing-aside gesture with her hand as she picked up her glass. "But surely such a handsome man must be married."

Kitty shook her head, looking gleeful. "Uh-uh—he's not."

Leila glanced at her in surprise. "Really? Then…surely, someone special—a girlfriend?"

"Not that I know of." The expression on Kitty's face reminded Leila now of the palace cats—she all but purred. "Lots of girls, I imagine, but, nope—no one in particular. Elena would have told me if there was."

"But that seems very strange," Leila said, frowning. "What do you suppose is the reason? There must be some reason why a man of his age—he is what, thirty?"

"Thirty-six," Kitty promptly supplied. "I know, because Elena told me he's six years older than she is."

Thirty-six…ten years older than I am. But that is good—

Startled by the thought, Leila guiltily slammed it into a drawer, hidden far away in the back of her mind.

"Perhaps," said Leila with a sniff, "he is not a good man."

"Cade?" The other woman looked taken aback, even mildly affronted. Then she chuckled. "I'm not sure how you mean that, honey, but if you mean 'good' like in decent, honorable—that sort of thing—then I can pretty much tell you there's probably not a better man alive. Cade Gallagher is so honest it's scary. Oh, I hear he's tough when it comes to business, but judging from the way I've seen him with Elena—" She interrupted herself to lean forward like a conspirator. "His parents are dead, you know, just like Elena's—they're all the family each other's got." She sat back with a little wave of her hand. "Anyway, as far as I can see, the man's got a heart like a marshmallow."

"Marsh...mallow?" The word was unfamiliar to Leila.

Kitty laughed. "It's a kind of candy—real soft and gooey, you know? And sweet."

Sweet? Leila chewed doubtfully on her lower lip. "Sweet" was not a word she had ever heard applied to a man before. Certainly not to one as rugged-looking as Cade Gallagher.

"Well," said Kitty with an air of finality, "I know Elena thinks the world of him—that's enough for me."

And, Leila realized suddenly, *I think Elena thinks the world of you, too.* She must, to have invited the woman to her wedding. This woman—Kitty—seemed like a kind person. A bit of a gossip, maybe, but Leila saw no real harm in that. The important thing was, she was Elena's friend. Elena trusted her.

Leila took a deep breath and made a decision. She sat forward, hands earnestly clasped. "Please—tell me about America. What is it like, between men and women? How is it when they are..." she waved a hand in a circular motion, searching for the word. "I am sorry, I do not know—"

"You mean, dating?"

"Yes." Leila let out a breath. "Dating." She had learned a little about the customs of Europe and England from classmates in boarding school, but what she knew of America came mostly from movies and very old television programs, and she was, she feared, badly out-of-date. "You must understand, here we have no such thing. What is it like? How, exactly, is it done?" And without her realizing it, her heart had begun to beat faster.

"What's it like?" Kitty gave a dry little laugh. "Not that I've had much personal experience lately, you understand, but from what I can recall, it can be anything from fun and exciting to downright awful. As for how it's done—honey, there've been about a bazillion books and magazine articles devoted to *that* subject."

"Oh, but please," Leila cried, "you must tell me. For example, must the man always be the one to…to…" Frustrated, she paused to frown and gnaw at her lip. She was not accustomed to feeling so awkward, and she did not like it one bit.

"Make the first move?" Kitty said kindly.

"The first move—yes!" Leila was almost laughing with relief. "Must the woman always wait for the man to do it? Or may the woman be the first one to speak?"

Kitty gave a merry laugh. "I guess that depends."

"On what?" She leaned forward, intent with purpose now.

"Oh, well…on your generation, for one thing. Now, *my* generation, they're pretty much stuck on the 'leave it to the guy to make the first move' tradition. Men my age seem to feel threatened by pushy women, for some reason." She sighed.

Leila wasn't exactly sure what was meant by "pushy

women," but she forged on, eager to get to what she really wanted to know. Breathlessly, she asked, "And…Mr. Gallagher?" It was hard to imagine such a man feeling threatened by anything, much less a mere woman.

"Cade?" Kitty had that look again, the one that made Leila think of the woman's animal namesake. She leaned forward as if she were about to reveal a great secret. "Just between you and me, I think that man focuses entirely too much on business. I think maybe if a woman wanted to get his attention, she might *have* to be a little bit pushy."

"Pushy?" Leila frowned. That word again. The pictures it brought to her mind didn't seem appealing to her.

"You know," Kitty said, lifting one shoulder just slightly. "Give him a little…nudge in the right direction. A *push.*"

"Ah," said Leila, feeling as if a light had come on in her head, "you mean, not a real push, but a suggestion. And this is…permissible in America?"

"I don't know about all of America, but in Texas it is."

"Thank you," Leila breathed. "That is what I wanted to know." She placed her glass on the table and rose to leave, preoccupied and just in time remembering her manners. Turning back to Kitty, she said automatically, "It was very nice talking with you. I hope I may see you tonight at the reception?"

"Oh," said Kitty, looking solemn, "you can count on it."

As Leila was turning away, she saw the other woman pick up the paperback book she had laid aside when Leila interrupted her. She thought it must not be a romance novel after all, but perhaps a very funny one instead. Because, as she found her place and began to read, Kitty was laughing to herself, and the smile on her face stretched from one ear to the other.

Chapter 3

The hum and clatter of sound from the reception hall receded as Cade strolled deeper into the gardens, and was gradually usurped by the quieter conversation of the fountains. The music followed him, though, carried on the soft evening air like a sweet-scented breeze. At least it was western music tonight. Not *country* western, that would have been too much to hope for—but the classical stuff, something vaguely familiar to him. Mozart, he guessed, or maybe it was Beethoven. He never could keep those guys straight.

He had the gardens to himself tonight. Everyone seemed to be inside the grand ballroom, nibbling fruits and exotic Middle Eastern tidbits and awaiting the arrival of the king of Montebello and his entourage, including the recently restored crown prince, Lucas, who not so long ago had been all but given up for dead. Elena had filled him in on that story, and thinking of it now, Cade could only shake his head. The whole thing sounded like something out of a spy novel to him.

He'd pay his own respects to the honored guests before the night was over, of course; he owed that much to Elena. But for now, he was seizing the opportunity for a much needed breath of fresh air. And some space—oh, yeah, that more than anything. There was something about this damned island, beautiful as it was, that gave him claustrophobia. He'd be glad when all the hoopla was over and he could get down to doing business with the old sheik. Hassan and Elena were postponing their honeymoon long enough to give him the intro he needed to smooth the way, but he was confident the negotiations would be easy sailing for all concerned.

As he stepped though the rose-covered arch that led to the promenade where yesterday he'd stood and listened to that strangely sinister conversation, he paused once again to light one of his cherished cheroots. This time, though, he didn't linger there but continued on down the tiled walkway, which was arrow-straight and flanked on both sides by rows of intricately carved columns and lit at regular intervals by torches. At the far end, through another arched portal, he could see where it opened out finally onto a cliff-top terrace overlooking the sea. Through the portal the sky still glowed with the last wash of sunset, and it seemed to Cade like the gateway to paradise.

He walked toward his destination slowly and with a pleasant sense of anticipation, savoring the taste of the cigar, enjoying the textures of the night and his aloneness in it, feeling the breeze curl around his shoulders like a cloak…stir through his hair like caressing fingers…

And something shivered down his spine. He'd felt something…something that wasn't really a touch. Heard something that wasn't *quite* a sound. And knew with absolute certainty that he wasn't alone in the promenade any longer.

He halted…turned. Froze. His heart dropped into his shoes.

Halfway between the archway and where he stood the figure of a woman paused...hovered...then once again moved slowly toward him. Tonight, she wore an evening gown of a delicate yellow-gold, something shimmery that seemed to glow in the light of the torches like a small pale sun. It had a high neck and long, flowing sleeves, a bodice that clung and skirts that swirled around her legs so that she seemed to float, disconnected from the ground, like a wraith or a figment of his imagination. Except that he knew she was only too real.

Strands of long black hair, teased by the same wind that made a plaything of her skirts, coiled around her shoulders and lay like a shadow across one breast. Something glittered in the twist of braids on top of her head...caught an elusive source of light and winked. He couldn't see her features in that purple dusk, but he'd known at once who she was. In a strange way, her body, the way she moved, seemed already familiar to him.

Leila almost lost her courage. The tall figure silhouetted against the evening sky and framed by gold-washed pillars seemed so forbidding, utterly unapproachable, like a sentinel guarding the gates of Heaven. But, oh, she thought as her heartbeat pattered deliriously in her throat, how commanding he looked in his evening clothes—how elegant, even regal.

And yet—the notion came to her suddenly, the way such insights often did to Leila—as elegant and at ease as he appeared, there was something about the formal dress that didn't suit him. As if his appearance of ease went no deeper than his skin...as if it were his soul that was being suffocated.

Almost...almost, she turned to run away, to leave him there with his solitude. For uncounted seconds she hovered, balanced like a bird on a swaying branch, balanced, she was even in that moment aware, between two futures for herself…two very different paths. One path was familiar to her, its destination dismally certain. The other was a complete unknown, veiled in darkness, and she had no way of knowing whether it might lead her to the freedom she so desired…or disaster.

She hovered, her heart beating faster, harder, and then, somehow, she was moving forward again, moving toward that imposing figure in evening clothes. She felt a strange sense of inevitability as the figure loomed larger, as she drew closer and closer to the American named Cade Gallagher. And it occurred to her to wonder if she had ever had a choice at all.

They were only a few feet apart now, close enough that one or the other *must* speak. But Cade only looked at her and went on quietly smoking…something too brown to be a cigarette, too slender to be a cigar. Reminding herself what Kitty had said, that in America—in Texas—it was permissible for a woman to speak first, Leila summoned all her courage and sent up a small prayer.

"Good evening—it is Mr. Gallagher, is it not?" She kept her voice low to hide the tremors in it. "May I call you Cade?"

"I wish you would." *His* voice was a husky drawl that shivered her skin as if someone had lightly touched her all over. He gave a bow, and she wondered if he might be mocking her. "Good evening, Princess—or is it, 'Your Highness'?"

"If I am to call you Cade, then you must call me Leila." She was glad for the shadowy torchlight that hid the blush she could feel burning in her cheeks. On the other hand, she hoped he *would* see the dimples there, and as she joined him, she smiled and tilted her face toward him and the light.

He waited for her to reach him, then turned so that they walked on together toward the terrace, side by side. Leila's heart was beating so hard she thought he must hear it.

After a moment he glanced down at her and said, "Shouldn't you be at the royal reception?"

She hesitated, biting her lip, wondering just how "cheeky"—it was a word she'd acquired during her school days in England—she dared be. Hoping he wouldn't think her insolent, she looked up at him through lowered lashes and colored her voice with her smile. "Yes, I should. And...should not *you* be, as well?"

He acknowledged that with a soft and rueful laugh. Emboldened, she added, "You are certainly dressed for it." And after a moment, bolder still, "You do look quite nice in evening dress, but..." She counted footsteps. One...two...

She felt his gaze, and, looking up to meet it, caught a small, involuntary breath. *To get his attention, a woman would have to be a little bit...* She smiled and said on the soft rush of an exhalation, "But, I liked what you were wearing yesterday—especially your hat. You looked quite like a cowboy."

She heard the faint, surprised sound of *his* breath as he looked down at her. "Yesterday?"

"I saw you in the garden," she explained with an innocent lift of her shoulders. "I was with my sisters, on the balcony outside our chambers. I could not help but notice you. You stood out, among all the others. I thought you looked...very American—like someone I have seen in the Western movies."

He gave a little grunt of laughter, but she didn't think it was a pleased sound.

She conjured up a new smile. "But tonight...tonight you look very different—elegant, very sophisticated. And, of course, *very* handsome."

He laughed uncomfortably. "Princess—"

She laughed too, in a light and teasing way, and before he could say more, hurried on. "But, you have run away from the reception and all the ladies who would admire you, to walk alone in the gardens…'' She left it hanging, the question unspoken.

Cade brought the slender cigar briefly to his lips before answering. "I needed some air," he said abruptly, and there was a certain harshness in his voice now. They had stepped onto the terrace that overlooked the sea. He made a gesture toward the emptiness beyond the marble balustrade. "Some space.''

A breeze from the sea lifted tendrils of hair on Leila's neck. She felt a shivering deep inside her chest. *Space…*

"Yes," she whispered, forgetting to flirt, for all at once her throat ached and she no longer felt like smiling.

They stood together at the balustrade in silence, shoulders not quite touching, and she felt the ache inside her grow. I shouldn't have done this, she thought in sudden and unfamiliar panic. *This is terrifying. Perhaps I am not cut out to be a pushy woman.*

Far below, waves collided gently with the rocky cliff, sending up joyful little bursts of spray. The rhythmic *shusshing* sound they made was familiar and soothing to her soul. She listened to it for several more seconds, then lifted her eyes to the almost invisible horizon.

"I understand, I think," she said quietly, leaning a little on her hands. "I come here often when I am feeling…" At a loss for the word, she gave a little grimace and shook her head.

"Cooped up?" Cade softly suggested, watching the horizon as she did. She looked him a question, not being familiar with the expression. He glanced down at her. "Walled up…fenced in—"

"Oh, yes!" She turned toward him, her breath escaping in a grateful rush. "That is it exactly—walled up and fenced in. But what is this…coop? I do not know—"

He shrugged and turned his gaze back to the sea. "It's

an expression they use where I come from. A coop is a
kind of pen. They keep chickens in it.''

"In Texas?''

"Yeah…'' He said it on a sigh. "In Texas.'' After a
curiously vibrant pause, one that fairly sang with unspoken
communion, he jerked himself upright and away from the
silence with a loud and raggedy attempt to clear his throat.
"Other places, too. Pretty much any place they have chickens.''

He couldn't believe he was having this conversation with
a *princess*. One that, even in a designer gown, really did
look like something out of *The Arabian Nights*. But talking
about chicken coops, dopey as it was, seemed infinitely
safer than that terrifying sense of…what in the world *had*
it been? Affinity, concord…none of those words seemed
adequate to describe what had just happened between them,
between himself and this woman from an alien culture…a
kind of *oneness* he'd never experienced before with another
human being. As if, he thought with a shudder, she'd somehow found, and for that one brief moment touched, his
innermost self. His soul.

"Texas.'' Her sigh was an echo of his. "It must be very
wonderful.'' Hearing a new lightness in her voice, he
looked at her warily. Torchlight played mischievously with
her dimples.

She's flirting with you, Cade. The thought made him almost giddy with relief. This was familiar territory, something he was pretty sure he knew how to handle.

He turned toward her and leaned an elbow on the balustrade, relaxed now, and casually smoking. "Some parts
of it are,'' he drawled, "and some aren't.'' He was thinking
about the West Texas oil country, and parts of the Panhan-
dle that were so flat you had the feeling if you got to running too fast you'd run right off the edge of the world.

Even such a thing as wide open spaces could be carried too far.

Maybe because his thoughts were back home in Texas and he was feeling a little bit overconfident, it was a few seconds before he noticed the intensity of Leila's silence. By the time he did, and snapped his attention back into focus on her, it was too late. He thought it must feel something like this, the first moment after stepping into quicksand—a disquieting, sinking sensation, but not yet sure whether he ought to panic or not.

When had she come to be standing so close to him? The sea breeze carried her scent to him, sweet and faintly spicy. The word "exotic" came to his mind. But then, everything about her was exotic. Was that why she seemed so exciting to him? The fact that she was different from every other woman he'd ever met?

Don't even think about it. She's absolutely off-limits.

Or was it simply that she was forbidden fruit? Off-limits. Inaccessible. Except that, at this moment, at least, he knew she was entirely accessible…to him.

To think like that was insane. And insanely dangerous. He was dealing with a tiger out of her cage, nothing less.

Except that she didn't look much like a tiger at the moment, or anything even remotely dangerous. She looked soft and warm and sweet, more like ripe summer than forbidden fruit. Torchlight touched off golden sparks in the ornaments in her hair and in her eyes. Gazing into them, he felt again the peculiar sensation of not-quite-dizziness, as if his world, his center of gravity, had tilted on its axis. Clutching for something commonplace and familiar, he took a quick, desperate puff of his all-but-forgotten cheroot.

Her whisper came like an extension of the breeze…or his own sigh. For one brief moment he wasn't certain whether it was her voice he was hearing, or merely the echoes of his own thoughts.

"Do you want to kiss me, Mr. Gallagher?"

Cade almost swallowed his cigar. *Do you want to kiss me?*

What on God's green earth could he say to that? Jolted cruelly back to reality, his mind whirred like a computer through countless impossibilities, distilled finally down to two: Lie and tell her he didn't, which would be unconscionably cruel; or tell her the truth, which would most likely land him in more trouble than he cared to think about.

It was probably gut instinct that made him do neither of those things, but instead try to laugh his way out of it. To make light of it. A joke.

Tossing his cigar over the balustrade with an exaggerated, almost violent motion, he snaked one arm around her waist. The other he hooked across her back at shoulder-blade height, and laying her against it, arched his body over hers in broad parody of some old silent movie clip he'd seen recently, he couldn't recall exactly where—The Academy Awards, maybe?—about an Arab sheik in flowing robes and headdress seducing a wild-eyed maiden in a tassel-draped tent.

"Kees you?" he intoned in a ludicrous and excruciatingly awful mishmash of several different accents—he had no idea where he'd gotten that from. "Oh-ho-ho, mademoiselle..."

Startled eyes gazed up at him. He felt a sensation of falling, as if the ground beneath his feet had dropped away.

What now? He had no idea what he was supposed to say next. That was the trouble with those silent movies, he thought. They were *silent.* Short on dialogue, long on action. And he was pretty sure he did know what action was supposed to come next.

Don't do that. You can't. You'd be crazy to do that.

Then came the smallest of sounds...the soft rush of an exhalation. Her breath was sweet and faintly wine-scented, so close he felt the stirring of it on his own skin. So near to his...her lips parted. Slowly, slowly her eyes closed.

Lord help me, he thought, and lowered his mouth to hers.

He had an impression of warmth and softness, of sweetness and innocence. Of purity. It occurred to him to wonder whether his might even be the first lips to ever have touched hers, and the thought both excited and shamed him. Is that what it's all about? he wondered. Is *that* why I want her so much? Nothing to do with exotic beauty and forbidden fruit, only the thirst of the conqueror for undefiled lands to claim as his own.

His thirst was in danger of blossoming into fullblown lust.

He felt the flutterings of her instinctive resistance. If only he hadn't! If only she'd responded openly, brazenly to his kiss, he might have been able to keep it as he'd intended it to be—blatantly mocking—and end it there. But that tiny faltering, that faint gasp of virginal hesitation... It stirred some primitive masculine response deep within him, so that her hesitation affected him not as a warning, but as a challenge. And an embrace meant only to lighten the mood and diffuse dangerous emotions became instead a seduction.

Instead of releasing her, his fingers stroked sensuous circles over the tightened muscles in her back and waist. Instead of pulling away from her, he gently absorbed her lips' quiverings and delicately soothed them with the warmth of his own mouth. And felt her relax...melt into his embrace...as he'd somehow known she would.

He shifted her slightly, to a more comfortable, more natural position, and felt her body align with his as if it had been custom-made for that purpose, a soft and supple warmth. He lightly sipped her wine-flavored mouth, and only then discovered—too late—that he was famished for the unique taste of her, that he craved her with every fiber of his being.

Tiny lightbursts of warning exploded inside his brain. Reserves of strength summoned from God knew where made it possible for him to tear his mouth from hers—for a moment, no more. He released a sound like the moaning of wind in old trees and buried his face in the graceful curve of her neck. Then...gently, carefully at first, he brushed his lips against the skin there, velvety soft and sweetly scented as rose petals.

The sound she made was breathy and frightened, but he felt the uniquely feminine, seeking arch of her body, and the hot rush of blood through his in automatic masculine response. With a growl of triumph, unthinking he brought his mouth back to hers. Still gently but inexorably now as water finding its own course, his mouth began to follow the shapes and contours of hers...his tongue found its way to the soft inside. She whimpered.

How can this be? Leila thought. *I cannot breathe, my heart is racing so. I feel as if I am drowning...dying...and yet I cannot stop myself—don't want to stop myself—or him. If I am dying, then this must be heaven, because I don't want it to stop...ever.*

Her skin felt hot and prickly all over, from the roots of her hair to the soles of her feet. And yet...she shivered. Her head—her heart—felt light as air, lighter than butterflies and wind-carried chaff, yet her body felt weighted, too heavy to move.

His body was a hard, unyielding weight against her breasts, breasts that had become so sensitive she could feel every ridge and fold of his jacket, the warp and woof of the cloth. Even the rub of her own clothing seemed an intolerable abrasion.

Panting, she tore her mouth free of his and arched her throat, offering that to him instead. And how had she known to do such a thing? Even as she wondered, she felt the press of his lips against the pounding of her pulse, and mounting pressure...and terrifying weakness.

And then the pressure was gone. From a great distance came a raw, anguished sound, and the weight lifted from her breasts. Her throat and lips felt cold, and throbbed with her racing pulse. Swamped with dizziness, afraid she might fall, she clung with desperate fingers to the arms that held her and fearfully opened her eyes. Eyes stared down into hers...eyes that burned with a golden gleam...eyes that burned her soul like fire.

"What—" She meant to whisper, but it was a tiny squeak, like the mew of a kitten.

His voice was so ragged she could hardly understand him. "Princess—I'm sorry. I can't do this. I can't..."

When she felt his arms shift, depriving her of their support, she gasped and caught at his sleeves. His fingers bit into the flesh of her arms as, grim-faced, he held her away from him, then with great care stood her upright and steadied her like a precariously balanced statue. Once more his eyes lashed across her, and she flinched as though from the sting of a whip.

"Dammit," he fiercely muttered, and then, as he turned, added with soft regret, "Another time, maybe...another place."

And he was gone.

Left alone, Leila stood where she was, trembling, hardly daring to move, until the scrape of footsteps on stone had been swallowed up in the *shushing* of waves and the whisper of wind.

Foolish...foolish... The whispers mocked her. *Serves you right. This is what happens to pushy women.*

But...what *had* happened, exactly?

Hugging herself, Leila whirled to face the glittering indigo vastness of sky and sea. She was shivering still, no longer with shock, but a strange, fierce excitement. Cade

Gallagher had kissed her! Kissed her in a way she was quite certain no man should ever kiss a woman who was not his wife.

And that she had allowed it…? Fear and guilt added layers to her excitement, but did not banish it. That she had allowed such a thing to happen was unpardonable.

She knew she should feel frightened, terrified, ashamed. So why was she smiling? Smiling, lightheaded, and absolutely giddy with excitement?

Another time…another place.

That was what he had said. She remembered his exact words. Understanding came; certainty settled around her, comforting as a cashmere shawl.

Back in his own room at last, Cade slipped out of his tux jacket with a grateful sigh. One helluva day, he thought as he tossed the jacket onto the cushions of the surprisingly trendy brown-and-white striped sofa. And thank God it was over. Tomorrow he'd be back in familiar territory, home country. The world of business was where he belonged, where he felt comfortable. It was what he was good at— doing deals, making plans, working out compromises. All this formal socializing, rubbing elbows with royalty—that wasn't his style. Oh, he knew a certain amount of that stuff was unavoidable from time to time, but he was always glad when it was time to roll up his sleeves and get down to the real work, down and dirty sometimes, rough as a bareknuckle brawl, but that was what he liked about it—the excitement of the game. That, and the satisfaction that came with winning.

Anyway, for sheer stress, all that was a piece of cake compared to what he'd just been through. He'd rather spend three days in cutthroat negotiations than three hours at a formal reception—and in this case, *formal* was putting it mildly. Not that it hadn't been impressive as hell, the palace ballroom lit up like Christmas, the food delicious, the music tolerable, if you went in for that sort of thing. And he'd never seen so many purple sashes and gold medals in one place in all his life, or so many beautiful people—especially the women. Everywhere he looked was a feast for a man's eyes. But there was something about it he couldn't quite put his finger on. Undercurrents.

Undercurrents. Yeah, he thought, that about described it, all right. Underneath all the bright lights and highbrow music, the dazzling smiles and graceful bows, elegant tuxes and designer gowns in rainbow colors swirled together like ribbons in a washing machine...under all that, like a subterranean river, ran a ribbon of tension, a hum of intrigue he could feel in his bones. He wondered whether it was something going on between these Tamiri people and their nearest neighbors, the Montebellans, or if it was just standard operating procedure for royal courts. Not unlike what goes on every day in Washington, D.C., he thought, or for that matter, any state capitol back home.

This thing with Leila Kamal, though...that was another story. *That* particular intrigue was entirely personal, and the tension a steel rod running straight down the back of his neck. It had made for one helluva nerve-wracking evening, trying to avoid eye contact—or any sort of contact whatsoever—with the woman, while being at the same time aware of her with every nerve in his body. Nervewracking...intense...but now, thank God, it was over. Finally, he could relax.

With another gusty exhalation, he peeled off his necktie and headed for the bathroom. There, while his fingers dealt with the studs on his shirt, his eyes gazed dispassionately back at him from the ornately framed mirror above the sink.

You were damned lucky, Gallagher.

Oh yeah. He knew just how lucky he'd been. He'd played with fire and somehow managed not to get burned.

That narrow brush with disaster had left him shaken, but he'd managed to put it behind him. All he needed now was a good night's sleep, and tomorrow some mutually advantageous wheeling and dealing with the old sheik, and he'd be himself again.

Stripping off his shirt, he briefly considered another shower. But he was tired, just wanted to hit the sack, so he turned on the tap above the sink instead. He was hunched over the bowl, cupped hands filling up with water to splash over his face, when he heard a light tapping on his chamber door.

What now? One of the servants, probably, they were always bringing him something—towels or fruit or herbal tea—though it seemed pretty late for that. Frowning, he turned off the faucet, grabbed a towel and went to open the door.

When he saw who was standing there, he wondered why he didn't have a heart attack on the spot. At the very least, he was pretty sure he knew now what it might feel like to be speared in the belly with an icicle.

Chapter 4

"**P**rincess—" It gusted from him before he could think. "What're you—why—" And while he was sputtering like that she slipped past him and into his room.

He had a fleeting impression of a light, spicy scent, hair that flowed down her back like an ebony river, a gown made of something pale and floaty—she'd glow in the dark like a candle!

He'd never felt more exposed, or more cognizant of the danger he was in. If anyone happened to walk by…if she so much as raised her voice, cried out, Cade's goose was as good as cooked. Even in this part of the world he doubted they still executed people for such transgressions, but at the very least, any hopes he had of doing a deal with the Tamari people would be out the window, and he might even be out—literally—himself. As in, given the bum's rush. Bounced unceremoniously out the door on his butt. Right now, this minute, in the middle of the night.

Plus, Elena was never going to forgive him—never.

With icy dread crawling down his spine, he gave his face an absentminded mop with the towel, glanced quickly up and down the corridor, then silently pulled the door closed. He felt as if the door of a trap had just slammed shut behind him.

Leila moved as if through a wall of suffocating heat—holding her breath, feeling her cheeks burn and sweat bloom on her forehead. Knowing instinctively the source of the heat, she kept her face turned away from him—as if that would help!

She reached with her hand to touch the back of the sofa and leaned against it a little, testing it for support, then brushed her fingers over the fabric to hide the fact that she'd done so. She heard the door close behind her and silence fill the room. In it the thump and swish of her pulse sounded loud as the storm surf striking the rocks below the cliffs.

"Princess—" His voice was harsh.

And though she didn't want to, she flinched. Still, as she turned she knew her smile would appear bright and determined. "I thought you were going to call me Leila."

Breath gusted from him, as if he'd been holding it in too long. "For God's sake, what are you doing here?"

But she could not answer. Suddenly she had no moisture in her mouth; she could not seem to move her tongue. Nor her eyes, either, for somehow they had become stuck to the naked masculine chest in front of her, and not even for her life could she tear them away. She did not understand—she had seen men's chests and torsos before…hadn't she? In pictures, at the very least. But if she had, it did not *seem* so. To her this felt like the first time she had ever laid eyes on such a sight…*ever*.

"Look…Leila—" He took a step toward her, face darkened, both hands upraised and fingers tensed, as though he wanted to grasp her with them.

Her breath caught and her heart gave a frightened leap. Even she could see that it was not a welcoming gesture. But not a violent one, either. She thought he seemed more distraught than angry, and her fear was not for her physical safety. He would not harm her, she was certain of that.

Just as she was certain now that she had made a terrible mistake in judgment. Somehow, because of the vast difference in their cultures, probably, she had misunderstood him. She knew that he had not meant what she had thought he meant. Not at all.

I shouldn't have come.

All of that passed through Leila's mind in the time it took her to utter a single dismayed gasp. In the next moment, memory—sensual, visceral, overwhelming—slammed her with the force of a physical blow. *Hard lips, smooth and gentle lips…liquid warmth, breath smelling of tobacco, trembling pressure and pounding pulse…*

Her body felt cold, and her legs as if they would not support her weight. She heard a rushing sound in her ears. *But I had to come…I had to. What else could I do?*

She took one step forward…and into a void.

Swearing vehemently, Cade caught her as her knees buckled. Then, since there didn't seem to be anything else to do, he scooped her up in his arms. *This is insane. Ludicrous.*

While casting frantically about for a place to deposit his unconscious burden, he caught a glimpse of himself and her in the gilt-framed mirror above the tile and marble fireplace—heaving breasts in a filmy gown against the backdrop of his own naked, sweaty chest…her pale throat a taut and graceful curve…raven hair cascading over his arms like a waterfall… Damn, he thought with a snort that was part irony, part disgust and most of all dismay. *I look like the cover of one of those romance novels women are always reading.*

He'd about decided to lay his swooning princess on the sofa when he felt her arms come to twine around his neck. He barely had time to register that fact before her hair began to stir against his skin, an incredible, unimaginable softness.

He shivered involuntarily and felt his nipples harden. As if in response to that, she turned her face toward him and touched him just there in a series of tender and tiny kisses, rather like a kitten, he dimly thought, making tracks across his chest. His heart, already beating hard, gave a lurch.

"Princess..." His voice was faint and airless. "What the hell do you think you're doing?" Her lips were working their way across his collarbone and upward along the side of his neck. His jaw muscles felt so rigid he half expected to hear them creak when he added almost desperately, "Hey—cut that out."

Poised to deposit her on the sofa, he halted, muscles quivering, beset by a new dilemma. If he put her down now, she would almost certainly pull him down with her, which would be nothing short of disastrous. If he went on holding her, with that unnerving weakness creeping through his body, he was afraid he might drop her. To head off that possibility, he brought one knee up under her bottom, braced his foot on the cushions, and tried to shift her to a more secure position in his arms.

Big mistake. Hadn't this happened to him once before?

Yes, and once again as on the terrace, he felt her body mold itself to his as if it had been custom-made for that purpose...an all-over body glove, silky-soft, supple as finest kid. Tiny puffs of her breath brought his sweat-damp skin alive with goose bumps. Her spicy, exotic scent made his head swim. The weakness in his arms oozed into his legs, while in the center of his body his heart was banging like an energetic and enthusiastic bass drummer, sending joyful, giddy impulses and inviting—no, *compelling*—the rest of his body to follow along.

His body's predictable response was, *Oh, yeah. I'm there!* And his heart chimed in with, *Sure would like to…maybe it would be okay…don't you think I could?*

To which the rational part of his brain emphatically replied, *No way, Jose!*

"Princess—" he began, but the rest was muffled. Leila's lovely and adventuresome mouth had reached its destination at last, and anything else he might have added was swallowed up in its sweet, intoxicating warmth.

For a moment…just a moment, it seemed to Cade he was fighting a losing battle. He thought how easy it would be…what a relief it would be…to just say the hell with it and give in. He thought it would be a little like drowning, to let himself go wherever this might take him, and damn the consequences.

He might have been able to do that—just maybe—if it hadn't been for the strident and insistent clamor of his reason. *Cade, you can't! She's a princess, most likely a virgin! You're a guest in her father's house! You have to stop this. Now!*

He wasn't sure how much longer he might have resisted the voices of sanity inside his head, or if in fact he'd ever have found the strength to end it. What saved him was anger. It came suddenly and unexpectedly, a bright and savage flare of resentment. *Foolish woman—what the hell does she think she's doing? Spoiled brat…she's going to ruin me—ruin everything!*

He let go of her abruptly, and felt her round and firm little bottom come to rest on his drawn-up knee.

"No," he said hoarsely as, jerky and shell-shocked, he peeled her arms from around his neck and thrust her from him. The places where she'd touched him felt like fresh abrasions.

Little by little, in ungraceful adjustments, he managed to stand her on her own two feet, and himself as well. And all the while she said not a word, while her eyes gazed up at him, black as ink, glistening dangerously. Her lips, pink and soft and still glazed from *his* mouth, parted slowly. If she speaks, he thought… Or worse, if she cries…

He grasped at his anger like a drowning man reaching for a life preserver and spoke in a ragged and guttural voice. "I said *no*. Do you understand me?" He pulled himself away from her, raked a distraught hand through his hair and fought to get his breathing calmed down. "This isn't going to happen, okay? Not tonight, not ever. I'm sorry—you have to go. Come on—*out*."

Since she didn't appear able or willing to move on her own, he took hold of her arm and gave it a tug. Just a small one. Then he watched in horror as her gown slipped down over one creamy-smooth shoulder. He let go of her arm in a hurry. "Ah, hell—Princess…" He closed his eyes and said it with a groan, almost pleading.

Then, through the pounding of his own pulses he heard a sharp, heartbroken sob…felt the rush and flurry of her passing…and at last, the click of an opening door.

Regret pierced his heart without warning, pierced it like an arrow and sent it plummeting into his belly. Belatedly he was aware of how young, how innocent Leila really was, and how grievously his rejection must have hurt her. He felt as if he'd kicked a puppy, or trampled a lovely blossom into the mud.

Hoping to explain, to soften it for her somehow, he lunged after her as she hurled herself through the doorway, out into the hallway—straight into the arms of her father, the sheik.

Sheik Ahmed Kamal had been feeling quite pleased with himself, and enormously satisfied with the way the weekend's events had unfolded. The wedding ceremony had been as solemn and dignified as should be—in spite of the tendency on the part of young people nowadays to want to adopt certain deplorable Western customs instead of adhering faithfully to traditional ways. The groom's banquet had been enjoyable for all in attendance, sumptuous and generous as was appropriate for a royal couple yet neither excessive nor ostentatious. The exhibition polo matches had been enjoyed by the many guests in attendance, *and* had resulted in gratifying wins for the Tamari team. Tonight's state dinner and reception honoring the king and the crown prince of Montebello had been a grand success.

Yes…and its aftermath even more so. Sheik Ahmed was, in fact, just returning from a most productive private meeting with his Montebellan counterpart, after having personally accompanied the royal contingent to their quarters in the guest palace on the other side of the gardens. He was in an expansive mood; his belly was full of good food and his mind full of plans for Tamir's future, plans that involved economic expansion in a number of areas near and dear to the sheik's heart.

Now, accompanied by his cadre of loyal bodyguards, he was making his way toward his private chambers at the end of a long, empty passageway adorned with mosaics and murals and softly lit by recessed lamps. He was looking forward to discussing the weekend's activities with Alima, his beloved wife, and afterward…a well-deserved rest.

And then—what was this? His youngest daughter, blinded by tears and with garments in disarray—garments, moreover, that would be appropriate only for a woman's chambers, or her husband's—his beloved child running headlong into his arms!

"Daughter, what is the meaning of this?" the sheik thundered, holding her at arm's length while he made hurried and necessary adjustments to her costume. He spared no

thought at all for his contingent of bodyguards; being both
well-trained and loyal, they had already turned their backs
and averted their eyes from the deplorable spectacle.

Besides, if the truth were known, at that moment Sheik
Ahmed's thoughts were in too much of a quandary to worry
about what his bodyguards might or might not have wit-
nessed. On the one hand, there was a father's understandable wrath at finding one of his offspring in a place and
circumstances she had no business being at such an hour.
On the other hand...the fact was, the sheik had a secret
softness in his heart for his youngest child, and seeing her
face so pale and frightened, her eyes overflowing with tears,
gazing up into his...

"Leila, explain yourself!" he bellowed, but his anger
was more show than substance.

Her lips opened, but she did not speak. He felt her arm
tremble in his grasp. About to repeat the command a bit
more gently, he hesitated. His focus wavered. A flash of
movement on the periphery of his vision caught his gaze
and jerked it away from his daughter's frozen face...and
beyond. His eyes narrowed.

In the space of an instant his fatherly anger, mostly bom-
bast, bluster and hot air, melted down and solidified into a
rage as cold and deadly as any he'd ever known in his life.

Cade had never seen murder looking back at him from
a man's eyes before, but he knew beyond any doubt he was
seeing it now.

Strangely, faced with his worst nightmare, he felt all fear
leave him. His body grew cold and his mind quiet. His eyes
never left Sheik Ahmed's face as he waited for what would
come.

Rotund and flushed with the effects of good food and
good living, the Sheik was still an imposing presence. His
snow-white hair and beard and magnificent hawk's beak of
a nose gave him an almost biblical majesty, and even

though he didn't speak loudly, his voice, welling from the depths of a barrel chest, sounded to Cade like the voice of doom.

"Young man, there was a time, not so long ago, when I could have had you executed on the spot. *Explain yourself.*"

A strangled cry from Leila tugged at Cade's attention, but it was only a flicker, and only for an instant. All of his attention was focused on her father.

Explain himself? Under the circumstances it seemed to him a more than reasonable, even generous demand. Certainly more than he'd expected.

Explain himself. *Well. Your Highness, I was just getting ready for bed, minding my own business, when your daughter, here, came knocking at my door, and the next thing I knew, she was throwing herself into my arms. Did I invite her? No sir, I did not. And...where did she get the idea to come to my chambers, Your Highness? You mean, did I entice her? Lead her on? Well...no sir, I sure didn't... unless you count kissing her earlier this evening until she couldn't stand up....*

Cade sighed inwardly. To explain seemed cowardly to him, and heartless, somehow. His mouth, opened to release the words that were poised on the tip of his tongue, firmly closed.

He looked at Leila, standing so straight and still beside her father. Her face was pale but proud, even with eyes lowered and veiled by tear-clumped lashes. He cleared his throat and determinedly began. "Your Highness, this is not what you think. Your daughter—" He glanced at her again, and saw her eyes go wide and stare straight into his...saw her lips part and her cheeks flood with pink. She reminded him of a doe he'd seen once, caught in a hunter's snare. And again he felt that awful sensation in his midsection, as if his heart had just been speared, and had landed with a thud in the bottom of his belly.

Every rational thought went out of his head. His mind was chaos, a whirlwind of remorse and shame. This was his fault. He'd humiliated this girl—and she *was* a girl. She was a princess and he'd humiliated her. She was almost certainly a virgin, and he'd kissed her frivolously, toyed with her emotions. And now, to make matters even worse, her humiliation was made public, since all at once the hallway around them seemed filled with people—bodyguards, servants, even Leila's mother with *her* servants, come to see what all the commotion was about. The damage he'd done to Leila—and to his own agenda, of course—seemed irreparable. *Unless...*

Just as suddenly as the chaos had come, now calm and certainty descended upon him. There was only one way to fix the mess he'd created. Cade knew precisely what he had to do.

He drew himself up, and with as much dignity as he could muster with his hair standing on end and without benefit of shirt, jacket and tie, looked Leila's father straight in the eye. "Sheik Ahmed, this may seem sudden, but I have fallen in love with your daughter." Ignoring Leila's shocked gasp, he rushed on. "I want to marry her." The gasps had found echoes throughout the gathering; he ignored those, too, as well as the sheik's sudden stiffening. "I respectfully ask your permission—"

"My permission!" Sheik Ahmed's voice shook. His wife laid a cautioning hand on his arm, and he whirled, blindly thrusting Leila toward her.

"Take her," he bellowed. "Take her away—and the rest of you—" he waved his arms, making shooing motions at the crowd. "Leave us!" Without waiting for his orders to be obeyed, he turned back to Cade, black eyes glittering with rage.

"*You.* You would *marry* my *daughter?*" With extreme effort, the sheik seemed to draw himself together and spoke more calmly though with no less anger. "Mr. Gallagher, I have made you a guest in my house, and you thank me by inflicting this gravest of injuries upon my family."

Cade frowned. This was not going quite the way he'd expected. "That was not—"

"*Silence!* And now, to that injury you would add insult? Do you think that I would allow *my* daughter to marry *you*—an infidel, an unbeliever, a man without honor?" There was a pause, during which Cade could have sworn the sheik grew in height at least a foot before his very eyes. And then, in a magnificent bellow, "I would sooner see her dishonored!"

Having delivered his exit line, Sheik Ahmed whirled—then spoiled the effect of it somewhat by jerking back to Cade. "You will leave my house," he growled, stabbing the air in his direction with a bejeweled finger. "Tomorrow—as early as can be arranged." Once more he turned, and stalked off down the now-deserted hallway, footsteps ringing on the tile floor.

Protected by an icy shell of calm he knew must be shock, Cade watched until the massive doors at the end of the hallway had closed upon the sheik's broad back. Then he retreated into his own chamber and carefully pulled the door shut after him.

On the whole, he thought as the quivery aftereffects of shock hit him, that had gone pretty well. At least he hadn't been executed on the spot.

Like a gracefully pensive statue, Leila stood in steamy and fragrant warmth and gazed at the familiar back of the woman who knelt beside the bath. Gazed at, but did not really see. Her mind was empty, as bereft of thoughts as her eyes were of tears. She did not dare allow herself to think, not even so much as a single thought; if she did, she feared the anger, humiliation and despair would simply overwhelm her.

Salma Hadi, her mother's most trusted servant and once upon a time Leila's own nanny, hummed nervously as she fussed over the bathwater, adding scent and soap bubbles, swishing the water with her fingers to test the temperature. The tune she hummed was simple and familiar, a children's play song she had sung to Leila long, long ago. Leila found it oddly soothing.

Pushing stiffly to her feet, Salma turned to smile up at her. Holding out her hand, she spoke in Arabic, the language of her youth. "Ah, yes, now it is good. Come, my treasured child, let me help you undress."

Mindlessly, Leila obeyed the familiar voice, lifting her hair to allow access to the fastenings of her gown. She stood, docile and numb, while well-remembered hands gently removed her clothing and twisted her hair into a pile atop her head, securing it there with jeweled clips and combs. Naked, she allowed herself to be taken by the hand and led to the edge of the bath.

"There, my sweet...gently...gently," Salma crooned. "The water will sooth you...take away the pain."

Leila gave her former nanny a puzzled look. *Pain? What pain?* Was Salma getting old? Losing her mind? The pain *she* felt was all inside, deep in her heart, and it would take much more than a hot bubble bath to make it go away.

"Thank you," she murmured as she lowered herself into the fragrant suds, for she had been taught never to take loyal servants for granted. "This does feel good." Closing her eyes, she lay back with a sigh and stretched herself languidly, like a sleepy cat. How good it felt to relax, after such a tumultuous day. How good it would be if she could simply go to sleep right here, and not have to think...

"Princess? Are you—"

There was concern, and something else—embarrassment, perhaps?—in Salma's voice. Leila opened her eyes. "Yes, Salma, what is it?"

The servant's round face was flushed, and her eyes glistened with kindness. "Princess, I have some oil—it is very soothing. When you have finished—"

"Oil?" Leila frowned. "What kind of oil? What for?"

Salma touched Leila's cheek with gentle fingers. "My little one…it is normal for a woman to have pain, the first time she…is with a man. But after a hot bath…the soothing oil…it goes away quickly—" She stopped, for Leila was shaking her head wildly. She continued in distress, "Princess, it is *all right*—" But Leila went on shaking her head, and brushing aside Salma's anxious fingers, covered her face with her hands.

Her face, her whole body burned with shame; even the bathwater felt cool on her fevered skin. Oh, how she wished she could just…sink to the bottom of the tub and disappear forever.

"Princess—what is it?" Salma's voice had risen with alarm. Lifting her hands heavenward, she uttered a rapid, wailing prayer, which she almost immediately interrupted to ask in a despairing whisper, "Oh, tell me—did he harm you? Are you injured, truly? Tell me—what has he—"

"No, no!" Leila cried, "you don't understand. He did nothing. *Nothing.*"

"Nothing?" Salma rocked backward, hushed and wondering. "You mean, you are not—he did not—"

"No," Leila moaned, putting her hands over her eyes once more, "he *would* not. Oh, Salma, it was awful. Just awful…" And all at once she felt herself gathered into loving arms, soapsuds and all, and she was sobbing like a little child on her nanny's shoulder. "Salma," she gulped, "I have been a fool…."

"Yes, my treasure," Salma crooned, rocking her. "Yes…."

* * *

Alima Kamal was worried about her husband. She had never before seen him so angry—his color was quite alarming. Hadn't the doctors warned him about his blood pressure, insisted he must lose some weight? And after such a weekend, so much excitement, too much rich food—and perhaps more of the mild Tamari wine than he was accustomed to—now *this*. What had Leila been thinking of, to do such a thing?

Ah—Leila. That was another worry entirely. She was in Salma's capable hands—that problem could wait until tomorrow.

At the moment Ahmed was in the bathroom, Alima having persuaded him that a warm bath might help him to relax—with the help of a little subtle bribery, naturally, in the form of the promise of a nice massage afterward. She had in mind an old family recipe of Salma's—passed on to her by her maternal grandmother—a mix of fragrant oils and certain herbs that were designed to soothe the mind as well as the body. She had used it on her husband before, with most satisfactory and highly enjoyable results, for her as well. Although, under the circumstances she didn't hold out hope for such a conclusion to *this* evening's activities. Ah, well… Alima sighed.

A discreet tapping at the royal bedchamber's heavy wooden door almost went unnoticed, so engrossed was she in her preparations. When it continued, now a little louder, she glanced at the antique French clock on the mantelpiece. Who would dare disturb the sheik in his chambers at this hour? With a mildly vexed sigh, Alima went to answer it.

"Salma!" Her heart gave a leap of alarm when she saw her oldest and most trusted attendant standing there, almost bouncing on her tiptoes with ill-concealed emotion. "What's wrong? Is Leila all right? Is something—"

"Oh, no, *Sitt,*" Salma interrupted breathlessly, "Princess Leila is fine. That is why—Oh, *Sitt,* please forgive me for disturbing you, but I must speak with you."

Casting a hurried glance toward the bathroom where, judging from the sounds coming from within, her husband—perhaps in anticipation of what was to come after?—seemed to be enjoying his bath more than he'd expected, Alima stepped into the hallway and pulled the door closed behind her.

Flat on his belly with his eyes closed, Sheik Ahmed drifted on waves of pleasure. *Ah yes...there...* Alima's strong fingers never failed to find the spot that needed them most.

She wanted something from him, of course. She only resorted to the oils and herbs when she was hoping to cajole him into giving her her way. He knew this, but it did nothing to lessen his pleasure. He trusted his wife implicitly. He knew she would never use the considerable influence she had on him lightly. If she was attempting to manipulate him now, it would only be for something she considered to be of utmost importance. Ah well...she would get to it in her own good time. And meanwhile, as far as Sheik Ahmed was concerned, getting there was the most enjoyable part.

"Ahmed, my beloved..."

"Yes, jewel of my heart? Speak to me."

They had been speaking Arabic, as they often did on intimate occasions, but Alima switched now to English. "Ahmed, Salma was here, while you were in the bath. She brought news of Leila—"

"Leila!" A snort lifted his head and shoulders from the pillows.

Gently but firmly, Alima pushed them down again. "Hush, my husband—please, hear me." After a pause, which she decided to take for acquiescence, she continued in a musing tone, "What she had to say was interesting. I think you will want to hear it."

Ahmed gave a resigned grunt. "Very well…if you must."

Bracing herself for the expected upheaval, Alima bore down with all her strength on one of her husband's most troublesome spots, took a deep breath, and said lightly, "It is possible we have misjudged Elena's friend from Texas." A growl resonated beneath her fingers. She hurried on. "It seems this American may not be entirely without honor, after all. I say this—" she spoke calmly, but her fingers were kneading her husband's tensed muscles as hard and fast as they possibly could "—because of what your daughter has confessed to Salma. In tears." There was that growl again. "Yes, *tears*," she said firmly. "But *not* because this man had *dishonored* her. Quite the opposite. Your daughter was in tears because he had sent her *away*."

Like a small mountain shifted by an earthquake, Sheik Ahmed rolled himself onto his back. Raising himself up on his elbows, glowering fiercely, he bellowed, "*Away?* What do you mean, he sent her *away?* Explain yourself!"

Alima sat with her legs tucked under her, head high and eyes downcast. Her heart was beating rapidly and her hands, clasped tightly together in her lap, were cold. She was desperately afraid, though not of her husband—she could never be afraid of Ahmed! This was another kind of fear entirely—the fear of a mother for her beloved child. Her youngest daughter's future happiness was at stake.

"Yes," she said on a soft exhalation, "I fear it was not the American who behaved badly this evening, but our daughter. And I—" Her voice broke—she had not planned it. "I must say that I am not surprised. I have been afraid something like this might happen. Oh, Ahmed—" She rose and turned quickly from him to hide the tears that had sprung unexpectedly to her eyes. "Leila is so impatient and impulsive—she has always been so."

"Yes." Ahmed actually chuckled.

Whirling back to him, Alima was just in time to see him rearrange his face in its customary glower. "Ahmed, she is a woman. She has the feelings, the needs, the *impulses* of a woman. Every day I have watched her grow more impatient, waiting her turn, waiting for her sisters to choose husbands…"

Yes, and impatient for other things, for other reasons, too, about which Alima knew she could never tell her husband. Ahmed was a good man and a progressive leader in many ways, but he would never understand how bright, intelligent women like his daughters might feel frustrated at being patronized, overlooked, discounted and ignored. Particularly Leila, whom everyone considered silly and shallow, and whom possibly only her mother knew was anything but.

And there was another thing Leila's mother knew. She had noticed the way her youngest child looked at the tall oilman from Texas. Tonight she had seen the soft shine in her eyes, the pink flush in her cheeks….

"Humph," said Ahmed. "I have been more than patient with Nadia, it is true…" He scratched his bearded chin thoughtfully. "Butrus wishes to marry her, and she seems willing enough." He shrugged and gave a regal wave of his hand. "Pah—I see no real value in this tradition of marrying off daughters in order of their birth. So—if you are certain that Leila is eager to marry, and impetuous enough to do something foolish, then the answer is simple enough. I must find her a suitable husband. And now, my beloved, if that is all that is troubling you—" He smiled, and his eyes gleamed wickedly.

Alima hesitated. This was the tricky part. She must be

extremely careful not to give herself away. Breathing a relieved sigh, she bowed her head and said, "Yes, my husband. You are wise, as always. Only—"

Still smiling, he caught her hand and drew her closer to him. "Only? What is it now, my love?"

Bracing her hands firmly on her husband's shoulders, Alima looked gravely into his eyes. "Only, I fear that it may prove difficult to find a man willing to overlook tonight's escapade. Perhaps we should consider—"

"Not the American!" bellowed Ahmed, rearing back in outrage. "A nonbeliever? *Never.*"

"Of course not," said Alima, laughing. "What an idea! No, I was going to say, perhaps we should consider someone older, someone who will give Leila the firm guidance she needs." She paused, then continued demurely, "I hear the Emir of Batar is looking for a fourth wife."

"The Emir of Batar! The man is older than I am," fumed Ahmed, looking horrified. "And I have it on good authority that he treats his wives shamefully. No, no—we must do better for Leila." He gave his wife an absentminded squeeze and turned away from her. "Let me think about it."

"Of course, my husband," murmured Alima, beginning to knead his shoulder muscles. "Perhaps this will help."

After several minutes, Ahmed spoke, slurring his words slightly. "I have ordered the American to leave tomorrow, as early as possible." Alima said nothing, but continued massaging his neck and shoulders. "Perhaps," muttered Ahmed, "that was a bit…hasty. And somewhat unfair, under the circumstances. What do *you* think, dearest one?" He turned to encircle her with his arms. She saw that his eyes were twinkling.

She lowered her lashes so he would not see the gleam in hers. "You know best, my husband."

"I believe I will speak to the man, first thing in the morning."

"Whatever you say, beloved," crooned Alima.

Chapter 5

Cade dropped his toiletry kit into his carry-on bag, added a half-empty pack of cheroots and the zippable daily planner in which he kept his business notes and appointments, then straightened for one last look around. Not that he was afraid he'd overlooked something; rather, his gaze was one of wonderment, reflecting his frame of mind. He was still having a hard time accepting what had happened to him. He tried to remember whether he'd ever suffered such a demoralizing tail-between-the-legs disaster before in his life. He couldn't.

Ah, the car, he thought when he heard the discreet knock on his door. He called, "Be right there," and grabbed up his big suitcase and moved it over beside the door. A little early, he thought, glancing at his watch, but so much the better. He'd have time to grab a bite of breakfast at the airport before his flight. He sure as hell wasn't about to eat anything here at the palace, or for that matter, impose on the Kamal family's hospitality in any way, for one minute longer than absolutely necessary. He'd seen enough of these royals to last him a lifetime. With the exception of Elena, of course. Though he sure wouldn't care to run into her, right now, either. He couldn't even begin to think how he was going to explain this to her.

He zipped up his overnighter, picked it up and placed it beside its bigger twin, then opened the door. The man who stood there, waiting at patient and respectful attention, wasn't wearing the white-and-gold uniform of the household servants, but a western-style suit, dark gray with an immaculate white shirt and blue-and-gray striped tie. He looked familiar—dark, swarthy, probably handsome, in an austere, arrogant sort of way. Undoubtedly Cade had been introduced to the man during the course of the weekend, which meant he was a member of the royal family or somebody high on the bureaucratic totem pole.

Probably a lawyer, Cade thought cynically. For the defense, he wondered, or the prosecution?

"The sheik wishes to speak with you," the man said, in clipped English. "If you will come with me, please."

What now? Maybe he's changed his mind about having me executed, Cade thought sourly as he gave his room one last look and with a fatalistic shrug, pulled the door shut behind him.

His escort didn't say another word as he led the way along the corridor, following virtually the same path by which the sheik had made his dramatic departure the night before. Cade made a conscious effort to relax, and tried not to think about the confrontation to come. Instead he made a point of noticing the arched passageways, the apparently ancient tiles beneath his feet and mosaics on the walls, and the lamps which, set into niches along the walls, added to the medieval look of it all. He half expected to see armored guards with swords and crossed pikestaffs barring entry through the massive carved double doors at the end of the hallway.

Instead, his escort merely knocked twice, paused, then pushed the doors open and gestured for Cade to enter ahead of him. Cade gave the man a nod and a sardonic, "Thank you," which went unacknowledged.

The sheik's office was huge, but was saved from seeming cavernous by the warm opulence of mahogany, leather and Persian carpets. Arched windows along one side of the room looked out on the sea; on the other, Sheik Ahmed waited behind a long mahogany desk. He wore an ordinary business suit this morning, but that didn't make him seem any the less imposing. He still looked positively biblical, Cade thought. Moses in a suit and tie.

The sheik had risen at Cade's approach. Now he nodded at the escort and said, "Thank you, Butrus. You may leave us."

As the man muttered and made his exit, the name came to Cade. *Butrus Dabir. The sheik's most trusted advisor, and according to Elena, one with designs on his daughter, Nadia.*

"Thank you for coming, Mr. Gallagher. Please sit down." The sheik indicated one of several leather chairs in front of the desk, waited until Cade was seated, then returned to his own chair. Like a genial host, Cade thought, except without the smile. In fact, he seemed almost…in anyone else Cade would have sworn he was…. No way around it. The reigning monarch of Tamir gave every indication of being embarrassed.

Sheik Ahmed picked up a pen and put it down. He leaned back in his chair and scowled at the pen with lowered eyebrows. At last, following an introductory rumbling sound, he spoke.

"Mr. Gallagher, I have asked you here so that I may offer you an apology. It seems that, in the heat of the, uh,

moment last night, I have made a too-hasty judgment. I
believe I accused you of being a man without honor,
whereas it seems that you behaved with more honor than
most men would have under the same…ahem…the circumstances. I hope that you will forgive my behavior, and that
of my daughter.'' And with that, half rising, the sheik
leaned across his desk to offer his hand to Cade.

Who was momentarily speechless, with his mouth hanging open like a schoolboy caught red-handed at mischief.
Whatever he might have expected, it sure as hell wasn't
this. Finally, though, there was only one thing to do, and
that was shake the sheik's hand and say thank you. So he
did it.

He was settling back in his chair, feeling dazed as a
poleaxed steer, when the sheik gave another rumble and
continued. ''Regarding your proposal of marriage to my
daughter…'' There was a pause while the sheik stared intently at Cade, eyes glittering from beneath lowered eyebrows. Much against his will, Cade's heart began to beat
faster. ''Mr. Gallagher, I am fully aware of the circumstances under which it was made, and I—that is to say,
your gallant attempt to salvage my daughter's honor is not
unappreciated.'' There was another pause. Again the
sheik's eyes pinioned Cade with the intent stare of a hawk
zeroing in on a cornered gopher.

Cade's mind was racing. What was going on here? The
old sheik had an agenda, that was clear enough. What
wasn't clear at all was exactly how Cade was supposed to
fit into it. Okay, he'd been cleared of dishonoring the princess, apologies had been made, he'd been let off the hook.
On the other hand, his banishment hadn't been lifted, not
in so many words. He had a very strong feeling that if he
said thank you now, shook hands and left this room, he'd
be taking that early flight home, no hard feelings, but no
business deal, either.

What was it the old fox wanted from him? He'd made his feelings on the marriage issue plain enough. So, what?

His heart was pounding, his mind in chaos. However, only his narrowed eyes betrayed the turmoil he was feeling as he calmly said, "Sir, I assure you—I didn't propose marriage to your daughter merely to save her reputation. My desire to marry Leila was—is—sincere."

God, what had he just said? *Marry Leila?* He felt a bright stab of panic before he remembered that he was safe. Her royal papa was never going to go for it anyway.

At the moment, though, the way the old sheik was staring at him was making him decidedly uneasy. Still intent as a hawk about to pounce, but now—there it was again, that odd little shift of embarrassment.

"Hmm, yes...I see." Sheik Ahmed tapped his fingers on the desktop. "Mr. Gallagher, you must understand that in our culture, such an alliance would be impossible..."

"I understand," Cade murmured, gravely nodding.

"Unless—" the sheik pounced "—you were to convert."

Cade's heart leaped into overdrive. "Convert?"

"To our ways, our culture." The sheik spread his hands and in the white nest of beard his lips curved in a smile. "Then there would be no objection to a marriage between you and my youngest daughter—from me, of course. Naturally, Leila would have to consent to such a match." He actually chuckled.

"Naturally..." Cade breathed. His head was whirling again. What the hell was happening? He gave his head a little shake and tried to smile. "Wow. Convert, huh? That's an...interesting idea. I'll...definitely have to..."

"Of course," Sheik Ahmed said smoothly, "I understand such a decision should not be made lightly. And I would fully understand if you wished to leave us, Mr. Gallagher, after the treatment you have recently been subjected to, from me and, uh...members of my family. However, if you should decide to stay..." another of those strategic pauses, another shrewd glare "...it is my understanding that my son, Hassan, and daughter-in-law, Elena, had scheduled a visit to the oil-producing regions of our country, and a tour of our facilities, before their departure on their...uh..." He frowned, searching for the word.

"Honeymoon?" Cade supplied.

"Yes, honeymoon." The sheik waved a hand and muttered something about "western traditions," then harrumphed and went on. "It is also my understanding that the three of you wished to discuss a possible business arrangement between your own company, Elena's and Tamir."

Cade, who was pretty much in shock at this point, could only nod and mutter, "Yes, sir, I had been looking forward to meeting with you on that subject—"

Sheik Ahmed gave another hand wave and leaned dismissively back in his chair. "I have decided to leave that aspect of my country's business dealings to my son. *And* his new wife, who, as the head of her own company, seems very knowledgeable on the subject. You may consider them my representatives. Any agreement you might enter into with them, especially as a member of the family, if you should chose that course—" the sheik smiled, showing strong white teeth "—would be honored fully by the government of Tamir."

Cade let out a gust of breath. He felt absolutely calm, now, clear through to his insides. The cards were on the table; he was pretty sure he knew both the game and the stakes. He also knew he'd been seriously outmaneuvered.

"I understand," he said as he rose to accept the sheik's proffered hand. "Thank you, Your Highness. You've given me a lot to think about. I'm looking forward to visiting your oil production facilities." He tried a strategic pause of his own, meeting the old sheik's glittery black eyes and locking on as their hands clasped across the mahogany desktop. His smile felt frozen on his face. "I'm sure we can work out something," he drawled, "that'll be to both our advantages."

"He is *what?*" Leila shrieked, slopping hot coffee into her saucer and very nearly her lap.

"He is going to convert," her mother repeated, her face so round and happy she looked like a child's drawing of a beaming sun. Leila felt as though *her* sun had just been covered by a huge black cloudbank.

She was on the terrace with Nadia, having a late breakfast—or perhaps an early lunch—while Nadia, who had already eaten, passed the time in her usual way, with her sketchbook. At their mother's interruption Nadia looked up briefly, then went back to making little pencil sketches of Leila.

While Leila mopped up coffee with her napkin, her mother selected the chair next to her and turned it so that it angled toward Leila before she sat. She took Leila's hand, holding it in both of her warm, soft ones. Tears sprang to Leila's eyes. She had to swallow hard to fight down the lump in her throat.

"Your father has given his permission for the two of you to marry," her mother said in a husky, excited voice. She gazed at Leila with shining eyes. "Oh, my child, I am so happy for you. Mr. Gallagher must love you very much, to honor you so."

Leila was glad she was no longer holding the cup of coffee in her hands; as badly as they were shaking, she would surely have dropped it—or perhaps hurled it into the nearest fountain. Inwardly she was seething with anger, with outrage. Remembering the way he had thrust her away from him, as if she were something vile. Remembering the humiliation. *How dare he!*

Why is he doing this? she thought desperately. What can he possibly hope to gain? Is he trying to humiliate me even more?

Because she knew, she *absolutely* knew, that whatever Cade Gallagher's motive might be for marrying her, it most definitely was *not* because he loved her.

"Mother," said Leila in a choked voice, "I do not want to marry Mr. Gallagher. I will not." A tear ran down her cheek.

Her mother made a distressed sound and brushed it away. "Oh dear—I thought you would be pleased. But tell me, why not?"

Why not? Because he made me feel like...like I never knew it was possible to feel. Because he opened a door and beckoned to me, showed me a glimpse of paradise, then slammed the door in my face. Because he made me want him...and I cannot stop thinking about him...and I know I will never be able to forget him. How can I forgive him for that?

"He is from America!" Leila cried, brushing furiously at both the tears and her mother's hand. It was the only thing she could think of to say. "From *Texas!*"

Her mother looked startled, but only for a moment. Then she put her arms around Leila and patted her on the back as she crooned, "Yes, of course...I understand. Don't cry, my sweet. Naturally you would not wish to marry someone who would take you so far away from your home...your family. I hadn't thought, but yes—you would have to live in America—in Texas! Your father and I would hardly ever see you. What were we thinking? Hmm. Well. Never mind."

She gave Leila one last little hug and rose. "Don't worry, my sweet, I will explain things to your father." She smiled and leaned down to kiss Leila's cheek. "To be honest, I think he will be glad that you will be staying right here in Tamir.''

When her mother had gone, Leila reached for her coffee cup, then pushed it savagely away from her.

Nadia put aside her sketchbook. "Have you suddenly lost your mind?" she asked mildly. Leila said nothing, but stared at her coffee cup with hot, tearless eyes. "Or," said Nadia, "are you merely being contrary?" She gave a sigh of exasperation. "Did I not hear you say, two days ago, how attractive you thought Mr. Gallagher? *And,* were you not talking about how much you wanted to go to America? *Especially* Texas? It seemed like an impossible dream, even I thought so. To have it realized would have taken a miracle. Now, it is as if you had rubbed a magic lamp! All your wishes have been granted. And you would turn them down? Leila—for mercy's sake, *why?*"

"Because I do not love him," Leila said flatly. Her voice was as dry as her eyes. "And he certainly does not love me."

With an exasperated noise, Nadia flung herself away from the table. "Leila, you are such a child."

Leila stared at her, stung. Although it was the sort of thing people were always saying to her, for some reason, this morning, it hurt more than usual. She swallowed, then said softly, "I do not think it is childish to want to be loved. *You* have known love, Nadia. Why should I not have the same?"

For a moment, as she gazed back at Leila, Nadia's face softened. For a moment. Then her eyes darkened with pain and she veiled them with her lashes before she turned away. "You don't know what you are talking about. Love brings only pain. Trust me—you do not ever want to know pain like that."

"I am sorry, Nadia," Leila whispered, belatedly remembering her sister's secret heartbreak.

"Besides," Nadia went on briskly, "we are not talking about love, but about marriage, which is a different thing entirely. Love is a terrible reason to get married. It is a recent idea, this notion that one must be in love in order to marry—don't you know that? And look at what *that* has done! So much unhappiness. Inevitably, love leads to disappointment, and disappointment to misery and even divorce. No, thank you."

"So," said Leila grudgingly, "what reason *do* you think people should marry for, if not love?" She was by no means ready to agree with such a cynical point of view, but there was no arguing with Nadia.

"Why, for practical reasons, of course." Nadia looked as annoyingly superior as an older sister can. "Marriage should be entered into as a business agreement—a contract, mutually advantageous, of course. I, for example," she said loftily, holding her head high, "have decided to marry Butrus. Why?" Ignoring Leila's gasp of surprise, she rushed on, ticking off reasons one by one on her fingers. "One, Butrus wishes to marry me in order to gain favor with Father, therefore, he knows he must treat me well—very well—because if I were to be made unhappy, Father would not be pleased. Two, as Father's advisor, Butrus is away a great deal of the time. So, I would not only have the status of a married woman, but at the same time I would be assured a considerable amount of freedom. And three, I wish to have children. Butrus is handsome and physically well made. So, we would have beautiful, healthy babies. And, he has rather nice teeth, I believe."

"Nadia," Leila said, giggling in spite of herself, "you sound as though you are buying a horse."

"It is very much the same thing," Nadia said airily. A moment later, though, she was serious again as she bent down to cover Leila's hand with her own and give it an urgent little squeeze. "Leila—for once in your life, use your head. *Think.* Cade Gallagher will make beautiful, healthy babies, too. And, he will take you to America—to Texas.'' She glanced quickly over her shoulder and lowered her voice. Even so, it quivered with passion. ''Away from *here.* Just think, Leila—in America you can do—you can become—anything you want to. *Anything.* Do you understand? The freedom...'' She straightened abruptly, biting her lip. ''*Think* about it, Leila,'' she whispered, and snatching up her sketchpad, walked quickly away without looking back.

Leila did not know how long she stayed there, biting her lip and stubbornly frowning at nothing. Bees hummed among the roses, birds came to drink and play in the fountain and a servant came quietly to clear away the remains of the meal. And still she sat...quivering with the burden of unshed tears.

It was the strangest meeting Cade had ever been a part of. Definitely not what he'd expected. Though he'd have had a hard time putting into words just what it was he *had* expected.

One thing, definitely—he'd expected to have at least one more chance to talk with Leila. Alone. But clearly, that wasn't going to happen. Instead they each occupied separate leather chairs facing Sheik Ahmed's long mahogany desk, with several feet of space between them. It might as well have been several miles. Like a cross between a biblical Moses and a junior high school principal facing down a couple of co-conspirators in mischief, Sheik Ahmed presided behind his desk. His wife, Alima, Leila's mother, sat in a comfortable chair near one of the casement windows that overlooked the sea. She wore a serene smile and held in her hands a small, leather-bound book.

As for Leila, she hadn't spoken a word to Cade, or even looked at him. She sat straight-backed in her chair with her head held high, the arch of her throat as pale as the marble columns that graced the palace gardens. There was only a quivery softness about her mouth to betray any emotion or vulnerability at all, but to Cade, that was enough. Disliking the queasy, seasick feeling he got when he saw…when he remembered…that incredibly ripe, incredibly fragile mouth, he'd stopped looking at her at all.

With a face as stern as an old-fashioned Texas hang-'em-high judge, Sheik Ahmed was speaking, "…and that you have entered into this decision of your own free will, and with pure mind and sincere heart?"

"Yes—" Cade cleared his throat. "Yes, sir, I have."

The sheik went on talking, something solemn about a man's heart being the province of God and therefore not to be questioned by man, but Cade wasn't listening. His mind was full of the incredible fact that he, Cade Gallagher, an American businessman living in the twenty-first century, had just agreed to an arranged marriage. *Arranged*—like in medieval times! How had such a thing happened to him?

Right now, more than anything, what he felt was dazed, bewildered, at a loss to explain how a man such as he, a master at navigating through the most circuitous and complex of business negotiations, could have gotten himself so completely boxed in. Because the truth was, he just didn't see any other way out of this. Not unless he was prepared to take it all back, right here and now, in front of Leila and both her parents. Say he hadn't meant the proposal of marriage to begin with, that it had been a mistake and he wasn't prepared to go through with it after all. Say it to her face.

There was no way. He could not do that. No way in hell.

Because if there was anything he'd learned as a kid growing up in Texas, it was to stand up and take the consequences for his actions like a man.

Consequences…. Elena had said something like that, hadn't she? They'd had only a few minutes together, while

Hassan was speaking to the foreman at one of the refineries they'd visited this afternoon about some sort of minor problem or complaint. Even now, remembering the disappointment in her eyes made Cade squirm. *"Cade, I warned you...."*

"You did," he'd acknowledged, and added, grimly joking, "Don't worry, I take full responsibility for my own stupidity."

But Elena hadn't smiled, and with a sad little shake of her head had murmured, "This isn't what I wanted for you, Cade." Her eyes had gone to where her husband stood with his back to them, deep in conversation with the refinery foreman. "I'd hoped...someday...you'd find someone you could love the way I love Hassan." Her voice had broken then, and Cade had snorted to cover the shaft of pain that unexpectedly pierced his heart.

Why he'd felt such a sense of loss, he didn't know. He'd never expected to experience that kind of love, anyway. The kind of love that lasts a lifetime. From his own personal experience he thought it doubtful love like that even existed.

As for his own feelings about Leila, since they were so confusing to him, most of the time he tried not to dwell on them at all. If he had to define them, he'd have said they pretty much consisted of a mix of anger and remorse. Yeah, she'd behaved like a moonstruck girl, but he was old enough, experienced enough, and he should have known better. He was responsible and it was up to him to make it right. But there was something else in the stew of his emotions that wasn't as easily defined, possibly because it was a whole lot less unfamiliar. The closest he would allow himself to come to defining it was *protectiveness*. With his own carelessness he'd hurt this child-woman immeasurably, and he never wanted to do so again.

Understandable enough. But even that didn't account for

the strange ache of *tenderness* that filled his throat sometimes when he looked at her—like now, as she murmured
affirmative responses to her father's questions.

*Do you agree to this marriage, Leila, and enter into it
of your own free will?*

Yes, Father....

But still, not once did she look at Cade. And he felt a
strange, unfamiliar emptiness inside.

Alima rose then, and came to her daughter's side. She
placed the leather-bound book on the shiny desktop. Sheik
Ahmed picked it up and handed it to Cade, explaining that
it was an English translation of the Quran, which he might
wish to study in his own time. Cade nodded, accepted the
book and murmured his thanks. The sheik then repeated,
in Arabic, the words of the *eshedu*, which Cade would be
required to recite later that evening, before the marriage
ceremony itself. Cade nodded again. Then Alima touched
Leila on the shoulder. Without a word, she rose and followed her mother from the room.

"Now, then," purred the sheik when the women had
gone, leaning back and lacing beringed fingers across his
ample middle, "let us discuss the *Mahr*... It is our custom
that a husband bestow upon his wife a gift. This may be
money or jewels, of course—" the sheik waved a hand in
a casually dismissive way "—or something of even greater,
if less concrete value. That is up to you. You will no doubt
wish to give the matter some thought...."

Once again, Cade could only nod. His heart was beating
hard, gathering speed like a runner hurtling downhill.

This is real, he thought. *It's actually happening. I'm marrying a princess of Tamir. And a virgin princess, at that.*

Leila gazed at her reflection in the mirror, eyes dark and
solemn in her waxy pale face. She saw her mother's hands,
graceful and white as lily petals as they plucked and

tweaked at the veils that covered her long black hair, veils that soon would be arranged to cover her face as well, until the final moments of the *nikah* ceremony later that morning when her husband would lift them to gaze at last upon the face of his wife.

At least, she thought, there would not be many people present to witness that moment. Only her parents and her sisters, Nadia and Sammi, of course, and Salma, and perhaps a few of the other servants who had known her since she was a baby. She was glad she would not have to face Elena, and especially Hassan. Salma had told her that they had left last evening for their honeymoon trip, right after returning from their tour of the oil refineries with Cade. Most of the guests who had attended Hassan and Elena's wedding had left yesterday, as well, and probably would not even know yet of Leila's humiliation.

Sadly, she thought of the wedding she had always imagined for herself, the most wonderful, beautiful occasion...even more glorious than Hassan's. Instead, it must be only a brief and private, almost secretive affair, with only her closest family attending. Papa would preside over the ceremony, of course. She would not even have a *Walima*, since she and Cade would have to leave for his home in Texas immediately after the *nikah* ceremony, and so how could there be a joyous celebration of its consummation?

Her stomach lurched and she swallowed hard. I wish I had some makeup, she thought. Lipstick, at least. *What will Cade think, when he sees me looking so pale?*

Does he think I am pretty at all?

Will he want to kiss me again, the way he did that night?

Her stomach gave another of those dreadful lurches. Oh, she thought, I do hope I'm not going to throw up.

Another time...another place...

She took a deep breath, and then another. *After tonight I will be his wife. Will he want me then?*

"Are you all right?" her mother asked, holding her hands away from the veils and looking concerned. "Do you need to sit down for a moment?"

"I am fine, mother," Leila said, trying a light laugh. "I was just thinking about Sammi and Nadia. Are they *very* angry with me?" Not Nadia, of course—she was the one who had convinced Leila to go through with this. But Leila had not told her mother *that*.

Her mother gave a rather unladylike snort. "Of course they are not *angry* with you." She paused to consider the effect she had just created with the drape of the veils, then threw Leila a quick, bright glance by way of the mirror. "They have been no more happy than you have, you know, with some of our more…restrictive ways. To have one such restriction done away with they see as a victory for themselves as well as for you."

Leila could only stare back at her, openmouthed with surprise. She had never heard her mother speak so freely. It occurred to her then, perhaps for the first time, that her mother was a person in her own right, a woman of intelligence, with her own thoughts, opinions, hopes and dreams. And she suddenly wished with all her heart, now that it was too late, that she could have talked with her about those things.

This time, the lurch was not in her stomach, but in her heart. She made an impulsive movement, a jerky half turn. "Mother—" she began, then paused, because Alima's eyes had darkened with worry…and something else. *Embarrassment?*

Her mother took a small step back and clasped her hands together in front of her ample chest. "Leila…my dear, you are the first of my daughters to marry. I am sorry—I do not know…exactly how…" She closed her eyes for a moment and bent her head over her clasped hands, as if in prayer, then drew a resolute breath. "What is it you would like to know? There must be questions you wish to ask. Please do not be afraid. I will try—''

A strange little bubble rose into Leila's throat—part nervousness, part excitement, a little guilt—but she bit it back before it could erupt in laughter. A wave of unheralded tenderness swept over her; she suddenly felt quite amazingly mature and wise. ''Mother,'' she said gently, ''I *know* about sex. Really. You do not have to worry.''

''Oh dear.'' Alima closed her eyes and let out an exasperated breath. ''I was afraid of that.''

''From *school*.'' Leila was softly laughing. ''It is all right. *Really*.'' She did not think it necessary to mention to her mother that most of her ''education'' on the subject of sex had not come from classrooms and textbooks, but from the lurid novels and how-to books smuggled in from time to time by Leila's classmates and examined late at night, by flashlight, under the covers, to the accompaniment of giggles, gasps of amazement and sometimes, outright horror.

Her mother sighed, reached for her and drew her close, in a way she had not done since Leila was a little girl. ''Then...you are truly all right? You are not afraid?''

As she fought back tears, Leila briefly considered lying. Then, trembling, she whispered, ''Mummy, I am *terrified*.''

''Oh, my dear one—''

''He is a stranger to me! *Who is he?* What is he like, this...Cade Gallagher? Mummy, I do not know him at all!''

''Then you will learn,'' said her mother in an unexpectedly firm voice, putting Leila away from her and making little brushing adjustments to her veils. ''And he will learn about you. And, God willing, you will continue doing so all the days of your lives. As your father and I have.''

''Mother?'' Leila brushed a tear. ''Did you know Father well before you married? Did you...love him?''

Alima considered that for a moment, and there was a

faraway look in her dark eyes. Then she smiled. ''I knew that he was a good man....'' Then she added more firmly, ''And I believe Cade Gallagher to be a good man, as well.''

She paused as Leila turned from her in frustration. Catching hold of her arm, she gave it a tug and said with exasperation, ''Leila, *you went to his room.* Have you forgotten? There must have been a reason. Perhaps you should try to remember what it was about Mr. Gallagher that made you do such an incredibly foolish thing! What made you decide, of all the men in the world, to pursue *him?*''

In the silence that followed, Leila heard her mother's words like an echo inside her head. *What was it about Mr. Gallagher? What was it...what was it?*

Once again she faced her own reflection in the mirror, but now her eyes saw another scene...a sunlit garden, bright with flowers and people and noisy with chatter and the shush of fountains...and a tall man in a pale gray suit and a western cowboy hat with his face lifted to follow the flight of a bird, smiling...eyes alight with wonder, like a child's. And she drew a long, unsteady breath.

Yes. That was it. The moment when I knew. Everything else came after....

For a long moment her own dark eyes gazed back at her. Then, carefully, she lifted the veils and pulled them forward so that they completely covered her face. They would not be lifted again until her husband drew them aside to look for the first time upon the face of his wife.

She turned to her mother and said in a voice without tremors, ''I am ready.''

It is true, she thought. *It is really happening. I am marrying Cade Gallagher from Texas. I am going to America.*

Chapter 6

"So this is Texas." Leila tried to keep any hint of disappointment out of her voice as she peered through the windows of the big American car at the jumble of tall buildings and looping ribbons of freeways filled with cars—so many cars, all moving slowly along like rivers of multicolored lava.

"It's *Houston*," her husband replied in that drawling way he spoke sometimes.

Glancing over at him, Leila saw that the corner of his mouth had lifted in a smile—a smile nothing at all like the one that had lit his face like sunshine when he turned in the palace garden to watch the flight of the bird. The one she held tightly in her memory as if to a sacred talisman. Nevertheless, she felt encouraged by it. She had seen him smile seldom enough in the twenty or so hours that she had been his wife.

His wife…I am a wife. He is my husband…. How many times had she repeated those words to herself, sitting beside him in airplanes and cars and airport lounges, standing with him in queues, facing him across restaurant tables? And still the words seemed unreal to her...totally without meaning.

Sitting beside him in the airplanes—that had been the worst part. Sitting so close to him, for hours and hours and hours on end! So close, even in the roomy first-class seats, that she could feel the heat of his body...smell his unfamiliar scent...and, if she was not *very* careful, sometimes her arm would brush against the sleeve of his jacket. When that happened, prickles would go through her body as if she had received an electric shock. Once...she must have fallen asleep, because she had awakened to discover that her head had been resting on his shoulder. Mortified, she had quickly made her apology, to which he had grunted a gruff reply. Then, looking uncomfortable and shifting restlessly about, he had offered her a pillow.

She had tried very hard to stay awake after that, and as a result now felt fuzzy-headed and queasy with exhaustion. But, she thought, mentally squaring her shoulders, I will not complain. She was a princess of Tamir, after all, and a married woman, not a child. And even as a child had been much too proud to show weakness or fear.

"It is not quite what I expected," she said lightly, letting her dimples show.

He threw her a glance, a very quick one since he was driving. "In what way?"

"I thought it would be more open—you know, like in the movies. Fewer people, fewer buildings... And," she added, gazing once more out of the windows, "not so many trees." In fact, she had never seen so many trees in all her life, not even in England. In some places they made solid curtains, like tapestries woven of green threads, on both sides of the highway.

Her husband laughed softly, deep down in his chest. She

had never heard him make that sound before, and she decided she liked it, very much. It made her feel warm, with quivers of laughter in her own insides.

"Like I said, this is Houston—that's *east* Texas. The kind of wide open spaces you're talking about, that's *west* Texas. Out in the hill country and beyond. I have a place— guess you could call it a ranch—out there." He threw her another of those tight, half-smiling glances. "Which I guess you'll probably see…eventually."

She caught her lip between her teeth to contain her excitement. "Are we going there now?"

He answered her again with laughter—indulgent this time. "Not hardly. It'd take the rest of today and most of tomorrow to drive out there. Texas is a bi-ig place."

"Yes," Leila said with a little shiver of suppressed delight, "I know." She felt her husband's eyes touch her, but did not turn to see what was in his glance.

Instead, looking through the window at the unending wall of trees, she asked, "You live here, then? In Houston?" And her momentary happiness evaporated with the realization that she knew so little about the man she had married—not even where he lived.

"Near there. We've got a ways to go, though, so if you want to, you can just put your head back and sleep."

"Oh, no," she said on a determined exhalation, "I don't want to miss anything."

"Wake up, Princess," said a deep and gentle voice, very near. "We're home."

Home. Leila's eyes opened wide and she jerked herself upright. Her heart was pumping very fast and she felt jangly from waking up too suddenly. She must have been disoriented, too, because the view through the car's windshield seemed oddly familiar to her, like something she had seen

in a movie. Not a western movie. Maybe one about the
American Civil War.

They were driving slowly down a long, straight avenue
with trees on both sides—not a solid wall, but huge trees
with great spreading branches that met overhead like a lacy
green canopy. Sunlight dappled the grassy drive with
splotches of gold, and somewhere in all those branches she
could hear birds singing—familiar music, but different
songs sung in different voices. Eager to hear them better,
she rolled down the car window, then gasped as what felt
like a hot, damp towel slapped her face.

Cade looked over at her and drawled, ''Might want to
keep that window closed,'' though she was already hurrying to do just that. ''You're probably not used to the humidity.''

A squirrel scampered across the road in front of them,
and Leila gave another gasp, this one of delight. Again
Cade glanced at her, but this time he didn't speak.

Now, far down at the end of the shaded avenue, the trees
were opening into a pool of sunlight. The driveway made
a circle around an expanse of bright green lawn bordered
by low-growing shrubs and flowers. On the other side of
the lawn, twin pillars made of brick with lanterns on top
flanked a shrub-and-flower-bordered walkway. The walkway led to brick steps and a wide brick porch with tall
white columns, and tall double doors painted a dark green
that almost matched the trees. On either side of the porch
and above it as well, large windows with many small panes
and white-painted shutters gave the red brick house a
sparkly-eyed, welcoming look.

Again, Leila drew breath and said, ''Oh...'' but this time
it was a long, murmuring sigh. She thought it a lovely
house—small compared to the royal palace of Tamir, but
plenty large enough for one family to live in.

Family. Are we, Cade and I...will we ever be...a family?

She felt a peculiar squeezing sensation around her heart.

Two people—a man and a woman—had come out of the tall green doors and were waiting for them, standing side by side on the porch between two of the white columns. Neither was tall, but the woman's head barely topped the man's shoulder.

He was thin and bony, with legs that bowed out, then came together again at his western-style boots, as if they had been specially made to fit around the girth of a horse. His white hair was slicked back and looked damp, and he had a thick gray moustache that almost covered his mouth, a stark contrast to skin as brown and wrinkled as the shell of a walnut. He wore blue jeans and in spite of the heat, a long-sleeved blue shirt. One gnarled hand, dangling at his side, held a sweat-stained cowboy hat.

The woman seemed almost as wide as she was tall, with a face as round and smooth as a coin. She had shiny black-currant eyes and skin the exact color of the gingerbread cookie people Leila had learned to love as a schoolgirl in Switzerland and England. Her hair, mostly black with only a few streaks of gray, was cut short and tightly curled all over her head, and she wore a loose cotton dress that was bright with flowers.

"That's Rueben and Betsy Flores," Cade said before Leila could ask, nodding his head toward the couple on the porch. "They take care of the place for me."

"They are your servants?"

He answered her with that sharp bark of laughter. "Well…they work for me. But they're more…friends. Or family."

"Ah," said Leila, nodding with complete understanding. Like Salma, she thought. "And…they live here also? With you?"

Cade shook his head. "They have their own place, down

by the creek.'' He stopped the car in front of the steps and turned off the motor.

Time to face the music, he thought. And inexplicably his heart was beating hard and fast, as if he was a teenager bringing a girl home to meet his parents. He took a sustaining breath and reached for the doorhandle.

But his bride's hand, small and urgent, clutched at his arm. In a low, choked-sounding voice she said, ''Did you tell them? Do they know?'' Turning, he saw panic in her eyes.

His throat tightened with that strange protective tenderness. ''It's okay, I called them from the airport in New York and filled them in.'' Except for the part about his new bride being a princess. And, he thought, even without that they're probably still in a state of shock. But impulsively, he put his hand over hers and gave it a squeeze before he reached once more for the doorhandle.

He went around the car and as he opened her door for her, leaned down and said in a low voice, ''I should warn you—Rueben's great with horses and dogs, but he's kind of shy with two-legged animals, so he probably won't say much. Betsy'll hug you. They were born in Mexico but now they're American through and through—I doubt they're much up on royal protocol.''

''That is quite all right,'' Leila said coolly. ''Since I am an American now, too.''

While he was still trying to think of a response to that, she belied it by extending a regal hand and allowing him to help her out of the car. She released him at once, though, and stood for a moment, squinting a little in the hot sunlight, smoothing the skirt and tugging at the jacket of the once-elegant, now badly wrinkled designer suit she'd worn all the way from Tamir. Then, before he could even think to offer her his arm, she slipped past him and started up the walk alone.

And for some reason, instead of hurrying to catch up with her, Cade stood there for a moment and watched the woman who was now his wife...slender and graceful in a travel-worn and rumpled suit the color of new lilacs, her head, with hair coming loose from its elegant twist, held proudly.

American? Well, maybe, he thought with something like awe. But somehow still every inch a princess.

As he watched his bride with dawning wonder, he was surprised by yet another alien emotion—an unexpected surge of pride. It made his eyes sting and his nose twitch, and he had to clear his throat before he went to join her on the porch.

He got there just in time to see her hold out her hand to Rueben and say in her musical, slightly accented voice, "Hello, I am Leila. You must be Rueben. I am very happy to meet you. Cade has told me so much about you."

It was a graceful little lie—he hadn't done any such thing. And he should have, he realized now. Lord knows he'd had plenty of time, all those hours on various planes and vehicles, waiting around in airports; time to tell her more than she probably wanted to know about himself, his home, his life. The truth was, he'd barely spoken to her at all during the trip home—just what was necessary between two strangers sharing the same space, no more. He tried to excuse his behavior now by telling himself it was because they'd both been in a state of shock, that he'd been trying to let her rest...sleep a little, which was hogwash. The reason he hadn't spoken was because he hadn't known what to say to her. He still didn't.

By this time, Leila had turned to Betsy, holding out her hand, face all decked out in dimples. "Hi, you must be—" was as far as she got, though, because just like he'd said she would, Betsy was already hugging the stuffing out of her, cooing to her like one of her little lost puppies.

And no sooner had that thought entered Cade's head than here they came—Betsy's mob of adopted mutts, barking and baying and wiggling and whining, falling over themselves and everybody else trying to be the first to slobber all over the newcomer.

In those first chaotic seconds Cade had his hands full, along with Rueben and Betsy, pushing and scolding and grabbing at collars. So he didn't notice right away that Leila had gone rigid as a post. By the time he did notice, she'd already started backing up, moving stiffly with tiny jerky steps, like a statue trying to walk. She kept backing up until she bumped into Cade's chest, then tried to back up some more, as if, he thought, she was trying to crawl inside his skin.

His first instinct was to wrap her in his arms and help her to do that any way he could. His heart was kicking like a crazy thing against her back and his skin had gone hot and prickly, as if he'd gotten too close to a fire.

Ignoring all that, he took her gently by her upper arms and moved her a couple of inches away from him, then leaned down to mutter gruffly in her ear. "They won't bite. They're just saying hello."

"Are they...yours?" Her voice was trying hard to be normal.

"Nah—they're Betsy's. She picks 'em up here and there. The woman can't resist a stray."

"I am sorry." The tiniest of tremors skated beneath his fingers. "I did not mean to be rude. I am not used to dogs—" she gave a breathless little laugh "—so *many* at one time."

Cade murmured, "Don't worry about it." His tongue felt thick and his thumbs wanted to stroke circles on the tender muscle hiding underneath the fabric of her jacket.

Meanwhile, Betsy and Rueben had managed to corral the dogs, not as many as they'd seemed, now that they were relatively still—only four, in fact. Somehow or other, Betsy managed to exchange her pair of dogs for Leila, and, cooing and fussing, maneuvered her through the pack and into the house. The front door closed firmly behind the two women, leaving Cade, Rueben and the dogs outside on the porch.

For several seconds the two men just stood there, saying nothing at all. Forgotten, the dogs scattered about their business, looking chastened or pleased with themselves, according to their various natures.

Cade cleared his throat and made a half turn. Rueben touched a hand to the top of his head and then, as if surprised to find it bare, resettled his hat into its customary place. He gave one shoulder a hitch. "Give y'hand with the suitcases?"

"Naw, in a little bit." Cade started down the steps, Rueben clumping stiff-legged beside him. Cade glanced over at him. "Things go okay while I was gone?"

Rueben hitched his shoulder again. "Sure. No problems."

At the bottom of the steps, both men turned by unspoken agreement and headed along the side of the house and around back toward the stables. "Suki have her foal yet?" Cade asked.

Rueben shook his head. "Two...maybe three more days."

"Yeah? How's she doing?"

"Doin' good...real good."

That was as far as conversation went, until they reached the stables.

Cade went to check on Suki first, naturally. She was his best mare—dapple gray with a black mane and tail, charcoal mask and legs, a real beauty—and this would be her first foal. Not that he was worried. If Rueben said she was doing okay, then she was. But he looked her over anyway, because it made him feel good doing it, and he and Rueben discussed her condition and care the way they always did, which was mostly mutters and grunts with the absolute minimum number of actual words. Then he went out to the paddock to look over the rest of his stock—two mares with spring foals and three more pregnant ones due later in the summer.

He was leaning on the fence railing watching the foals trotting around after their dams, fuzzy little brush tails twitching busily at flies, when Rueben came to join him.

"Doin' real good," he said.

Cade nodded. He'd been wondering why the sight wasn't giving his spirits a boost the way it was supposed to.

"So," said Rueben after a silence, "you got married, huh?"

Cade surprised himself with a hard little nugget of laughter, which he gulped back guiltily. "Yeah...I guess I did."

"Pretty sudden."

He didn't try to stop the laugh this time. "You could say that."

Rueben mulled that over. "Pretty girl," he said after awhile, nodding his head in a thoughtful way.

Cade nodded, too. "Yeah..." and he changed the nod to a wondering little shake "...she is that."

"Seems nice," said Rueben. He stared hard at the toes of his boots, then kicked at the dirt a couple of times, and finally turned to offer Cade his hand. "Congratulations."

They shook, and Rueben gave his shoulder a hitch. "I'm gonna go get those suitcases now." He walked rapidly away in the bowlegged, rump-sprung way older men do when they've spent a good part of their lives sitting on the back of a horse.

Cade thought about going to help him, but for some reason didn't. He stayed where he was, leaning on the fence, watching the foals cavort in the sunshine, smelling the familiar smells of grass and straw and horse manure, feeling the humidity settle around him like a favorite old shirt. This was his world. It was where he belonged. It was good to be home. *Home...*

And then he thought, *What in heaven's name have I done?*

Having suffered through the pain of his parents' divorce at an age when his own adolescent struggles were just getting underway, he'd come to believe with all his heart and soul that if two people got married it ought to be forever. It was why he'd never been tempted to try it himself—he just didn't think he had it in him to make that kind of commitment. And here he was, not only had he gone and committed himself, but to a girl ten years younger, from the other side of the world, with whom he had nothing in common with, and barely knew!

He patted his shirt pocket, looking for the comfort of a cheroot, which Betsy wouldn't let him smoke in the house. Then, remembering they were still packed away in a suitcase, he gazed up into the milky haze and sighed.

It wouldn't have been so bad, he thought, but...well, it was what Rueben had said. Leila was a *very* pretty girl—downright beautiful, actually—but more than that, yes, she was *nice.* Sure, she was a princess, and spoiled and pampered and very, very young. But she had a bright and buoyant spirit. And he'd come to realize, even in the short time he'd known her, that she also had a kind and loving heart. She deserved someone who would love her back, someone who would make her happy. As he was certain he never would.

His chest swelled and tightened, suddenly, with that familiar surge of protective tenderness, and he brought his closed fist down hard on the fence railing. *Dammit,* he thought, I can't do this to her. *I can't.*

At the time, he remembered, it had seemed to him he'd

had no choice. Converting...marrying Leila...it had looked like the only reasonable course of action open to him. But that had been back *there,* in *The Arabian Nights* world of Tamir. Here, with the green grass of Texas under his boots, he knew it was impossible. Not so much the conversion—he'd never had any particular religious beliefs one way or another, so what difference did it make what label he carried? But marriage, now, that was different. Marriage involved somebody else, not just him. In this case, a nice, lovely girl. A princess. *And a virgin princess, at that.*

His fist tightened on the fence railing. Somehow or other, he was going to have to find a way out of this—for both their sakes. And in the meantime...well, the very least he could do, Cade figured, was see that the virgin princess came out of this marriage in the same condition as when she went in....

It was late—almost midnight—and Leila was growing more nervous and apprehensive by the minute. Surely, she told herself, Cade would come soon. He *must* be tired after such a long journey. Why did he not come to bed?

This was his bedchamber—bed*room*—she must remember to call it that, now that she was to be an American. Betsy had told her so. "And yours, now, too," the round, kind-faced woman had said, and had given Leila's hand a happy squeeze.

Betsy's husband, Rueben, had brought her suitcases here along with Cade's, and then Betsy had helped her with the unpacking until it was time for her to go and prepare the evening meal. She had even rearranged things in the dresser drawers and spacious closets to make room for Leila's things. So few things, really—she had left Tamir in such a hurry. The rest of her belongings would be packed into boxes and shipped to her later, though where she would find room for them all here was a mystery to her.

But would she even need so many things...so many beautiful clothes, hats, designer shoes...now that she was married to Cade Gallagher and living in Houston, Texas? She didn't know. There were so many things she didn't know.

It had all happened so fast. She had barely had time to say goodbye to her mother and sisters, to Salma, and Nargis. Thinking about them now, she felt a frightened, hollow feeling, and for one panicky moment was afraid she might begin to cry. She took several deep breaths and blinked hard until the feeling went away. *I must not cry—what would Cade think?*

Perhaps it was just that she was so tired. It seemed a lifetime since she had slept. Cade's bed—big and wide and covered with a puffy comforter in masculine colors, a burgundy, blue-and-green paisley print—looked inviting. But Leila didn't dare to lie down. She didn't dare even sit. In fact, she had taken to pacing, not so much out of nervousness, although she definitely was, but because she was afraid if she stopped moving she would fall asleep. She had refused wine at dinner for the same reason—even the mild vintages at home made her sleepy.

Cade, she had noticed, drank strong black coffee with his meal, and afterward a small glassful of something the same golden brown color as his eyes. Bourbon, he said it was, when she asked. After that he had excused himself and gone into his study—to make some phone calls, he told her.

Betsy had shown her Cade's study, on her tour of the house. To Leila it had seemed the most fascinating of rooms, full of photographs and books and all sorts of personal things that belonged to Cade. There had been a photograph of Cade with his mother and father, taken when Cade was very young, and Leila remembered that Kitty had told her that Cade's mother and father were both dead. She had felt a warm little flash of sadness for the eager-looking golden-haired boy in the picture. There had been a black-and-white photograph of a bearded man dressed in overalls, standing amongst a forest of tall wooden oil derricks—Cade's grandfather, Betsy had told her, and he had been a "wildcatter." *What was a wildcatter?* Leila had longed to ask that question and so many others, to study the pictures and ask about them...to learn more about the stranger who was her husband.

But there had not been time, then. And after dinner Cade had gone into his study and Leila had dared not intrude.

Instead, she had gone alone to this, the bedroom they would share, to prepare herself for bed. And for her husband.

Butterflies. Oh yes, they were all over inside her, not just in her stomach, but everywhere under her skin. They had caught up with her in the bathroom she and Cade were to share, as she arranged her personal things, her bottles and jars of powders and scents, oils and lotions, her hair brushes, toothpaste and shampoo. There were two sinks, one of which, she assumed, was meant to be hers. The other, barely an arm's length away, was Cade's. And yes, there were *his* personal things, neatly arranged around it.

Daringly, unable to help herself, she picked up a bottle labeled Aftershave Lotion and sniffed it. So this is my husband's scent, she thought. But it was not yet familiar to her. She closed her eyes and tried to imagine him there next to her, brushing his teeth, shaving, patting the spicy lotion onto his smooth, clean skin...and all the while the butterflies frolicked merrily.

She tried to relax away the butterflies in a warm bath scented with jasmine, but although the water made her limbs and muscles feel warm and limp and heavy, the hard fluttery knot in her belly remained. And there was something else—a new, squirmy, quivery feeling between her legs. When she put her hand there and pressed against the quivering, she felt her pulse in the soft places beneath her fingertips, a slow, heavy pace.

She thought, then, about what Salma had told her, that there might be pain the first time she made love with a man. She thought of the bottle of soothing oil her former nanny, with tears in her eyes, had pressed into her hands as she was helping her to pack. A cold little gust of homesickness and dread swept through her, taking away the butterflies and leaving a great hollow void in their place.

I must not be afraid. A woman's first duty as a wife was to please her husband sexually. How could a man—how could Cade—find pleasure in sex if he knew that his wife was afraid? Clearly, there was only one thing to be done. *I must think of some way to not be afraid.*

And no sooner had she thought that, lying there in the water's warm embrace, with the sweet scent of jasmine melting into her pores and seeping into her senses, then here came the memories...vivid, tactile memories... sweeping away all thoughts of Salma and pain and homesickness and fear.

Cade's chest...a landscape of gentle hills and unexpected valleys her lips had explored like a greedy treasure hunter on the trail of lost gold...smooth, warm skin and a musky scent, unfamiliar but intoxicating as wine...the hard little buttons of his nipples...an intriguing texture of hair that tickled when she touched it with her nose....

The throbbing between her legs became heavier. She arched and squirmed sinuously as, under the water, her hands slid over her body, unconsciously following the same paths as the images in her mind. But, oh, what a difference there was between her own curves, and the hard planes and sculpted hollows of the male body she remembered...the body that invaded her thoughts, quickening her pulse and heating her cheeks at the most unexpected and inappropriate times. Cade's body. And now, her husband's.

My husband...will he desire me now? Now that I am his wife? Will he kiss me again the way he did that night on the terrace?

Her heart gave a sickening lurch, as though it were trying to turn upside down inside her chest. Trembling like someone just risen from a sickbed, Leila climbed out of the bathtub and wrapped herself in a thick, soft towel. She dried herself quickly, ignoring the shivers, then bravely tossed aside the towel and naked, faced her blurred reflection in the steam-fogged mirror. With her lips pursed in a thoughtful pout, she turned this way and that, trying to see herself from all angles. Yes...her breasts were full and yet still firm, with the nipples tightened now into hard, tawny buds...hips also full, but, she thought, not *too* wide...slender waist and firm, flat stomach...thighs well-muscled—probably from horseback riding—and her buttocks, what she could see of them, round and smooth, and, she hoped, not *too* big.

Almost as an afterthought, with a defiant little flourish, she pulled out the combs and pins that held her hair high atop her head and let it tumble, thick and dark, down her back and over her shoulders. As she watched it her breathing quickened. Her lips parted and a rosy flush spread across her cheeks. The eyes that looked back at her in the mirror seemed to kindle and glow, as if from a fire somewhere in their depths.

He kissed me. He desired me then, I know he did.

Confidence welled up in her like a fountain, and her thirsty soul found it more intoxicating, more erotic than wine. *He desired me once, and I will make him desire me again.*

Buoyed on a magic carpet of restored self-confidence and new resolve, Leila brushed her teeth and her hair and rubbed her skin with scented oil until it felt soft and smooth as silk. She put on a modest but alluring gown in a soft, shimmery blue-green—the color of the water in a shallow cove near the palace where she and her sisters liked to swim and sunbathe. Somewhere along the line she noticed that the butterflies had come back, although now it did not seem at all an unpleasant sensation.

I am ready, she thought as she paced nervously, glancing from time to time at the clock on Cade's bedside table. *Ready for my husband...*

It was half past midnight when she heard the creak and scuffle of footsteps outside Cade's bedroom door. Her heart skittered and bolted like the squirrel she had seen that afternoon in the lane as she watched the doorknob slowly turn and the door swish inward, silent and stealthy as a thief in the night, to frame the tall, imposing figure of her husband.

For a moment he hesitated, looking as if he wasn't sure whether he'd got the right room. Then he stepped through the doorway and carefully closed the door behind him. All the while his eyes never left her face, and they reflected the glow of the lamps she'd turned on low beside the bed so that they seemed to catch fire and flare hot as he looked at her.

Her stomach gave a lurch as the magic carpet of confidence she'd been riding on went into a steep crash dive.

Chapter 7

She was every man's dream. And Cade's worst nightmare.

He'd just about driven himself crazy, trying to think what he was going to do about this, his so-called wedding night. How did a man avoid consummating a marriage that never should have happened in the first place, without seeming to reject the woman he'd married and had already thoroughly humiliated once?

In the end, it had seemed to him that the best course of action was also the easiest one: Do nothing at all. If he stalled long enough, he reasoned, Leila was bound to fall asleep, as thoroughly jet-lagged as she must be. Then he could tiptoe in, snag his overnight bag and sneak off to the guest room, and his excuse would be that she needed her rest and he hadn't wanted to disturb her—what a considerate guy he was. Tomorrow morning early he'd be off to work, and after that—well, he had the pretty good excuse of a prior commitment, a weekend hunting trip to the ranch with a client he was trying to woo. No reason he couldn't arrange to fly out a day early, if the client was willing.

On Sunday when he got back, he'd sit Leila down and have a serious talk with her, and they could both try to figure out what they were going to do. By then, he told himself, they'd both be rested up and thinking clearly, and between them they ought to be able to come up with a way out of this farce with a minimum amount of embarrassment for all parties concerned.

It had seemed so reasonable to him, sitting there in his study sipping bourbon and enjoying a cheroot he knew he was going to catch hell for from Betsy tomorrow. He'd dozed a little bit in his chair and woken up stiff and groggy to find that it was well past midnight. Thank God, he'd thought, figuring there was no way in hell Leila would be awake at that hour. It ought to be safe to venture into his own bedroom.

Reeling with the effects of travel fatigue and whiskey, he'd mounted the stairs and made his way down the hallway, conscious of the silence all around him and his heartbeat ticktocking away like an old-fashioned grandfather clock. He was used to the silence of an empty house, but it was odd, he thought, how weighty silence seemed in a house that wasn't as empty as it should be. He was thinking about that, about the usual silence and emptiness of his house at night, when he turned the knob and pushed open his bedroom door.

Then his only thought was: Oh God, what now?

There she was, not only awake but looking like the overture to some erotic dream, a vision in sea-green silk that covered every inch but failed to disguise one centimeter of her curves, her hair cascading down around her shoulders like midnight rain. Every man's dream…his worst nightmare.

He didn't know how long he stood there in the doorway looking at her. Just looking at her, with all sorts of emotions shooting off in every direction inside him so that for a moment his brain function felt more than anything like an explosion in a fireworks factory. *Now what?* What was he supposed to say to her? He couldn't think of a thing.

It came to him gradually, as the shock subsided and his mind began functioning again, that he'd made a serious miscalculation. With all that had happened, he'd forgotten that, from almost the first moment he'd laid eyes on Leila Kamal, he'd wanted her.

He remembered it now. He remembered that the idea had amused him at the time, that he'd laughed at himself for his adolescent foolishness. He wasn't laughing now.

"You're still up," he finally said—as inane an observation as ever there was.

"I waited for you." She said it without a trace of seduction in her voice, facing him bravely with the light from a bedside lamp shimmering in her hair and making deep, dark mysteries of her eyes. She looked so incredibly beautiful…and nothing at all like the buoyant, flirtatious girl he remembered meeting in Tamir. Right now what she looked like more than anything was a virgin waiting to be sacrificed.

"You shouldn't have," he said, but in a gentle tone to temper the abruptness of it. He launched into his prepared justifications as he came into the room, keeping at a wary distance from her like a hiker circling a pit of quicksand. "Look…Leila. You've had a long day—you must be tired. I know I am." He stifled an ostentatious yawn. "I, uh…had a few things I needed to take care of—business things that couldn't wait." He brushed them aside with a diffident wave of his hand. "Things pile up when I'm away. I'm going to be doing a lot of catching up during the next several days.…"

"Oh yes," she murmured, "I understand."

For some reason her acquiescence annoyed him, made him feel fraudulent and unworthy. He cleared his throat and ventured a look at her, squinting as if she were a light too bright for his eyes. He continued almost defiantly, "In fact, there's something—this weekend I have a thing I'm supposed to do—I promised a client I'd take him hunting out at the ranch."

A frown appeared between her eyebrows. "The...ranch?"

"Yeah—I told you about it—west Texas?"

"Oh—yes, yes—I remember." She sounded eager, now. "And you will fly there in your airplane?"

His insides writhed with guilt. Furious with himself for it, furious with her for making him feel it, he fought the urge to fidget and cleared his throat instead. "I'll be leaving tomorrow, actually. Straight from work. So I won't be—"

"Tomorrow?" He could hear a different breathiness in her voice now...unmistakable touches of panic.

"Look—I'm sorry. It's been scheduled for a while. It's a client—I couldn't very well cancel at the last minute." Cade chose that moment to escape into his bathroom, too cowardly to risk another look at her. He didn't need to see the shock, dismay and disappointment he knew would be written all over her face...that incredibly expressive face that sometimes seemed to him like watching a video tape on fast forward.

Just inside the bathroom doorway, again he stopped dead.

In only a matter of hours his bathroom had become an alien place. A lush and steamy greenhouse garden, redolent of all sorts of flowery, exotic scents, where jewel-toned bottles sprouted like mushrooms from the marble countertops and a rainbow of fabrics intertwined with the more subtle hues of damp towels bloomed in tropical profusion over every available surface.

Closing his mind to both the chaos and the disturbingly evocative smells, Cade set about gathering up the toiletries Betsy had unpacked for him, putting them back in their travel case. And while he was doing that he went on glibly talking, telling Leila in a logical, reasonable way how he thought she should spend the time while he was gone, catching up on her rest, settling in, getting to know the place...

But not too well, he reminded himself. No sense in her getting too settled in and comfortable here. This "marriage" was only going to be temporary, after all.

Listening to himself talk like that, without Leila's disturbing presence to distract him and just the sound of his own voice and his reassuringly normal reflection glaring back at him from the mirrors, he could feel his selfassurance coming back. Everything he said sounded reasonable and sane—even logical and wise. And why shouldn't it? He was Cade Gallagher, successful Texas businessman, a self-made man who'd had his first few million under his belt before his thirty-fifth birthday. A man with a far-ranging and well-earned reputation as a dealmaker, a man who knew how to play the game—and win.

Play the game...and win.

It came to him then, a flash of self-awareness like a spotlight trained on a dark corner of his soul, just what had happened to him back there in Tamir. In the first place, he'd gone to Elena's wedding with a business deal in mind. Once there, he'd gotten so caught up in the game and so blinded by the idea of winning, he'd lost his perspective. In order to win the game he'd let himself be coerced into marrying a woman he didn't love, with whom he had nothing whatsoever in common.

But the truth was, he didn't need this "win." He didn't need the old sheik's oil deal. He'd made his millions right here in Texas, and there was plenty more where that came from.

He'd been an ambitious fool and had paid the price, but

all was not lost. He could still get out of this. He could still get his life back.

Just as long as he did not consummate this marriage.

That was it—the key to his deliverance. Because, from what he'd learned of Leila's culture so far, it seemed to him that when it came to marriage, it was all about the *consummation.* Even the *Walima,* the marriage feast, was to celebrate, not the wedding, but the consummation. The way Cade saw it, so long as he didn't make love to his wife, he wasn't even really married.

No problem. So what if she was one of the most beautiful and seductive women he'd ever seen in his life? He was thirty-six years old—a grown man, not a randy teenager. The image that looked back at him in the mirror was confident and mature…eyes world-weary, smile wry, eyebrows set at a sardonic tilt. Yes, he told himself, he had more than enough willpower, he ought to be able to resist one little black-eyed virgin princess.

He picked up his toiletry kit and turned around. And there she was, the virgin princess herself, standing in the bathroom doorway, filling it up so his only escape was going to have to be either through her or over her. Unless she moved out of his way, which she was showing no inclination to do.

As a test of that theory, he took a step toward her. Sure enough, she didn't budge an inch. Instead she watched him with great luminous eyes, and he saw her lips slowly part.

Apprehension shivered through his insides. He took another step…and another. Only a foot or so separated them now. And then she did move, but not away from him. Instead, she lifted one soft, scented hand and laid it alongside his jaw, a touch as cool and light as a flower. His heart began to pound.

''Leila—'' With no spit at all in his mouth, it was all the sound he could manage.

She didn't say a word, just touched one petal-like finger to his lips and shook her head. For a long and terrifying moment she looked deeply into his eyes, and he no longer felt the least bit logical or wise. Then she stretched way up on her tiptoes and kissed him.

His heart and stomach performed impossible acrobatic maneuvers and shimmers of panic danced behind his closed eyelids. His confidence had already evaporated. He snatched at a breath that seared the inside of his chest while every impulse and desire in him pleaded with him to give in…to kiss her back and then some. To carry her to his bed and make love to her for what was left of tonight and let tomorrow and the rest of his future—and hers—take care of themselves.

He might have done it. He wasn't sure what would have happened, in fact, if he'd had both hands free. As it was, while one hand, already tingling with anticipation of the feel of her, hovered indecisively inches from her shoulder, his other hand, filled with the small leather case that held his toiletries, made a lump, a slight but significant barrier between his chest and hers. One she couldn't ignore.

She drew back, one of her hands still resting on his shoulder, and looked down at it. After a long moment, her eyes came back to his. "I do not understand," she said in a husky voice. "These are your personal things. Why do you need them? Where are you taking them? Now… tonight?"

The air seemed to back up in Cade's chest. His tongue felt thick as he tried to explain. "I…uh, I thought I'd, you know, sleep in the guestroom—it's just across the hall…" Why did he feel like an inept thief trying to explain the goodies in his sack, an unprepared schoolboy without his homework?

"But, this is your bedcham—*bedroom*." She wasn't touching him at all, now, but somehow he knew she was trembling. "Betsy told me. If you do not wish me—" She broke off suddenly, as if she'd been choked, and swallowed hard several times. Then he saw her body stiffen and her chin lift, and his own heart sank. With her face now pale and frozen as a statue, she said in a proud and quiet voice he'd never heard before, "If you do not wish me to sleep here with you in your bedroom, then you must tell me. It is I who should move to the guestroom, not you."

"It's only for tonight," he heard himself say, as his free hand doublecrossed him by lifting to her cheek. He felt himself brushing it with the backs of his fingers, and it was hot and smooth, like the skin of a ripe peach. What the hell was he doing? And why had he ever imagined this would be easy?

"We are both so tired," he gently explained, "and I'm pretty sure if we share a bed tonight, neither of us will get any sleep. There'll be other nights...." Was it a lie? He didn't even know for sure. And if it was, why did it come so easily to him? He wasn't—or never had been—a dishonest man. "We'll have plenty of time. When I get back. Tonight...you just rest, okay?" He ducked his head and touched his lips to her forehead. He'd never felt so confused and ashamed of himself. "Get some sleep," he said huskily, and walked away and left her there.

Leila woke up in a very large bed and for a moment could not think where she was. She felt sweaty and her heart pounded the way it had sometimes done when she was a very little girl, waking from a nightmare she could not remember.

But she was not a little girl, and there was no Salma to stroke her hair and kiss her cheek and tell her everything was all right. And besides, she remembered it all, now. She was in Texas, in America, and the wife of a man named

Cade Gallagher, whom she did not know. And did not understand at all!

In Tamir he had kissed her. She understood that well enough. He had desired her then—surely she had not been wrong about that. And now that she was his wife, he did not seem to want to kiss her at all.

And yet...he had been kind to her. Considerate, yes, and even tender. She stretched languorously, pushing her arms amongst the pillows, then lightly touched the place on her forehead where he had kissed her. The memory of his lips, how warm and smooth they had felt against her skin, made a startling little shiver go through her.

And—she realized it now, though she'd been too humiliated at the time to appreciate the fact—he'd actually proposed marriage to her to save her from public disgrace! A foolish thing to do, but in a way very sweet....

Sweet? She remembered now—that was what Elena's friend Kitty had said about Cade. That he was sweet, like a... what was it? *A marshmallow?* Leila actually giggled; it had seemed then, and still did seem a very unlikely way to describe a man.

Maybe—the thought came suddenly—it was not such a good thing for a man to be *too* sweet. At least, not *all* the time.

But her outlook was brighter as she threw back the covers. She felt much more like her usual buoyant self. It was as Cade had said, that they both had been very tired yesterday, from all the traveling and the emotional stress of what had come before. Her husband had been right, and wise, to postpone consummating their marriage until they had both had a chance to rest and—how had he put it?— yes, *settle in.*

Little shivers rippled through her as she dressed for the day in cool gray slacks and a simple white blouse. *It is true—it has really happened. I am in America—in Texas!*

A married woman! Over and over she said those words to herself, adding to those another, perhaps incongruous thought, *I am free!*

She realized that for most women marriage might mean the opposite of freedom, but for her it seemed to promise endless possibilities. Yes, she was a wife, and she would work hard to be a good one. *But she was in America.* Here she could do anything—go to college, become a doctor, or a teacher—perhaps even a lawyer, or the head of her own company, like Elena. No longer would people laugh indulgently at her and treat her like a child. She was Mrs. Cade Gallagher, and she was in America. *She was free.*

She told herself these things, but in a state of fearful wonderment, not quite able to believe they were true—like a caged bird who hasn't yet realized that the door has been left open, or a child too young to grasp the fact that the wonderful new toys in the gaily wrapped packages are hers to keep. This is my house, she thought as she walked slowly down the curving staircase, trailing her fingers on the polished wood banister. *This is our home...mine and Cade's.* The thought produced more of those happy shivers, and she was biting her lip and smiling as she went into the kitchen, like a child with a secret.

Betsy was standing at the sink, stemming strawberries and singing along with the music from a radio turned down low. When Leila said "Good morning!" she turned with a little cry and a smile of welcome that made her cheeks look round as pomegranates. "You're awake! I bet you're hungry. Sit down, sit down—I'll make you some lunch."

"Lunch!" Leila looked for a clock. "What time is it?"

Betsy leaned sideways to peer at a digital clock on the back of a gleaming white stove. "Almost two."

"Two! In the afternoon? But—I have never slept so late!"

"Jet lag," said Betsy, waving a hand. "Take you a couple days to adjust. Here—have some strawberries. They're pretty good right now—don't even need sugar. I thought I'd leave a bowl in the fridge for you—they'll be good for your breakfast tomorrow, too.'' She pushed a blue bowl heaped high with the berries over in front of Leila and put a fork beside it.

Leila picked up a berry with her fingers and closed her eyes as she bit into it, wondering how Betsy could have guessed that strawberries were one of her favorite foods.

''I guess Cade told you he's not going to be home tonight—got a business trip this weekend.'' Betsy sounded wary.

''Yes, I know.'' Leila picked up another berry. ''This afternoon I think I would like to see the outside—the horses.''

''You sure?'' Betsy seemed relieved as she cocked an eyebrow. ''It gets hot out there, middle of the afternoon.''

''That is good, I like the heat,'' said Leila, showing her dimples. ''It will make me feel as if I am at home.''

Betsy gave her a doubtful, sideways look as she opened the refrigerator. ''If you say so, hon.''

Leila ate a delicious meal of strawberries and a chicken salad made with strips of roasted sweet red peppers and pecans, sitting in a breakfast room with a wall of windows that looked out on a swimming pool surrounded by lawns and flower gardens. Beyond that she could not see, because of course there were more trees, making walls of green all around the garden. She also drank a very delicious iced beverage made with tea and lemon and a great deal of sugar. If I am not careful I will get fat, here in America, she thought.

When she had finished her lunch, Leila opened a door in the breakfast room and stepped out onto a flagstone patio. Once again she gasped involuntarily when she felt the slap of hot, wet air, and heard Betsy call out from the kitchen, "I told you."

I keep forgetting about the humidity, Leila thought as she forced herself to breathe the thick, soupy air. But it was only a small thing, and she would get used to it.

She lingered at the pool, pausing to trail her fingers in the clear, tepid water and sniff some roses that had no scent. Then she set off briskly, following a flagstone pathway that led along the side of the house and through a wrought-iron gate. Just past the gate she came to the corner of the house, and there the walls of greenery ended. Interrupted by only a few very large trees and bisected by a curving gravel lane, the grassy ground swept away to the stables, which were made of wood, painted white with green trim. Beyond the stables were fields and paddocks of emerald green, ringed by white-painted fences, and in the paddocks she could see horses—mares with foals!—and Rueben, leaning on the fence, watching them.

Her heart quickened with excitement and she no longer noticed the heat and humidity. As she hurried along the gravel lane she was thinking, *These are Cade's horses— my husband's horses.* And, with a sense of awe, *Mine, too.*

As she came nearer to the paddock where the man stood vigil, she could see that it held only a mare with a mottled gray body, darker face and legs, and jet-black mane and tail.

"She is very beautiful," she said as she joined Rueben at the fence, keeping a respectful distance between them. She did not ask what was obvious, even to her, but after a moment said, "She will have her foal very soon, I think."

Rueben glanced briefly at her, as if she had surprised him, then looked back at the mare and nodded. "Maybe today...maybe tonight. Maybe tomorrow."

Leila didn't say anything, but her insides had those joyful shivers again. The birth of a foal—she had never seen such a thing. It must be the most wonderful thing that could happen, she thought. She wondered...she hoped...if she was very careful not to get in the way, if Rueben might let her watch.

But that would be later. Right now there was something else she wanted to ask him, and after a long and oddly comfortable silence, she did. "The horses that are here—are there any that may be ridden?"

He gave her that look of surprise. "You like to ride?"

"Oh, yes," Leila breathed, "very much."

Rueben lifted up a shoulder. "Okay, sure—we got a couple that're real gentle..." Leila didn't tell him that "gentle" was the last thing she wanted. "Not right now, though," said Rueben. "Too hot. Maybe this evening. Tomorrow morning."

"Thank you," said Leila. "I would like that very much. And...where can I ride? Only here, in the pastures...?"

"The pastures, sure." Rueben gave his shoulder another hitch. "There's a trail, too. Goes down along the creek."

Leila nodded, but didn't say anything. She was looking at the neat green paddocks with their white rail fences, and remembering her dream about riding across endless plains with the wind in her face and her hair blowing free. So, here I am in America, in Texas, she thought. But...where are the vistas?

"You want to ride, tell me," said Rueben. "I fix you up."

"Thank you," said Leila softly. She turned away from the paddocks and walked slowly back to the house.

She woke in the darkness and was strangely wide awake and rested. Jet lag, she thought, stretching her body in the great wide bed she had yet to share with her husband. *My days and nights are turned around.*

Knowing it would be useless to try to sleep any longer,

she threw back the covers and got out of bed. Without turning on the light she made her way to the window and stood with her arms around herself, looking out on the shadowy, dark landscape.

"This is Texas...America."

She said the words deliberately as she had been saying them over and over to herself all day, but they failed to give her those joyous and optimistic shivers. Around her the house was empty and still, and there was a hollow feeling of loneliness inside her. She missed Tamir, and the palace that was always so full of people—her family, the servants. She remembered that she had sometimes had to steal away to secret corners of the gardens to find moments to herself. Now, as the silence of the house pressed in around her, she would have given almost anything for the sounds of laughter...people's voices.

But...there—surely that was a light! She peered into the thick gray darkness, trying to see through the deeper blackness of trees, remembering that earlier she had seen glimpses of the stables through the leaves and branches. Excitement gave a kick beneath her ribs. Rueben had told her the mare, Suki, would have her foal soon. *Maybe today...maybe tonight...*

Without stopping to think whether or not she should, Leila turned from the window and was already pulling her nightgown over her head. She dressed quickly in the same slacks and blouse she'd worn that day, slipped bare feet into her shoes and ran down the stairs. At the back entrance she remembered just in time to turn off the security alarm before opening the door.

This time she was ready for the warm, wet slap of humidity. What she hadn't expected was the noise. Inside the well-insulated and air-conditioned house she hadn't realized how loud the night was, in this place of so many trees and lush vegetation, so many ponds and fields and streams.

All around her the night was filled with sounds—busy sounds, ratcheting, chirping, hooting, clicking, screeching sounds.

After the first surprise, Leila decided she liked the racket. *And here I thought that I was alone.* She almost felt like singing along with the night creatures herself as she found her way along the flagstone path. To be out alone in the night gave her shivery feelings of excitement, anticipation and a delicious sense of adventure.

She unlatched the gate and slipped silently through. And her nice little shivers exploded all through her muscles like slivers of steel. Her scalp bloomed with prickles and her heart rocketed into her throat. All of a sudden the night was full of large warm bodies, wiggling, snuffling shifting bodies, pressing in on her from all sides. As her back slammed against the gate she sucked in air and whispered, "Oh— good dogs…nice…dogs…"

Something warm and wet slapped the back of her hand— then the other hand as well. She moved her fingers and felt them burrow through silky-soft fur. She could hear coming from the squirming, waggling shapes little whines and whimpers and panting sounds that sounded like laughter. Friendly sounds.

Taking a deep breath and summoning her courage, she pushed away from the gate and took several tentative steps. The dogs moved with her, arranging themselves in front and in back and on both sides of her, keeping just out of range of her feet as she walked. Just like my father's bodyguards, she thought, as the last vestiges of her fear slipped away.

The dogs followed her to the stable door, but made no move to go inside with her. Clearly, they knew this was not allowed.

Although the lights were on in the stable, no one was inside. Finding her way through a stall filled with sweet, clean straw, Leila found herself in the paddock where she had seen the mare, Suki, that afternoon. There, in a corner of the paddock just to the left outside the doorway in which she stood, by the light leaking through the stall's half doors, she could see the mare's pale shape lying on the darker grass. Rueben was there, too, crouched on one knee with his fingers braced on the ground, like a runner at the start of a race.

Leila ventured toward them as silently as she knew how. Rueben glanced at her as she crouched down beside him, but without much surprise—almost, it seemed to her, as if he had expected her to come.

"She's not doin' so good," he said in a low voice.

"What is the matter?" Leila breathlessly whispered back.

"Got halfway and quit. Happens sometimes. I think she'll be okay, though—just have to give her a little help."

"Help?"

"Yeah…gonna pull a little bit. She should start pushing on her own then."

"Should she not be inside, in the stable?" Leila's heart was beating very hard.

Rueben lifted one shoulder in his familiar shrug. "She's where she wants to be. Horses are meant to have their babies in the open. It's their nature. If the weather's bad, I bring her inside. When it's nice like this, I let her choose." He pushed himself up from his crouch. Leila did the same.

"What can I do to help?" she whispered.

He nodded toward the mare, who had her head up and was quietly watching them. "You can keep her calm, if you want. Just pet her…talk to her. Rub her under her jaw, like this…"

Leila nodded and began to move cautiously toward the mare's head, crooning to her softly in Arabic, the language her nanny had used to soothe her when she was a baby.

Her heart hammered and her lungs ached as she felt the slick, warm horsehide beneath her fingers, and smelled the familiar salty horse-smell. The mare gave a little whicker of uncertainty as Leila began to stroke her sweat-damp neck, but didn't try to rise. "Beautiful, noble lady..." Leila murmured. "You must be strong...you must have the courage of a lioness."

The mare grunted. Leila felt the surge of powerful muscles, and then a groan that seemed to come from deep inside the mare's belly.

"That's it—she's pushin' good now," said Rueben after a moment, panting a little. "Okay...okay—that's good. Let her go—she'll do it herself now, I think."

Leila pushed herself away from the mare's surging body and scrambled around to join Rueben just in time to see the foal's body slither onto the grass like a puddle of spilled ink.

"Nice filly," said Rueben. "Nice big girl."

"Is she all right?" Leila asked fearfully. The foal had not moved. Leila's heart was knocking painfully; she felt as if she could not breathe. "Is she...dead? She is not breathing."

"She'll be okay." Rueben pulled his white T-shirt off over his head. "Here—wipe her head a little bit," he said as he tossed it to her.

Then she was on her knees in the wet grass, trying not to shake as she wiped frantically at the film of mucus that covered the foal's mouth and nose. Sweat trickled down her sides, dripped from her nose and ran stinging into her eyes. She kept making desperate little whimpering noises, but didn't realize then that she was crying. Not until the foal suddenly jerked her head up and shook it hard, her long ears making a slapping sound against her neck.

"She'll be fine now," said Rueben, as Leila collapsed

backward onto the seat of her pants with a loud, quivering sob.

But she was laughing, too. Laughing and sobbing as she gathered the newborn foal's head into her arms and pressed her cheek to its soaking wet hide.

Chapter 8

Betsy and Rueben were in the kitchen when Leila came down to breakfast the morning after the birth of the foal. She'd heard their voices and didn't mean to listen in, but then she'd heard her own name and naturally that made her hesitate.

"I wish you could have seen her, Bets. That black hair of hers—you couldn't tell which was her and which was the filly."

Rueben's chuckle was lost in a loud metallic clang. "I wish *he* could have seen her, that's what *I* wish. He should have been here." Betsy's voice sounded angry. "Ooh, sometimes that man... Brings home a new bride and then goes off and leaves her!"

"He said it was business." She couldn't see it, but Leila knew Rueben had lifted a shoulder in his special little shrug.

"Huh. He couldn't cancel it? Just once? What kind of thing is that to do? Go off and leave his bride all alone... And such a nice girl, too. Really sweet, you know?"

Leila had gone into the kitchen, then, and her cheeks were hot and her heart beating fast.

Now it was Sunday afternoon, and Leila was lying on a chaise longue beside the pool, remembering that conversation from two mornings ago, and the moment that followed when she had walked into that room that was flooded with sunlight and the warm smells of coffee and bacon and toast.

Rueben had been at the sink preparing a large plastic bottle with a long red rubber nipple on it for the new foal, because, he said, the mare's milk wasn't comin' in so good yet, and maybe Leila would like to help him feed the baby in a little while. Betsy's eyes had lit with welcome and her smile had been warm.

Leila remembered the strange little lump of yearning that had come into her throat just then, the sting of lonely tears that she had blinked hastily away. Because she understood that she had interrupted a moment of special intimacy between these two long-married people—she knew because she had encountered such moments between her own parents, many times before. There was such *ease* between them. She could hear it in their voices—trust and understanding, respect and friendship. It was, she thought, just what a marriage should be like. It was what she wanted *her* marriage to be like.

But…what of her marriage? Would she and Cade ever know that kind of ease? Right now such a thing seemed impossible.

Hopelessness settled over her, more oppressive than the midday heat. She'd managed to keep it at bay the past two days, spending most of her time in the stables with Rueben, working with the new foal. Oh, and she'd been riding, too, and was getting more and more comfortable with Western-style saddles. At night she watched old movies on television until she fell asleep on the sofa.

But now, lying on her stomach beside the swimming pool with the sun like a hot anvil between her shoulders and her forehead resting on her hands, she could not stop the tears from seeping between her eyelids. She had never, even as a child in those first wretched months of boarding school, been so lonely.

Because today was Sunday, Rueben and Betsy had the day off. Rueben had come early to feed the horses and then had gone off to his home on the other side of the pasture, taking the dogs with him. Betsy had left fruit salad and cinnamon rolls for Leila's breakfast, and deviled eggs and sliced ham and tomatoes stuffed with tuna salad and sliced strawberries to eat with ice cream for later. She would be cooking at home today, she had told Leila, because her kids were coming over. According to Betsy, she was going to have a "houseful." *You should come on down,* she had said to Leila. *You should come and join us.*

But Leila had not wanted to intrude on their day off, on their family's time together.

Now she thought that she had been very foolish to say no. Proud and foolish. Because of course she would not have been intruding at all. If there was one thing she had learned in these past few days, it was that Rueben and Betsy Flores had hearts as big as the wide-open spaces Leila had come to Texas expecting to find. They would welcome her with open arms, she was sure of it. And if she was feeling lonely and sorry for herself right now, then she had only herself to blame.

She could hear them down there now, on the other side of the pasture. If she stilled her own breath she could hear distant music—sometimes Mexican music and sometimes American country and western music. She could hear shouts and laughter.

Finally she could stand it no longer. She rolled over and sat up. A particularly loud burst of laughter at that moment settled her resolve; she would *not* play this role she despised—the pitiful abandoned bride. She was Princess Leila of Tamir. She had been invited to a party, and she would go.

She was in America, now. She could do whatever she pleased.

She rose and dressed quickly, putting on a brightly colored wraparound skirt and a loose-fitting T-shirt over her modest one-piece bathing suit. She had braided her hair for swimming, one long braid that hung straight down her back. It would do fine as it was, although she did dip her hands in the pool and smooth back the loose wisps of hair around her face. Then she slipped into her sandals and set out.

She walked briskly, following the well-trodden path she had seen Rueben use, past the stable, along the paddock fences, then through a gate and straight across the pasture. Almost at once she could feel her spirits lift; it was not Leila's nature to be gloomy for long. And it was not so humid today. There had been a little rain in the night, and this morning some leftover mist and fog, but that had blown away in a light cool breeze and now the sky was a bright blue patterned with a few billowy clouds. The pasture was spotted with little yellow flowers, and white butterflies fluttered dizzily among them as if they had been sipping fermented honey. Once a bird flashed by in front of her, a stunning streak of blue that made her gasp in wonderment.

The pasture sloped gently downhill. Soon, in the little valley just beyond the lower fence, Leila could see trees, and the pale gray roof of a long, low house made of red bricks. Near the house, in the shady spaces between the trees, she saw a volleyball net, a metal stove for cooking outdoors and long tables laden with food. And people. People seemed to be everywhere, gathered around the stove and the tables or sitting in chairs under the trees. Some held babies, or watched indulgently while small children played on the grass near their feet. Older children darted here and there among the adults, and a few were hitting a ball back and forth across the net.

All four dogs bounded out to greet Leila as she came through the gate from the pasture. Then someone else noticed her and called out, "Ma—you got company!"

A door to a screened porch opened and Betsy came out, wiping her hands on a huge apron. When she saw Leila she threw her hands up in the air and gave a squeal of welcome. "Oh, good—you changed your mind. I'm glad you came. Come here—come and meet my kids. Hey, everyone, look who's here—it's Cade's new wife! Everybody—this is Leila."

There were squeals of amazement and surprise: "*What? Cade got married?* When did that happen? I don't believe it!"

Shouts of welcome: "Hey, Leila—you're just in time, food's almost ready. Hey, Leila, come on down! Hi, Leila, hope you like chili…"

Betsy began to point to people left and right and call out names. A few of the children she got wrong, which made her clap a hand to her forehead while everyone laughed and teased her about losing her memory. Leila's head was spinning. How many children did Rueben and Betsy have? She had lost track of who was married to who, and she knew she would never remember anyone's name, but it did not seem to matter. She knew nobody really expected that she would.

A brown, stocky boy of about ten, wearing only a pair of blue jeans that had been cut off above the knee, came running up just then, yelling, "Gramma—Gramma—can we go swimming?" He was flushed and sweaty from playing volleyball and wore an expression of extreme pain on his face as he pleaded, "*Please?*"

Betsy gave him a stern look, which it was clear no one believed. She called across the yard to where Rueben and several younger men were gathered around the metal cook stove. "Hey, guys—how soon is dinner gonna be ready?"

Somebody lifted the lid of the stove, peered into it then yelled back, "'Bout half an hour…maybe little bit more."

Betsy put a heavy hand on the boy's head and glared at him. "Okay, but just a quick one, you hear me? If your momma says okay…"

The boy was already dashing off across the grass, yelling at the top of his lungs, "Mom—Gramma says it's okay! Hey, you guys, did you hear that? We can go swimming!"

"Where do they swim?" Leila had not seen a pool. Perhaps she should invite the children to swim in Cade's—in *her* pool.

But Betsy waved a hand toward a thick, dark bank of trees. "Oh, there's a place down at the creek where they like to go. Been there a long time."

"That's where I learned to swim," said one of Betsy's daughters, and another chimed in, "Yeah, I think we all did."

Leila gazed at them with a combination of fascination and doubt. She and her sisters had enjoyed swimming in the sea, in a secluded cove near the palace, but she could not imagine how one would swim in a murky creek, among all those trees. "May I…see this place?" she asked, both hesitant and eager.

"Oh, *sure!* Yeah, go on—it's nice!" several voices immediately responded, and Betsy added, with another wave of her hand, "Go right on down—the kids'll show you. Just follow all the hollering."

Leila hesitated only a moment more, her lower lip caught between her teeth and her breath quickening. Then she set off after the disappearing children, and after the first few steps broke into a light, skipping run.

Following shrieks and shouts of glee, she made her way
along a well-worn pathway across the lawn and into the
trees, and soon came to a place where the creek widened
into a small pond, where large rocks and very old trees
fought each other for space along the mossy banks and
sunlight sparkled on the dark surface of the water. Leila
caught her breath and laughter bubbled up in her throat as
she watched children of all shapes and sizes hurl themselves into the water from the rocks and low-hanging
branches, arms waving, legs pumping, smooth brown bodies gleaming in the sun. Entranced and envious, she
crouched down on one of the rocks with her skirt over her
knees and her arms wrapped around them and watched the
children surface, slick and agile as otters, blowing and wiping water from their faces, laughing and splashing one another.

"Look," one of them cried suddenly, pointing at Leila,
"it's that lady."

Several of the children drifted toward Leila's rock to
gather in a half circle around her, curious and friendly as
a school of dolphins.

"Hey, are you gonna swim with us?"

"You can come in—it's deep enough. See?" To dem-
onstrate, several of the children sank beneath the surface,
like dolphins sounding, to rise again seconds later blowing
water and wiping grins with their small brown hands.

"Come and swim with us, lady. It's not too cold—a little
bit, but it's fu-u-n!" And again they subsided, amidst
waves and splashes and shrieks of laughter.

Oh, Leila thought, if only I could!

And then she thought: Why can't I? There were no men
around, only children, and besides, she was in America
now. Such things were permitted here.

Almost as quickly as the thought formed in her head, she
was slipping off her sandals and pulling her T-shirt over

her head, and her teeth were clamped on her lower lip to hold back laughter. The wraparound skirt was still settling into a multicolored puddle on the rock as she jumped. She felt for only an instant the rush of soft air, and then the water's cool and delicious embrace. Her lungs contracted; her feet met the sandy bottom of the pond. She pushed herself upward and exploded from the surface with a gust of breath and a cry of delight. Several of the children paddled around her, blending their giggles and squeals with hers and looking as pleased as if Leila were a protégé of whom they were especially proud.

"See?" they cried. "We told you—it's fun, huh? And look what I can do—can you do this? Watch me—I can do a backward somersault, can you?"

And for a short and wonderful time, Leila became one of them, those anonymous, exuberant children. Never in her life had she felt so free, not even when she herself had been a child such as they. For a short and wonderful time she did not think at all about the stranger she had married who did not seem to desire her, or the home and family she had left behind.

It seemed as if Cade had been hit with just one surprise after another. Ever since, returning from his hunting trip several hours earlier than expected, he'd walked into his house and found it empty. That had been the first surprise. The second had come when he'd realized how much he minded.

It wasn't that he wasn't used to coming home to an empty house; most days, by the time he got home from work, Rueben and Betsy would be long gone and his dinner left for him, wrapped and microwave-ready in the refrigerator. And he *sure* didn't plan on getting used to having a little wife waiting for him, either. The wife was a temporary circumstance; he'd already made that decision, it was just a matter of finding the right time and place to finalize everything with Leila.

So why today did his house seem to ring with silence? What was this strange heaviness he felt in his chest as he wandered from room to room, calling the name of someone he hadn't even known ten days ago? Could it possibly be…disappointment? Had he actually been looking forward to seeing her again?

Ridiculous. The denial came so quickly it bordered on panic. Hell, he told himself in disgust, I'm responsible for the girl. If she's run off, or been kidnapped… *Ridiculous.*

Nevertheless, it was with as much relief as exasperation that he discovered the towel-draped chaise longue beside the pool and the backyard gate open. That, together with the salsa music he could hear pumping up from the Flores' place gave him the obvious answer. Rueben and Betsy were having one of their family barbecues, and Betsy, being the mother hen she was, would have insisted on inviting Leila. Mystery solved.

Less easy to explain—if Cade had bothered to try—was the fact that he didn't even take time to shower and shave and change out of his ranch clothes before setting out for the Flores' place. Before going to find his wife.

Nobody noticed when he came through the pasture gate; everyone in the Flores' yard was gathered around the food tables, loading up their plates with hot dogs and hamburgers, spare ribs and chicken, potato salad, cole slaw and, of course, Rueben's special five-alarm Tex-Mex chili.

Cade had been to enough of Rueben and Betsy's gatherings to know that for the next ten or fifteen minutes or so, nobody was going to be paying attention to anything but food, so instead of announcing himself right away he paused and leaned a shoulder against the trunk of a pin oak tree.

He was feeling just a tad wistful, as he always did when

he saw their family together like this and thought about how lucky Rueben and Betsy were. They'd known each other forever, just about, had grown up together and knew each other so well. Theirs was a great marriage. A great family. The kind of marriage, the kind of family Cade would have chosen for himself, if he'd had any say in the matter. The kind he'd never had, and finally accepted he probably never would have.

Definitely not with Leila.

He straightened abruptly and lightened the heaviness inside him with a breath while his eyes searched for her in the crowd.

She wasn't easy to find. Naturally, with that black hair of hers she'd blend right in with this Flores bunch as if she belonged there. When he finally did spot her, in the thickest part of the crowd around the food table, it was because he'd heard somebody call out her name.

"Hey Leila—you ever eat chili?"

"Chilly?" Her voice was unmistakable and instantly recognizable to him—another surprise—and musical as a flute. "I do not think so. This means cold, no?"

There was laughter, and someone yelled, "I don't *think* so!"

Then there was a clamor of voices explaining, urging Leila to try some chili...some warning her not to. Cade had moved unconsciously closer, alert as a bird dog on point as he tried to see what was happening in the center of the knot of people gathered around the chili pot. He was a little apprehensive, too—Rueben's chili was notorious. After eating a bowlful Cade didn't stop sweating for hours. And he was used to the stuff.

An expectant silence had fallen around the food table. Cade found that his heart was beating faster. He really did wish he could have seen Leila's face when she tasted that chili.

And then the knot of people seemed to loosen and shift, as if everyone had decided to give her a little more breathing room. And suddenly he *could* see her face—perfect oval, breathtakingly lovely, smooth and fresh as a child's—as she lifted a spoonful of the rich, red-brown chili to her mouth. Cade's heart gave a kick, then seemed to stick at the bottom of his throat, thumping away to beat the band while Leila chewed and the suspense grew. Cade held his breath along with everyone else while a tiny frown etched itself between her eyebrows. Then she tilted her head, and her lilting, slightly husky voice carried even to where he stood.

"It is very good...." she said, still with that uncertain little frown, and now she was turning her head, as if she were looking for something, there on the table "...but I think I would like—yes, *there*—what are those little yellow peppers called? Jalapeños—yes. I think I would like some more jalapeños in mine, please."

There were shouts of amazement and laughter from everyone, and smatterings of applause which Leila acknowledged with a winsome display of dimples. Cade let out the breath he'd been holding. He was smiling in spite of himself. The suspense had broken, so why was his heart still beating so hard and so fast? And why this growling in his stomach when he wasn't hungry?

"Hey, Cade—hey, Ma, look who's here! Come on over, Cade, grab yourself a plate."

His cover blown, he grinned, shrugged and pushed away from the tree trunk. But while the grin, shrug and a little deprecating wave of his hand were for the assembled crowd, his gaze stayed where it had been, on Leila. So he knew exactly the moment her body stiffened and the dimpled smile froze on her face, when the liveliness drained out of her so that she seemed to become a flat black-and-white photograph of herself.

So, he thought dismally, she isn't exactly happy to see me. Did that surprise him? Why would he expect her to be? But his heartbeat now was a slow, dirge-like pulse, and his breath tasted bitter in his throat.

The knot of Flores' family loosened and Leila came toward him, carrying her plastic plate in both hands, carefully, like a child. And it seemed to Cade that she carried herself the same way. *With constraint.* Yes, that was the word he was thinking of—as if she held her natural exuberance under a tight rein. But a moment ago with the Flores bunch she'd been lighthearted and free as a bird, so it was pretty obvious she felt that constraint only because of *him.*

He felt heavy, suddenly. And his heart hurt, as if the heaviness was right there, pressing in all around it.

"I did not expect you until later." Her voice sounded breathless, although her face remained pale and calm.

He shrugged that aside. "Hunting was lousy and the power went out at the ranch, so we decided to leave early." He nodded his head toward her. "Looks like you've been having fun."

It had just occurred to him that she was wet, under the loose oversized T-shirt she was wearing. Her hair hung in a thick, sodden braid down her back, except for tiny spikes and tendrils around her face and neck that had begun to dry. The T-shirt clung to the dark wetness of the bathing suit, outlining her breasts in bold relief, and it came to him with a small sense of shock that until that moment he'd had no idea what her body was actually shaped like. That one glimpse made him feel the way he did when he was good and hungry and smelled Betsy's bread baking in the oven.

"I have been, yes." Leila said, responding to something he barely remembered saying, and she was nodding earnestly, obviously completely unaware of the direction his

gaze—and his thoughts—had been taking. "Betsy and Rueben have such a nice family, have they not? They have
been very kind to me, all of them. Even though," she
added, showing him a brief glimpse of dimples, "I do not
think I will remember any of their names."

"I see you've been swimming," Cade said bluntly.

Her eyes flicked downward toward her own chest, then
jumped quickly back to his. Her lips parted in dismay. Letting go of her plate with one hand, she plucked the shirt
away from herself as color blossomed slowly in her cheeks,
going almost imperceptibly from delicate to sublime, like
a sunrise.

"Yes—with the children. In the creek. Was this all
right?"

"What? Sure, it's all right."

"You do not mind?" Again her voice sounded breathless.

"Why should I mind?" His voice sounded angry, though
he wasn't. And damned if his heart wasn't beating too fast
again. As if they were having an argument. Which they
weren't, not as far as he was concerned. He wasn't so sure
about her.

"I am very glad you do not." Her head was high and
her eyes seemed to flare and blaze like coals, with something that looked like defiance—though he couldn't think
what she might be in defiance of. *He'd* never told her she
couldn't go swimming—or anything else, for that matter.
And he had no intention of ever doing so. He was her
husband, dammit, not her father, even if she was ten years
younger than he was.

"Because I liked being with the children," Leila went
on. "Very much. I like children. I would like—" She broke
off and looked away, and her throat moved with a swallow.
He knew she'd meant to say more, but had no idea what it
might be.

I want to have children. A lot of children—like Betsy and Rueben. I want to have your children, Cade Gallagher.

A little shudder quivered through Leila as she realized that she had almost said such a thing out loud. Perhaps, she thought, it is wrong for a wife to be too proud with her husband. But she was not only a wife, she was a princess, and she could not—she would not say such a thing to a man, husband or not, who did not seem to want to make babies with her at all.

"Have you been to this place where the children swim?" she asked after a moment, watching him from under her lashes. "Did you swim there also, when you were a child?"

"What?" Cade was staring at her with that fierce, rather puzzled frown. "Oh—no. I only bought this place about six years ago. Rueben and Betsy came with it—Rueben had worked for the previous owner forever. Most of their kids grew up in this house. But no, I never swam there when I was a kid."

In spite of the photograph she had seen in his study, Leila could not imagine Cade as a little boy, with knobby arms and legs and a lean brown body, golden hair dark and slick as a seal's, leaping and splashing and squealing with pleasure, like Betsy's grandchildren. Not this man, with a face so rugged and shoulders so broad, in his cowboy hat and blue jeans, and whiskers beginning to show on his chin. What was it Samira had called him? Oh yes. *Imposing.* It would be hard, she had said, not to be intimidated by such a man.

But Leila Kamal would *not* be intimidated, not by *any* man.

"You do not have to be a child to enjoy this swimming place," she said with a lift of her chin. "I am not a child."

He did not answer. For a long moment he just looked at her, and she realized suddenly that her mouth and throat felt dry. She saw Cade's throat move as if he had swallowed, and then she wanted to swallow, too. She felt hot in spite of the wet bathing suit she wore under her clothes, a peculiar heat that filled all her insides in ways that even Rueben's famous Texas chili had not.

"Hey, Cade, come on, man—better get yourself a plate, before it's all gone."

Leila jerked as if she'd been roused from a daydream. Rueben was coming toward them across the grass, carrying a long fork with two prongs and leather strips hanging from the handle. He looked younger today, she thought, less shy than he usually did.

Cade put out his hand and shook the older man's. "Ah, thanks, Rueben, but I better take a raincheck."

Rueben looked at him as though Cade had gone insane. "What, are you kidding me? We got plenty—steaks, chili...come on, you gotta eat something."

Cade was laughing, but also shaking his head. "No, really—I had a sandwich at the airport. I just came to collect my...wife." Leila glanced at him curiously. His smile seemed as though it had been carved from wood.

Rueben nodded toward Leila. "Hey—she tell you already?"

"No...tell me what?" Then Cade caught a breath and snapped his fingers. "Suki had her foal."

"Yup," said Rueben. "Nice little filly. Think she's gonna look just like her mama."

"How is she? Everything go okay?" This was man-talk, and Leila saw that Cade had already turned toward Rueben, automatically excluding her.

Leila was used to that kind of treatment. But before she could even begin to feel her usual frustration and resentment, Rueben had begun to back away. "Hey, let *her* tell you about it," he said. "She was there." Then he glanced over at Leila and, to her complete amazement, *winked.* "Lucky she was, too. Suki couldn't of done it without her.

"Well—hey, I gotta get back to my burgers—see you in the morning, boss." And he hurried off to join his family, agile in spite of his funny disjointed walk.

Leila looked at Cade, who was frowning at her as if she were a strange creature, perhaps in a zoo. He cleared his throat. "What the hell did he mean by that?"

Leila smiled, showing her dimples. "Oh, I think he was making a joke." But pleasure was flooding through her, warming her insides the way a hot drink does when the weather is cold. "I helped a little—but only a *very* little. I only spoke to her—in Arabic. I think she liked that—"

"Who, the foal?"

"No, Suki—the mare. And I petted her while Rueben pulled on her feet—"

"Suki's?"

Leila gave a little crow of laughter. "The *foal's*. Then, after she was born, I had to wipe her nose and mouth so she could breathe. And later I fed her with a bottle because her mother did not have milk for her right away. But she is fine now. And—oh, Cade—she is so beautiful. You must see her. May we go to see her now?" And she checked in surprise, because they were standing in front of the pasture gate and she had not even realized that they had been walking.

Just then someone noticed them leaving. Many voices called out goodbyes, and Leila waved and answered with thank-yous and promises to come back and visit again some time. Cade waved absently as he opened the gate and held it for her.

"Maybe you'd better tell me about it," he said gruffly as they started up the gentle slope, walking together, side by side. His feelings were mixed, and very confusing.

He kept glancing at her as she talked, stimulated in unexplainable ways by that little burr of roughness in her voice, entranced by the way her dimples came and went, like a baby playing peek-a-boo. His heartbeat had quickened again, and he knew it was not from the exertion of the climb. He told himself he was glad to see the color back in her cheeks and the bounce in her step. He told himself he was happy to see the dimples again, and hear the musical peal of her laughter. But there was a place inside him…a kernel of disappointment…a leaden little cloud that wouldn't let him forget. *It's not me. It's not me. It's Suki and the foal that's made her happy, not me.*

Happy? What about that? *Was* she happy? Whether it was Rueben and Betsy's clan, or Suki and her foal that had made her so or not, right now it sure as hell seemed as though she was. Uncertainty filled Cade's belly. His resolve to undo this crazy marriage, based as it was on the justification that Leila wasn't and could never be happy with him, trembled.…

She stopped in the stable long enough to fill a can with grain for Suki. Cade stood in the doorway of the stall and watched her cross the grassy paddock, graceful as a nymph in her long wraparound skirt and sandals, T-shirt knotted at one hip, dark braid swaying as she walked. She approached the dappled gray mare confidently, murmuring in a musical language he assumed must be Arabic. How exotic she is, he thought. And yet…somehow she wasn't. That sunny paddock, beautiful gray mare and beautiful woman, spindle-legged black foal butting at her back… Cade had never considered himself a connoisseur of art, but he thought if someone were to paint this scene, it would look incredibly beautiful…and exactly right.

"She thinks I am her mother," Leila said to Cade as he joined her, laughing as the foal again butted impatiently at her hip. "Because I fed her with a bottle. No, no, little one, you must drink from your own mama now." And she bent down to encircle the foal's neck with her arms and press her face to the fuzzy black hide.

The hollow feeling in Cade's belly pushed into his chest, and he struggled to haul in a breath for which he had no room. "I've been thinking," he said, and because it was a lie—the idea had only that moment come to him—his voice was scratchy and filled with gravel. Still cradling the foal, she looked up at him, waiting with bright and expectant eyes. "I haven't given you your bride gift—what do they call it?—the *mahr*?"

She nodded, frowning a little. "The *mahr*, yes."

Cade tipped his head toward the foal. Nerves jumped in his belly. "She's yours, if you want her. For your bride gift."

He was unprepared when Leila sucked in air in a cry that sounded more like grief than joy. Unprepared, too, for the tears that suddenly glistened in her eyes. She looked so stricken, in fact, that he tried to apologize. "I know it isn't jewelry, or money—"

"I have no need for jewelry or money! Oh, Cade—she is so beautiful—this is the most wonderful bride gift—more wonderful than I ever dreamed of." She buried her tear-wet face in the foal's coat, then as quickly was smiling up at Cade again. "I will name her—*may* I name her?"

"She's yours," Cade said gruffly. "You can do anything you like."

"Then I will name her Sari," she said with a fierce, impassioned joy. "In Arabic it means, 'most noble.'" She turned to face him squarely then, smiling with a radiance that took his breath away. "Thank you, Cade. Thank you for my bride gift." And she stepped forward, put her hands on his unshaven jaws, and kissed him.

Chapter 9

Her lips were warm and soft, but with an enticing little bite to them that he recognized, even in that moment of shock, as Rueben's chili. But there was something else, too, a salty coolness he knew could only be tears. It was that as much as anything, he thought later, when he was capable of it again, that reminder of her vulnerability, the fragile state of her emotions he'd violated once before, that made him stiffen when she touched him. That made him hold himself rigid while his insides quivered with unanticipated longing, his arm muscles tensing until they ached with the control it took to keep from wrapping them around her.

"You're welcome," he said as he took her by the arms and held her where she was, a few critical inches away from him. Any closer, he knew, and he'd never be able to resist her. If he let her body touch him he was finished. "I'm glad you like her."

His thoughts were as bleak as his words were gentle, and as uncompromising as his touch. *It's gratitude, nothing more. It's the gift—it's the horse she loves, not me.*

* * *

I don't understand him, this man I have married, thought Leila. He seemed so kind...yes, even sweet—Kitty had been right about that. But at the same time, so distant it seemed impossible that she would ever know or understand him.

What if I can't? What if I never do?

The thought filled her with the cold emptiness of panic. She could not endure such *aloneness* for long. And what must she do then, go running back to Tamir, to her mother and father, like a little child with a bumped knee? To even think of such a thing made her cheeks burn and her heart quicken. *No—I cannot. I will not go back.*

No, she was not ready to give up. Not yet.

Tonight, she had decided, she would try again to seduce her husband. Except...no, she did not think *seduce* was exactly the correct word. She had looked it up in her English dictionary, and it seemed to mean that she would be trying to make Cade do something bad. What could be bad about a man making love to his wife? No—she did not like this word, seduce. Not at all.

So, what *would* she call it, this business of trying to make her own husband desire her? And more important, how could she accomplish it? She had not had any success at being pushy, so it was clearly time to try something else. But what? Leila was not accustomed to having to work to get her way. All her life she had been the baby of the Kamal family, the palace darling. All that had been required in order to wrap her family and servants around her little finger was to flash her dimples, be her winsome and charming self.

Be herself? Was it possible? Could her own winsomeness and charm be enough to win over such a man as Cade? Leila didn't know, but since nothing else seemed to be working, it was definitely worth a try.

Yes, she thought, watching herself in the bathroom mirror as her small white teeth pressed into her lower lip and her dimples magically appeared. *Tonight*... Tonight, she would make herself so appealing, not even Cade would be able to resist her.

Cade was accustomed to fixing his own Sunday evening meal. He'd eat it alone in the kitchen, sometimes standing at the counter, or, if he'd remembered to pick up a Sunday paper, at the table in the breakfast room with the sports and business sections spread out in front of him. Tonight was no different, except that he had company.

Leila had come in while he was filling his plate from the array of covered containers and foil-wrapped packages Betsy had left for him, looking scrubbed and delectable in a belted robe the soft pink of wild roses. He'd tensed automatically when she first appeared, armoring himself against her appeal and gearing up to do battle with the unwanted desire for her that was beginning to gnaw at him like a hunger in his belly.

But she hadn't made any attempt to touch him again, or even get close to him, leaning instead against the counter and nibbling strawberries while she chattered on about the day she'd had. He thought he should have found her presence annoying. He wished he did. With all his heart he wished he didn't enjoy the sound of her voice so much. He wished his mouth wouldn't water at the sight of those soft lips of hers lush with strawberries.

She followed him into the breakfast room and sat down across the table from him, so he never did get to his newspaper. Instead, while he ate he listened to Leila telling him all about swimming with the children at Rueben and Betsy's, and how much she'd enjoyed meeting all the Flores family. She asked him all sorts of questions, and seemed so interested he told her everything he knew about Rueben and Betsy—how they'd grown up together in the same small village in Mexico, had married as teenagers and come to the United States not long after that, like so many others, to find work. How they'd been lucky enough to both find jobs with the same estate, Betsy as cook and housekeeper, Rueben as caretaker and horse wrangler. How they'd raised eight kids in the house down by the creek, and sent every one of them to college—they'd all graduated, too, except Tony, the youngest, who was still at Texas A&M studying veterinary medicine.

While he was telling her all this, he couldn't help but notice how the glow in her eyes had grown misty, and that her smile seemed wistful, even sad. It had a bad effect on him, that smile. It made him ashamed of himself. It made him think about his behavior toward her—especially the way he'd treated her since he'd married her and brought her here, to this place so far from her home and family. God, how lonely, how homesick she must be. No wonder she'd enjoyed Rueben and Betsy's bunch so much. And she'd never once complained. He—Cade—was a jerk, a selfish, thoughtless SOB, thinking only about how he was going to get out of this marriage mess, and nothing at all about what *she* must be going through.

Being thoroughly ashamed of himself didn't exactly put him in a frame of mind to be sociable, so as soon as he'd finished eating, he excused himself rather abruptly and shut himself up in his study to brood. It didn't take him long to discover that being exclusively in his own company wasn't doing much to improve his mood, and that it probably wasn't going to get any better until he'd figured out a way to make it up to Leila.

Meaning to step out into the backyard for a cheroot, he found himself climbing the stairs instead. He halted in front of the closed door to the bedroom that wasn't his anymore and raised his hand, only to discover that it still held the unlit cigar. He tucked it in his shirt pocket, then knocked.

So was his heart, knocking so loudly he barely heard Leila's musical, "Come in."

She was sitting on the bed—his bed—half-sideways to him with one leg drawn up, giving him enticing glimpses of smooth legs that were either naturally tawny or lightly tanned. There was the promise of other intriguing secrets in the deep vee of her robe, but they were screened from his view by her upraised arms, from which the sleeves of her robe had slipped down to reveal still more of that silky, cream-with-a-dash-of coffee skin. Which was more of her skin than he'd ever seen before at one time, come to think of it. His memory chose that moment to replay the thought that had struck him down at Rueben's, the incredible fact that he'd never actually seen his wife's body.

What was more incredible was the realization that, of all the women's bodies he'd seen in his life, in all stages of sexy and alluring undress, he'd never been so turned on as he was by those tiny, half-imagined glimpses of golden-tan skin.

With all that going on in his mind, it took him a minute or two to realize that what she was doing was braiding her hair. A tortoise-shell brush lay on the bed beside her and a length of pink ribbon was draped across her lap. She looked flustered, as if he'd caught her in a private act. She murmured something he couldn't hear and struggled to bring the braid over her shoulder so she could finish the task, and he murmured something back that was meant to tell her she didn't need to rush on his account. She watched him come toward her with apprehensive eyes. He wondered if she could hear his heart thumping.

She pulled her eyes away from him. Holding the braid with one hand, she picked up the length of ribbon with the other.

"You need some help with that?" His tongue felt thick; his voice sounded furry. Her eyes jerked back to him as he sat on the bed beside her and reached out a hand to take the ribbon.

For a moment she seemed mesmerized, gazing at him without comprehension. Then she gave herself a shake and murmured, "Oh, yes—thank you..." Her eyes dropped behind the veil of her lashes as she watched his big-boned hands tie the delicate piece of ribbon around the glossy rope of her hair. Her lips parted. She seemed to be holding her breath. He knew *he* was.

He tried to clear his throat. "Just out of curiosity, how were you going to manage this before I happened along?"

She gave him a sideways, upward look through her lashes. "Like this—" Her dimples winked at him as she demonstrated, with lips tucked between her teeth, how she would have held the braid in her mouth while she tied the ribbon around it.

He finished the task and held it up for her inspection. "Okay—how's that?"

"That is very nice, thank you."

For some reason he didn't relinquish the braid right away, but held it for a moment, staring at it and measuring the warm, damp weight of it in his hand. He had a sudden powerful urge to yank off the ribbon he'd just finished tying, unravel and bury his face in the soft, fragrant mass of her hair. *Your hair is beautiful.* He wanted to say that to her, but he didn't.

Instead, as he felt the smooth rope slide through his fingers, he cleared his throat and said, "I've been thinking..."

With a single graceful motion the braid disappeared over her shoulder. "Yes?" Her eyes waited, expectant, vulnerable.

He knew he should be more careful with her. He knew he ought to move away, at least. But he seemed to be drowning in those midnight eyes. For one panicky moment he couldn't remember what it was he'd wanted to say to her.

"I've been thinking," he said firmly, and struggling against the spell of those eyes was like swimming up out of a whirlpool. "It's been almost a week since we left Tamir. I thought you might be feeling…you know, a little homesick." She straightened almost guiltily and gave her head a little shake, ready to deny it, but he checked her with a gesture. "Hey, it's natural you'd be missing your family. What I thought, is, maybe you'd like to give them a call."

She tried to catch back the cry with her fingertips, but it was too quick for her. Above her hand, her eyes were suddenly bright with tears.

"I should have thought of it before this," Cade said gruffly. "I guess I was just so busy…business…catching up…" He felt thoroughly ashamed of himself. "Anyway, if you like, we can make the call right now. It would be…" he frowned at his watch "…early in the morning in Tamir."

"I would like that…very much." She'd turned a shoulder to him and was trying to wipe away a tear without him noticing. Then she jerked back to him, eyes wide and stricken again. "But I do not know the number. Is that not terrible? I do not even know my own telephone number!"

"I doubt you've had reason to call it," Cade said dryly.

"Not since school, that is true. That was so long ago."

"It doesn't matter. I just happen to have it, right here."

He reached into the pocket of his shirt for the slip of paper he'd written the number down on and found his forgotten cheroot there instead. Distracted, he handed the cigar to Leila while he retrieved the paper and reached with the other hand for the cordless phone on the bedside table. He dialed the number, and while he waited for the overseas connection he looked over at Leila and saw that she was still holding his cigar. Sort of rolling it between her fingers in an exploratory way, holding it to her nose and sniffing it.

Just as he was about to take it off her hands he heard the phone ringing on the other end, and immediately after that a voice saying, "Royal palace, family residence, may I help you?"

A few minutes later Leila was laughing and sobbing joyfully into the phone and didn't even notice when Cade walked out of the room. He had a knot the size of a fist in his belly, and just about the last thing on his mind was that damned cigar.

He went straight down to his study and poured himself a double shot of bourbon. He couldn't have felt worse if he'd been torturing kittens. What kind of man am I? he wondered as he gazed morosely into the amber depths of his whiskey glass. What kind of selfish idiot was I, to have convinced myself I could marry a girl from a completely alien culture, haul her thousands of miles away from her home and family and expect her to be happy? The look of sheer joy on her face when he'd handed her the phone, her radiant, tear-wet eyes, haunted him.

I have to make it right, he thought. Somehow.

Half a bottle of bourbon later, she was still haunting him, but in a vastly different way. As the level of liquid in the bottle dropped, so, it seemed, did the focus of his thoughts. The image he couldn't get out of his mind now wasn't her eyes, or even her dimpled smile. It was those taunting glimpses of creamy skin vanishing into the shadowed slashes of her robe, one at her breasts, the other her thighs. And he kept coming back to the fact that she was his wife, and he'd never seen either of those parts of her, not to mention others even less accessible.

She's my wife, dammit. And I want her.

Oh yeah, he kept coming back to that, too, like a little kid nagging in a toy store.

A few more sips of bourbon and he was starting to rationalize pretty effectively, with much the same sort of creative thinking he recalled employing as a teenager. Then he'd been under the influence of hormones, not whiskey, but the effect was the same. He began to convince himself that she *wanted* him to make love to her. After all, back there in Tamir she'd asked *him* to kiss her, hadn't she? And she'd come to *his* room, hadn't she? Hell yes, she had. She wanted him, he wanted her, they were married—so why *shouldn't* they have each other?

It began to seem ridiculous to him that he'd been married nearly a week and hadn't yet made love to his wife. He couldn't even recall his reason for not doing so—something about her being a virgin?—but whatever it was he was sure it couldn't have been very important. Not nearly as important as how full and hot and hard he was right now, and how much he wanted her.

But then, high on hormones, the teenage boy he'd been hadn't given much thought to tomorrow, either.

That's it, he thought, enough of this bull. She ought to be about talked out by now, homesick or not. He knocked back the last of the whiskey, plunked down the glass and marched out of his study and up the stairs. He almost barged right into his bedroom without knocking, but at the last minute thought better of it and tapped softly with one knuckle. When he got no answer, he opened the door part way and poked his head through the crack, calling her name. Then he stopped. He let out his breath in a long slow hiss, like something deflating.

His princess bride was lying on his bed, curled on her side with one hand under her cheek, the other cradling the telephone against her breasts. She was sound asleep. And those elusive legs of hers, slightly bent at both hip and knee, had escaped the confines of the robe through the front overlap and were finally displayed for him in all their glory. It was a sight to make a man's mouth water and his belly howl.

He tiptoed over to the bed and stood looking down at her...this lovely, exotic creature he'd married. The hormone-and-whiskey high was ebbing, and he felt a strange, indefinable sadness, an ache of longing he neither liked nor understood. It scared the hell out of him, as a matter of fact. What did it mean? Was he *falling* for this girl? God help him if he was, because things were complicated enough the way they were.

He was easing the phone out of her grasp when he made another unsettling discovery. Pillowing her cheek, her hand was still curled around his forgotten cheroot. What did *that* mean? His heart skittered and bounded like a startled rabbit. He flicked the comforter over those delectable legs, turned off the lamp and went out and closed the door behind him, feeling shaky and weak in the knees.

He woke the next morning with a severe headache and a sense of having escaped unthinkable disaster. No question about it, he was going to have to get this marriage thing solved right quick. Before he got himself in so deep he couldn't get out, at least not without permanent damage to his heart.

Meanwhile, he was swearing off bourbon.

When Leila woke up Monday morning, Cade had already gone—to his offices in Houston, Betsy told her. And after that, she said, he was going to fly up to Dallas to meet with some people about a refinery he was going to rebuild and modernize for them out in a place called Odessa. There was a lot of planning to do—probably take several days, she said, so Cade would be staying in Dallas most of the week. Betsy's face looked stern as she told Leila this, as if she were angry.

Later, she heard Betsy talking to Rueben in the kitchen. "...makes me so mad. Why is he acting like this? What did he marry her for, if he's just going to leave her alone all the time? Why doesn't he sleep—" And she broke off quickly as Leila came into the room.

I don't know why either, Leila wanted to say. Although, unlike Betsy, she did know why Cade had married her. He had married her because she had disgraced herself, and he felt sorry for her. And because he did not want to displease her father, the sheik.

And now she was trapped, every bit as trapped as she had been in Tamir, only worse. There, at least, she had been surrounded by people who loved her, even if they did treat her like a child most of the time. Here, she had only a husband who did not love her at all, and Rueben and Betsy, who were kind.

"Just give him some time," Betsy told her with a sigh, as if she were talking about one of her own children who was misbehaving. "He's real busy right now, but he'll come around. You just have to give him time."

Yes, Leila thought, but I do not know how long I will be able to stand this loneliness.

She kept busy during the day, working with the foal, Sari, reading books beside the pool and swimming. Once, two of Betsy's grandchildren knocked at the back door and said, "Can Leila come out and play with us?" And so she enjoyed a wonderful afternoon swimming with them in the creek.

But the thing she liked the most, besides working with Sari, was following Betsy around the house, asking questions about Cade. She especially liked the photograph albums Betsy gave her, and spent hours poring over them staring at the grainy black-and-white or faded color photographs of Cade when he was a boy, and the people who had made him who he was.

One album was older than the others, made of black paper pages between stiff leather covers. It had been Cade's mother's, Betsy told her, and the pictures were of her father, who had been the "wildcatter." There were many pictures in the album like the one Leila had seen framed in Cade's study, of grimy men with blackened faces standing beside wooden derricks or oil well pumps that reminded Leila of giant insects. Betsy explained that a wildcatter was someone who searched for oil, and that Cade's grandfather had found a lot of it, back in the nineteen-twenties, and had become very rich.

"Ah," said Leila, nodding. But she was puzzled, too. For some reason it had not seemed that Cade had always been rich.

But then Betsy explained that Cade's father had been a gambler and an alcoholic, and had lost almost all of his wife's money before she divorced him, when Cade was twelve. And then had died a short time later.

Leila's eyes had filled with tears when Betsy told her of Cade's mother's death only a few years after that, in a tragic accident. There was something about the pretty blond woman with the kind eyes and gentle smile that reminded her of her own mother. Even now, Leila could not imagine her world without her mother in it, and to think that Cade had been no more than fifteen… The photographs of Cade at that time showed a solemn-faced boy with broad shoulders that looked as if they carried a great weight, and now she understood why.

Earlier, though, there were pictures of a younger, much more carefree Cade with his mother and a handsome dark-haired, hawk-nosed man, and a little girl who looked familiar. Leila looked closer, then gave a cry. "But this is Elena!"

Yes, Betsy told her, and the man was Elena's father, Yusuf Rahman. Betsy's mouth tightened when she said that name.

"Then...Cade's mother and Elena's father were lovers?" In the photographs they seemed close, like a family, Leila thought.

But Betsy shook her head and said, "You'd have to ask Cade about that."

She had gone on about her dusting, and her whole body quivered with indignation and disapproval—though it was not, Leila understood, of *her.* She already knew, from things Elena had told her, that Yusuf Rahman had been an evil man, that he had even killed his own wife, Elena's mother, and would have killed Elena, too, if Hassan had not shot him first. She had not known how close that evil had come to touching Cade's life as well.

She had gone on to study the photograph albums alone after that, and if she felt disappointed it was because she wished she *could* ask Cade, as Betsy had suggested—about many things. She liked listening to Betsy talk about Cade's background and family, but she wished she could have talked of those things with her husband instead.

Someday he will talk to me. I must believe that. And maybe then I will understand why he does not want to love me.

Cade returned on Friday, just as Rueben and Betsy were about to leave for the weekend. They were all in the kitchen when he came in. Betsy was showing Leila the food she had prepared for their weekend meals, and Rueben was sitting at the small kitchen table drinking a glass of sweetened iced tea. Cade nodded at Rueben, who nodded back.

"Huh," said Betsy as she closed the refrigerator door with a loud smack, "what're *you* doing home so early?"

Even Leila recognized the sarcasm, and not for the first time she thought how different Rueben and Betsy's position in this house was from that of the servants back home in Tamir.

Cade pulled out a chair and sat down at the table. He *looks very tired,* Leila thought, watching him draw a hand over his eyes and rub them briefly. Her heartbeat stumbled as those deeply shadowed eyes slid past her...but when he spoke his words and half smile were for Betsy. "Got any more of that tea?"

Betsy gave him a look, but did not say anything as she took a glass from the cupboard and poured tea from the pitcher in the refrigerator. Then she handed the glass to Leila. Leila took it, not comprehending; *she* had not asked for tea. Betsy jerked her head toward Cade and made a motion with her hand that he could not see.

Then she understood. Of course—she was to serve her husband. *What a lot I have to learn about being a wife,* she thought. When it came to food and drink, Leila was accustomed to *being* served, not the other way around.

Her heart hammered and her hands shook as she placed the glass of iced tea on the table in front of her husband. His eyes flashed briefly at her from their shadows as he mumbled, "Thanks." Leila nodded and retreated until she felt the cold edge of the tile counter at her back. She slumped against it because her knees felt weak and she was grateful for the support, but she remembered her pride and straightened just in time. *A daughter of Sheik Ahmed Kamal does not slump.*

Betsy asked again why Cade had come home so early, and what his plans were for the coming weekend. He took a long drink of iced tea before he answered. "I thought I'd fly out to the ranch...do some repairs. That was more than a little bit embarrassing last week, having the power go out, with a client."

Leila felt strange, as if she were standing all alone on a great empty stage, and thousands of people were looking at her. She heard herself say in a loud, clear voice, "I would like to go with you." The strangeness dissolved and she saw that there were only two people looking at her—Cade with silent shock, and Betsy with a little smile of approval. Rueben, with his back to her, drank tea with a noisy clanking of ice cubes.

Leila stepped forward, and her stomach quivered with butterflies. "I would like to see this ranch that I have heard about," she said, and there was no quiver at all in her voice. "I would like to see more of Texas."

Cade was opening his mouth to speak, and she knew that he was going to say that she could not go. She did not know what she would do if he told her that. I will not be left alone again, she thought, trembling now with anger. Anger and a new determination. *I will not be abandoned again.*

"That's a good idea," said Betsy. Cade shut his mouth on whatever it was he had planned to say and glared at the short, brown woman. She glared back at him. Her arms were folded on her great soft bosom, and her round face looked as though it had been carved from wood. "You should take your wife—show her the ranch. Have a nice weekend together—just the two of you."

The silence in the kitchen was profound. It seemed to Leila that they must all hear each other's hearts beating. Then Rueben gave his shoulder a hitch and said, "Yeah, you should take her."

Cade flashed him a look of pure shock. Leila held her breath while seconds ticked by. She knew that this was important—maybe the most important moment of her life, a crossroads. If he refuses me, she thought with cold resolve... If he leaves me again...

His eyes came back to her. She felt them as a strange kind of heat, a melting fire that spread through her chest. "It's pretty primitive out there," he said. "Not very comfortable. Are you sure you want to go?'' And she knew that she had won.

She gave a happy sigh. ''*Very* sure.''

The twin-engine Cessna 310 arrowed upward through the East Texas haze and leveled off above the outer limits of Houston's suburbs. This early in the morning there were no thunderheads to reckon with, so Cade set a course straight across the checkerboard of farmland and small towns toward the hill country west of San Antonio. Flying time to the ranch was anywhere from an hour and a half to two hours, depending on wind conditions.

He looked over at his passenger. She hadn't said much since he'd buckled her into her seat, just kept looking out the window with her face pressed right up against the glass. Reminded him of a little kid staring through the walls of an aquarium, oblivious to everything except what was going on in the alien world on the other side.

Not completely oblivious. As if she sensed his look, she glanced over at him. ''America is so...*big*,'' she said, her voice breathless and wondering. She sat back in her seat with a happy-sounding sigh. ''It is just as I imagined. And all of this—'' she turned once again to the window, as if she couldn't help herself ''—is still Texas? It must go on forever!''

''Not quite,'' said Cade dryly, ''but just about.''

She was silent, gazing down on the crazy-quilt landscape. Then she said, ''I understand why you felt 'cooped up' in Tamir.''

Cooped up. He felt a strange little shiver go through him—not déjà vu, exactly, just an instant of total sensory recall. Hearing those words, for a moment he was back there in Tamir with Leila, the night of the state reception. She was flirting with him on the terrace overlooking the sea, and he was feeling again that unnerving and mystifying sense of accord with a woman as exotic and alien to him as anyone he'd ever met. Thinking about it, and about everything that had happened to him since, he wondered now if it had all begun with that moment. He sure as hell hadn't felt like himself since.

"Yeah," he said in a gravelly voice, "Pretty hard to feel cooped up out here."

"You would think so…" Her voice was wistful and soft, and he wondered how words so gentle could cause such a fierce and painful wound, right in the vicinity of his heart.

There was no more talking after that. Leila gazed out the window and Cade was left alone with his remorseful thoughts. And some that were wistful, too. He kept thinking about those days and nights in Tamir, remembering the gardens, the scent of flowers and the music of fountains, a princess's enchanting smile. And it seemed to him that there had been a magical innocence about that time, remembered, like a fairy tale from his childhood, with a sense of regret, an awareness of having had something precious that was now lost. Something he wished he could find again, and had no idea how.

Time went quickly, and in no time at all the Cessna was circling over dun-colored hills dotted with gray-green live oaks and darker splotches of juniper. There was the pale ribbon of road—smoother-looking from up here than the corduroy it was—and the landing strip with its wind sock hanging limp at this time of morning. Cade pointed them out to Leila—the maintenance shed next to the runway, then the slate-gray roof of the farmhouse, and on the other side of the house, shielded from the landing strip by a grove of live oaks, the barn and corrals. She didn't reply, just gazed down at everything in silent awe.

And suddenly, in his mind he could hear Betsy saying,

"…show her the ranch. Have a nice weekend…just the two of you."

Just the two of us. The whole weekend.

The knot in his stomach felt a lot like fear.

Chapter 10

"Well—this is it." Cade dropped the key into his pocket and pushed open the door, then reached around it to a light switch. "Okay—at least we have power." He looked sideways at Leila and made a motion with his head. "Sorry about the mess. I wasn't expecting to bring company this trip, or I'd have had Mrs. MacGruder—that's my next-door neighbor—she takes care of things here for me—feeds the horses, things like that. I'd have had her come in and clean."

"I can clean," Leila said, stepping over the threshold. She heard Cade make a disbelieving sound as he picked up the thermal cooler containing food that Betsy had sent with them and followed her into the living room. She tore her gaze from the room to give him a look. "Do you think I cannot? Because I am not required to clean does not mean I do not know how."

"Oh yeah?" Cade lifted a skeptical eyebrow at her as he passed. "So tell me—where did you learn how to clean house?"

"Well...not *house,* exactly." Her smile was brief and distracted; there was so much to see. "In boarding school, we were required to clean our own rooms and make our beds, so I do know how to sweep and dust. Frankly, it is not that difficult."

Cade grunted. Through an open double doorway she saw him put the cooler on a table in what could only be the kitchen. "Well, I told you it was primitive."

"I do not think it is primitive at all." Leila had visited some of the poorest parts of Tamir with her mother and sisters. She knew what primitive was. She clasped her hands together to contain her excitement. "I think it is...perfect."

In fact, she had fallen in love with the house at her first glimpse of it. It was made of yellowish-brown stones, with a wooden veranda that ran straight across the front and a roof made of dark gray composition shingles, which Cade told her had replaced the original wooden ones. And the room she was standing in seemed so familiar to her she was sure she must have seen one just like it—perhaps more than one—in western movies. At one end there was a large fireplace made of the same stone as the outside of the house, with a sofa and several comfortable-looking chairs gathered in front of it. The floors were made of wood, covered with rugs made of cloth that had been tightly braided and then coiled. There was a set of antlers, perhaps from a deer, above the fireplace, and, oddly, the actual skin of a cow thrown over one of the chairs, like an afghan.

She let out her breath in a happy gust. She thought it was just what a house on a ranch in Texas *should* be.

She went into the kitchen where Cade was taking things out of the cooler and putting them into the refrigerator. He looked around at her, or rather, at the overnight bag that was hanging from her shoulder. "I'll show you where to put your things, and then we can have some breakfast."

Leila nodded. Once more she was too busy looking to reply. The kitchen had white-painted cupboards and blue linoleum on the floor, and a yellow plastic cover on the table that was covered with tiny blue and white flowers. Directly opposite the wide door from the living room, another door with a window in the top opened onto what appeared to be a screened-in porch. Just to one side of the door, a window above the sink looked out on dusty-looking trees, and beyond that, the barn and corrals she had seen from the airplane. Her heart quickened when she saw movement in the corrals. *Horses.*

"Bedrooms are in here." Cade was waiting for her in another doorway that opened off the kitchen to the right. He moved aside to let her pass, and she found herself in a small hallway with an open doorway—including the one in which she stood—in each of its four walls. Through one she could see a bathroom, with a deep iron tub with feet shaped like claws. The other two were bedrooms.

"Take your pick," he said, waving her toward them. "I think they're both about the same."

Leila peeked into both rooms, then walked through the doorway closest to her and placed her bag on the bed. She noticed that it was a much smaller bed than the one in Cade's room in Houston, but she did not linger and look as she had in the other parts of the house. There was nothing personal here, nothing to tell her which room Cade used when he visited the ranch. She felt a strangeness in being there with him so close behind her, and yet, so very far away. With so much unsaid between them there was awkwardness in the silence.

But, she thought, that is why I am here, because these things must be spoken of—they *will* be spoken of. *But not now. This is not the right time.*

Leaving her bag on the bed, she fixed a smile on her face and turned. "You said we could have breakfast? That is good, because I am hungry.'' She had eaten some toast with her one cup of coffee before leaving that morning, but it seemed a long time ago. "What must I do to help?" She felt strange little showers of shivers inside and rubbed her arms, though she wasn't cold.

"You want to *help?*" Cade looked at her, again with that *so* superior half smile that so clearly said he didn't see how she could. Leila was beginning to be very annoyed by that smile.

Back in the kitchen, he opened a drawer and took out a metal tool, which he placed on the countertop. Then he opened a cupboard and took out a large brown can. "If you want to help, why don't you open that while I get the coffeemaker going."

Leila picked up the tool, which was unlike anything she had seen before. It had two legs that opened when she pulled them, like a pair of scissors. Obviously, she was meant to use the tool to open the brown can, which contained coffee, she could see that. *I will not ask him. I will not.*

My God, thought Cade, she doesn't even know how to use a can opener. He wondered if she'd ever seen one before.

"It's…a can opener," he said gruffly, moving closer to her.

She glanced up at him—a patient look, as if he had said something stupid. "Yes, I know. It is just that I have never seen one…like it…before." There was a smudge of color in each cheek, and he wondered if it was pride, or embarrassment.

"It's, uh…pretty much just your classic can opener." He edged closer still. "They're kind of a basic necessity around here, since about the only things we can leave in the house are canned goods. Power's unreliable, so we can't leave anything in the freezer. And then there are the mice…''

"Mice?" She was gazing at him, not with the maidenly horror he'd expected, but with a bright and childlike delight. "Oh, do we have mice? I would very much like to see one." She tilted her head and dimpled thoughtfully. "I do not think I have ever seen a real mouse before."

Why am I not surprised? Cade thought. Aloud he muttered, "They're a damned nuisance."

"Perhaps you should keep a cat."

"Who'd take care of it when there's nobody here?"

"Perhaps…your neighbor, what was it? Mrs. Mac-Gruder? Since they must come to tend the horses anyway?" Her eyes were wide and ingenuous. He wondered how he'd come to be close enough to her to see himself reflected in their depths.

"What, once a day? Nah—animals need attention. You can't just leave them on their own all the time."

"Oh yes," she said softly, "that is true." And she looked at him just long enough before she said it that he felt a mean little stab of guilt.

"Here, why don't you let me do that?" he said roughly, reaching for the can opener.

She held it out of his reach. "No. I would like you to show me how to do it." And she added as a breathless afterthought, "Please."

Cade was awash with feelings he didn't know what to do with. Part of it was anger, or something close, and part was the kind of thing he imagined he might be feeling if he were trapped on a rocky shoal with the tide rising fast. And part of it, if he was honest with himself, was just plain old sexual excitement. It was her body heat, her woman's scent, partly familiar, partly exotic. He should never have let himself get so close to her. He was having trouble keeping his breathing quiet so she wouldn't hear how fast it was. He hoped she couldn't hear his heart hammering.

"Okay, here's what you do—here, let me show you." He reached again for the can opener.

And again she pulled it away, out of his reach. "No—I want to do it. Just please show me how."

What could he do? Gingerly as a rattlesnake wrangler, he reached across her and covered her hands with his. "First you open these up..." God, he could hardly breathe. "Then, you chomp down on the edge of the can—like this, see? That little hiss means you broke the seal. Then, you turn this..."

He felt like he was going to pass out, honest to God—just like the way he felt when he hadn't eaten in way too long. Only he didn't think he'd ever known hunger quite like this, couldn't remember ever wanting a woman the way he wanted this one. No, not wanting, *needing*. Like, if he couldn't have her right now, this minute, he might keel over right there on the floor.

It occurred to him that her hands weren't moving.

"I think we are finished," she whispered, and she was looking at him, not the can.

Oh, yeah, Cade thought, we're finished, all right. All his high-minded resolve? Dead...cooked. This was going to happen, and there wasn't a thing he could do to stop it.

It had come down to a matter of seconds...heartbeats. He could feel her heat and her scent seeping through his shirt and into his skin. His nerve-endings were learning the shape of her breast. She looked up at him and he stared down at her parted lips, and his throat was parched, thirsty almost to the point of madness for the taste of her.

The taste of her. He remembered it now. Oh yeah, it all came rushing back to him. And he knew in that moment that he'd never stopped thirsting for the taste of her.

He made a sound...whispered something, maybe her

name. His head dropped lower, closing that taunting distance between himself and the thing he craved....

A loud banging noise made him jerk upright with adrenaline squirting through his system like ice cold fire. The door—dammit. Someone was knocking on the back porch door.

A moment later, before the shock of that had begun to subside, there came a lighter tapping at the kitchen door. It opened, and a short, bandy-legged man with a completely bald head and cheeks as red as Santa Claus stuck his head in. His neighbor, of course. Deb MacGruder.

"Hey, how you folks doin'? Heard you come flyin' in."

It was impossible to stay irritated at ol' Deb, who had to be one of the nicest people ever put on this earth, and Cade didn't even try. Hoping he didn't look or sound as jangled as he felt, he invited the man in, introduced him to Leila and relieved him of the plastic grocery bags he'd brought with him.

"Edna sent you over some fresh eggs and a jug a'milk—figured you could use some." Cade noticed then that ol' Deb was sort of fidgeting and looking sideways at Leila and blushing like a tongue-tied teenager, and when he glanced over at her, he understood why. She had her dimples turned on, full wattage, and was looking about as lovely and charming as it was possible for a woman to look. Deb rubbed a hand over his sunburned scalp and coughed. "I, uh...put up some of the mares in the corral, just in case the two of you were wantin' to do some ridin' while you're here." He sounded as if he thought the possibility remote, under the circumstances.

But Cade heard a gasp from somewhere behind him, and Leila's voice, breathless and excited. "Oh, yes, thank you!"

And he realized that he ought to be feeling grateful. He'd been given a reprieve. All was not lost, after all.

Sure, he thought, what he had to do was keep his wife out riding all day until they were both so worn out and saddle sore they wouldn't be thinking about doing anything tonight except sleeping.

And tomorrow, well…that was another day. He'd cross that bridge when he came to it.

"Hey, what do you think you're doing? Come back here!"

Leila's answer to that was a peal of laughter. Crouching low over her mount's neck, she urged the mare to full gallop. Sure-footed like all of her breed, the roan mare's hooves seemed to fly over the hard ground. Dark shapes of the trees Cade had called junipers flashed by on either side of her, and their spicy scent rose into the muggy air.

At the top of the gentle rise Leila had a brief and exhilarating glimpse of forever, and then her heart lurched into her throat as the mare plunged over the top of the hill and skidded down…down into a sandy valley. With a squeal of sheer exuberance she urged the mare on across the sand and up the slope on the other side. And there she finally halted, with the wind whipping her hair and the view before her stretching all the way to the base of billowing black clouds. Laughing and out of breath, she waited for Cade to catch up.

"What the hell were you doing?" she heard him bellow as his horse's chestnut head with a white blaze appeared atop the rise. A moment later she saw Cade's face, and it was dark and stormy as the thunderclouds that filled the sky above their heads. "What're you trying to do, get yourself killed?"

Somehow, though, Leila knew the light in his eyes was not anger, and she tossed back her hair and smiled as she called back, "Killed? No, no—I am *living!*"

"Huh!" Muttering soothing things to his mount and patting her sweat-soaked neck, he brought her beside Leila's. "Living?"

"Oh, yes—do you not know? I am living a dream. *My* dream." She threw her arms wide and lifted her face to the sky. "I have dreamed of this—riding like the wind…land that goes on forever."

"Yeah, well, the land may go on forever, but my piece of it doesn't. You see that down there?" He jerked his head toward the limitless horizon, and he was throwing his leg over the saddle in a dismount that Leila was sure only a man with long legs and the body of a cowboy could accomplish gracefully. "That's where my property ends. If you'd decided to keep on going to the next hill over there, you *and* the mare would've run right smack into a barbed wire fence."

Leila was quite sure nothing of the sort would have happened, and that either she would have seen the fence in time to stop, or the mare would have. And then, most likely, they would have jumped over it.

But a wife must not argue with her husband. "Please, do not be angry with me, Cade. If you only knew—"

"I'm not angry with you," he muttered as he ducked under the chestnut mare's neck and came into the space between the two horses. "Here—your stirrups are too short. Put your leg up."

"Oh, but I like them this way. I am learning to ride Western style—Rueben has been teaching me—but I am not very good at it. He said I should get used to it a little at a time."

Cade gave his head a shake. "Looks like you were doing okay to me." He tipped back the brim of his hat and squinted up at her. "Where did you learn to ride like that?"

She felt a warm little rush of pride, felt it spread right into her cheeks. "My brother has horses—I told you that, remember? At the polo match. Arabians, like yours. I used to ride a lot when I was younger, before—'' She did not say, *Before I became a woman, and no longer had the freedom of a child.* "Before I got too busy with other things."

"Huh." He made a thoughtful sound and grudgingly added, "Well. Doesn't look like you've forgotten how." He looked at her for a long, silent moment, one hand on her saddlehorn, his arm resting on her horse's neck. He jerked his head and said, "Come on—get down for a bit. We'll give the horses a breather."

"A...breather?"

"A rest. Then I think we'd better be heading back. I don't like the looks of that sky."

Leila nodded and began to dismount. Then she stopped. She could not possibly manage the kind of graceful one-step dismount that Cade had used. Her stirrups were too short and her legs were, too. To dismount as she usually did, she would have to hold on to the saddle and lay her stomach across it while she freed her foot from the stirrup, then slide to the ground. But if she did that now, with Cade standing where he was, her backside would be only inches from his face. She was wearing jodhpurs, the only riding clothes she owned, and although they were not tight they did fit closely. If she was bending over, as she must, they could hardly help but outline her figure very clearly. The thought made her cheeks burn and her heartbeat quicken, but...not at all unpleasantly.

"Here—I'll give you a hand." He held out his arms to her, ready to help her dismount. His face had no expression at all. Even his eyes told her nothing; they were hidden in the shadow of his hat brim.

With pounding heart she considered her two choices. And then, with a sense of giving up a tiger in favor of a lion, she put her hands on his shoulders. She felt his hands, strong on her waist. Her throat closed and her breathing stopped.

Cade thought, what am I doing? He knew he should be more cautious around her, but something inside him was clearly enjoying this flirtation with disaster. He was like a child playing with matches, one old enough to understand the danger and arrogantly sure of his ability to avoid it.

Ah, but what a waist she had…slender and supple in his hands. Not so delicate and tiny he imagined his hands could span it, but firm and strong, with muscles that tightened under his palms as he lifted her down from the saddle.

He sensed a stiffening in her, too, that was more than the physical tensing of muscles, and to his profound regret, he thought he knew what it was. Not fear, exactly—he could see that she desperately wanted to feel at ease with him. It was as if she dared not allow herself to be. What she reminded him of—and his heart ached to realize it— was something he'd seen in Betsy's adopted strays, the guarded hopefulness of a once-friendly dog only lately grown used to unkindness.

Guarded. Yes. He understood, now, that where once she had been open to him, innocently eager and certain of her welcome as a well-loved child, now she was fortified against him. Against his rejection of her, at least. Pride had taken the place of innocence—she would not allow him to hurt her again.

The thought made him feel dismal and defeated, the more so because of the intensity with which he wanted her, right then, at that very moment. He remembered that night on the terrace overlooking the Mediterranean, his awareness that she was "forbidden fruit," and his wondering if she might have been the more desirable to him because of that. And if that was true, then what did it say about his character? Was he, Cade Gallagher, who prided himself on his honesty, on his sense of honor and responsibility, after all no more than a spoiled, contrary kid, wanting what he couldn't have?

A sound interrupted his dismal reflections—the soft rumbling of a cleared throat. Then it seemed that the thunder picked it up and carried it off into a darkening sky like a rolling echo, while Cade gazed down into the flushed face and luminous eyes of the woman he'd married, and felt that same rumbling in the back of his chest...the bottom of his belly.

A dust devil danced across the crest of the hill and swirled beneath the horses' feet. While the animals side-stepped nervously, it sprang like a teasing sprite into the sky, and Leila's laughter rose after it as, taking no chances, she held on to her hat with both hands. The hat reminded Cade of the one he'd retrieved for her from the polo field, and he could see from the way she suddenly went still and the way her eyes clung to his that she was remembering that day, too.

The dust devil had gone on its way, but the wind still tugged at him, nudging him as though it was trying to get his attention. It came to him in a fierce little gust of exultation: *She's not forbidden fruit. She's my wife. My wife!*

The thought crossed his mind that, as reprieves went, that one sure hadn't amounted to much.

He watched himself insert a wondering, wary finger under the cord that was supposed to keep her hat from blowing off, and slowly...slowly pull it out from under her chin. Questions sprang into her eyes, but she held them back with strong white teeth pressing into the softness of her lower lip. Moving as slowly as he did, she lowered her hands and let him take the hat. But he could see she had no idea what he meant to do. She couldn't hear the blood rushing through his body, like the sound of wind inside his head, or the merciless pounding of his heart.

Her eyes never left his face as he looped the string of

her hat over the horn of her saddle, then slowly took off
his own hat and hung it right over hers. His breath felt
heavy, and seemed to stick in his throat. Nerves jumped
and quivered in his belly. And still she didn't know.

He put his hands on the sides of her head and smoothed
back her sweat-damp hair with his thumbs. Tiny wrinkles
appeared in her flawless forehead, like ripples in satin. He
gazed at them, fascinated, while his thumbs stroked gentle
furrows above her ears. And *now* she knew.

A faint sound…a tiny movement drew his gaze, and he
saw that her lips had opened. He knew the question that
must be poised there—he'd heard it once before. *Do you
want to kiss me?* He also knew that she would never ask
him that question again.

Remembering the sweetness of that time, the innocence,
pain stabbed at him, ruthless and brutal. *What have I done
to her?* With a guttural little cry, he lowered his mouth to
hers.

The first shock that came to him then was how familiar
she seemed. As if, during all the time since he'd last kissed
her, his unconscious mind had gone right on learning the
shapes, tastes and textures of her. He wondered now if he'd
dreamed of her, those nights in the guest room or in the
hotel room in Dallas, when he'd woken up with the sheets
in a tangle and his body in a sweaty fever, aching with
unfulfilled desire.

How unbelievably good her mouth tasted to him—his
very favorite food when his belly was empty…cool pure
water when he was dying of thirst. Like a starving man, he
tried to remind himself to go slowly, to not be greedy, lest
he overwhelm himself and her. And so he separated his
mouth from hers and pulled back a little…but only a little,
and only long enough to savor the misty puffs of her ex-
halations, so soft and sweet he thought it must be like a
flower breathing. He thought of that, and of their own vo-

lition, just before they touched hers again, his lips formed themselves into a smile.

So caught up was he in his own sensations, he didn't notice right away that she was trembling. When that awareness did penetrate the blissful fog he was in, he felt a bright stab of pain. Like a shaft of sunlight, it melted away the insulating blanket of reason he'd kept wrapped around his emotions, and he felt the burn of desire...unsuppressed, unshielded, inescapable.

He had no defenses for it. He wanted her. Wanted her under him, her thighs making a cradle for him, and her breasts pillows for his chest. He ached to be inside her, to feel her soft, enfolding warmth around him. He wanted...he *needed* her, more than he needed his next breath.

A shudder rocked him from head to toe and a groan rumbled deep inside his chest as he let go of her head and wrapped his arms around her, enfolding her and bringing her body against him with all the restraint he could muster. It cost him dearly, that restraint; he could feel himself tremble. But oh, how good it felt to hold her, that marvelous body he'd never seen, so strong and supple he could feel every line and curve even through the clothes she wore. Avidly, he skimmed her body with his hands like a blind man exploring a new and wondrous gift. Eyes closed, he immersed himself in the sensual banquet of her body...the warmth and textures of her...the taste and smell, even the whimpering, whispering sounds—

No—that wasn't Leila. The horses. Close on both sides of them, they were tossing their heads and sidestepping, whickering nervously. An instant later there was a deafening *boom.* Cade jerked as if he'd been shot.

For one moment, Leila wondered if *she* had been shot. For this was just what she had always imagined it would feel like to suffer calamitous injury—a cold emptiness and no pain at all, only a trembling that would not stop.

"Are you okay?" Cade was holding her by the arms, looking down at her with dark, smoky eyes.

"Yes, of course." And she could not imagine how her voice could sound so okay when she was anything but. It was the night on the terrace all over again; she could not imagine how she would stand alone if he let go of her. Deciding she did not want to find out, she reached behind her with a surreptitious hand and grasped a stirrup for support.

"That lightning was close. We'd best get off of this hilltop before the next one comes." His voice sounded as if he needed to cough.

Leila nodded. Without another word she turned her back to him and reached up to grasp the saddlehorn as he bent down to make a stirrup for her with his hands. A moment later she was sitting in the saddle, calmly adjusting her hatstring under her chin as thunder rumbled and growled in the vast roiling sky above her head. *That is how I feel,* she thought, gazing up at it. *So much darkness and tension and tumult.*

She was glad to follow Cade down the slope into the sandy wash, then quickly up the other side...glad to break into a gallop when the first raindrops came. She had known thunderstorms, of course, but to actually be outside in one was very different from watching from the calm and safety of the royal palace, or Cade's solid brick house near Houston. Suddenly those endless vistas she'd longed for, that vast sky that had seemed to promise freedom and limitless possibilities, now was filled with violence and danger, forces powerful beyond imagining. It was awe-inspiring, yes, but frightening, too. And Leila was glad. Glad that her mind was all taken up with awe and fear and coping with powerful forces of nature, and that, for the moment, at least, there was no room left for thoughts of Cade, and what had just happened to her.

The first little shower passed quickly, hard pelting drops that stung like pebbles. But the storm seemed to be following them—chasing them, Leila thought. Spiteful Nature, bellowing and grumbling at two thoughtless trespassers and hurling handfuls of stinging raindrops at their backs. The day seemed to grow darker, until it seemed as though day had become evening. She could see the lightning flashes now, not just hear the thunder that came after, and she was glad when they reached the live oaks that told her they were coming close to the ranch.

They had been moving at an easy gallop, a gait Cade had told her was called a lope, riding single file, following a well-worn path through the trees because the sandy ground there was all but covered with clumps of low-growing cactus. As she followed along behind Cade, for some reason—perhaps because they were nearly home and shelter was not far off—Leila's thoughts began to creep back to the terrifying thing that had happened to her, there on the hilltop. Her thoughts were still full of awe and fear and powerful forces of nature, but now those things had a name, a face—*Cade's.*

She stared at his back as they loped along through the twisty, gray-green trees, thinking how strong and powerful he looked, with his broad shoulders and long, lean body, admiring the way he sat so tall and straight, with his butt firm in the saddle, the American—the *Western*—way. Like a cowboy. And her heart began to pound almost with the same rhythm as the horses' hooves. What is happening to me? she wondered. Something had happened to her when he kissed her, something awesome and frightening. Something wonderful. She had trembled with it.

And then, like a lightning bolt, it struck her. *It happened to him, too. I know it did. Because I felt him tremble, too.*

Seized by a tremendous exhilaration, she urged her mount forward until she had caught up with Cade. There was barely enough room on the path for two horses to go abreast, but she nudged her roan mare right up beside the chestnut, until her leg brushed Cade's. She looked over at him, not smiling, her gaze intent and searching. He looked back at her....

There was almost no warning at all. Just a sizzling sound. An instant later a flash and a tremendous *Cr-ack.*

Leila's mount tensed, then lunged forward in full stampede. It took Leila only a few seconds to bring the terrified animal back under control, and as she was walking the mare in calming circles, crooning to her in Arabic and patting her sweat-slick neck, Cade's chestnut mare came galloping past her, eyes wild, white-ringed with panic.

Without Cade.

Chapter 11

Leila stared after the riderless mare, refusing to accept the evidence of her own eyes. Then her heart grew cold and she wheeled the panting roan sharply on the narrow path and raced back the way she had come. As she rode she called Cade's name and whispered prayers under her breath. *Oh please, God, most merciful God, please let him be all right...*

She found him without any trouble at all. Cade was only a short distance from the path, lying on his back on the ground with the upper part of his body raised and his weight on his elbows. Once she was assured—both by his position and the glare of helpless fury on his face—that her prayers had been answered, Leila's next impulse was to laugh. As she had laughed when her brother Rashid had been thrown from his pony once while they were racing on the cliffs overlooking the sea. Oh, how she had laughed to see the regal and arrogant Rashid flat on his backside in the grass! But crown prince or not, Rashid was only her brother. Cade was her husband! She should not laugh at her husband!

Horrified—and helpless to stop it—Leila clapped a hand over her mouth as she reined the roan mare to a halt. She was snuffling with mirth as she hurled herself from the saddle.

"Cade—what has happened? Are you all right?"

"Not…really." His voice sounded airless and strained, and she realized that he was trying to hide a grimace of pain.

She started to go to him, feeling even more terrible for laughing when he must be hurt after all. But he threw up a warning hand with an urgent gasp. "No—don't come any closer. There's cactus everywhere." His lips drew back over tightly clenched teeth. "I think I must have landed in a patch of it."

This time her hand flew to her mouth in time to muffle her horrified cry. "Oh, Cade—what must I do? How can I help you?" She was bending over him, having disregarded his warning and picked her way through the cactus to his side.

He shifted in an experimental way and then grunted. "Not…much you can do to help. Unless you think you could throw me over your shoulder and carry me home." He flicked her a glance and a crooked, embarrassed smile.

Cade Gallagher—*embarrassed?* Only this morning such a thing would have seemed impossible to her, but now…oh yes, she could see it very clearly. Her so very imposing, intimidating, commanding husband was embarrassed. Quite humiliated, in fact.

Realizing that, she felt a surge of feeling so alien to her that it was a minute or two before she understood what it was. *Power.* For the first time in her life, Leila felt…powerful.

"No, I do not think I would be able to carry you," she

said as a strange, protective tenderness began to layer itself with the newfound strength inside of her. "But perhaps the horse—"

He snorted disgustedly. "Don't think I'm going to be sitting on a horse—or anything else—not until I get these damn spines out of my backside, anyway."

Leila smiled, gently sympathetic. "I was not suggesting that you should sit. But I think, if you were to lay yourself on your stomach across the saddle—"

"Hell no!" He reminded Leila very much of an unhappy child. "I'm not about to be carried home like a sack of oats—no way."

She lowered her eyes. "I am sorry. I was only trying—"

"Look—" He touched her cheek, and she felt a stirring of pleasure, understanding then that he was only gruff with her because he was so frustrated. "I told you—there's nothing you can do, okay?" But he made a liar of himself by adding, "Just...give me a hand up."

"Forgive me, but I must ask," said Leila, when he was more or less on his feet again and working himself carefully inch by inch upright. "If you cannot ride, how *do* you propose to get back to the ranch?" Before he could answer, she touched her fingertips to her lips and exclaimed, "Oh! And your poor horse, will she be all right? Should I not go and look for her?"

He gave her a sideways, reproachful look. "My 'poor horse?' Hell, she's long back at the barn by now. *Bibi.*" He snorted, then muttered, "Never did like that horse."

"What happened to her? I heard such a loud noise—"

"Lightning struck a tree," said Cade, and his voice was tight with pain as he cautiously eased his weight from one foot to the other. "Pretty close by, too. Didn't you feel it?" As if to underline the question, thunder grumbled and rolled across the grove of trees, and leaves rustled in the rising wind.

"Well, yes, but then I was too busy trying to control my Kamilah, here—yes, and you are my 'perfect one,' yes, you are…" Leila crooned, as the roan mare, perhaps recognizing her name, began to nibble at her hair. The mare had been waiting on the path—like cow ponies, all of Cade's horses were trained to "ground tie," or stand still when their reins were dropped to the ground—and she was growing impatient for Leila's return. "Kamilah was also very frightened—weren't you, my sweet? She tried to run away." Leila took great care not to mention the fact that *she* had not landed in the cactus.

Nevertheless, Cade gave her a dark look and grunted like a bad-tempered camel. "At least yours took off in a straight line. Mine went sideways. Next thing I knew, my butt was bouncing through the cactus." He paused as if listening to the words he had just spoken, then grinned crookedly at her, in a way that made her heart feel fluttery and soft. "This is probably going to seem funny as hell to me someday, but right now it hurts too damn much to laugh."

Leila didn't feel like laughing, either. She realized that what she wanted more than anything in the world was to put her arms around him—or at least touch his face…stroke and soothe him. But she sensed that would be the last thing he would want from her now. Still, she could not resist asking, in a voice husky with concern, "Are you…in very much pain?"

Then, of course, being a man, he must try to be heroic and act as though he was not. "Oh, hell—I'll live. I guess I've been in worse shape." He paused in the middle of hobbling back to the path to tilt his head sideways. "Been awhile, though."

Leila gave a small gasp. "Do you mean that this has happened to you before?"

"No, no—" his laugh was dark rather than humorous

"—I was thinking of the last time my dad tanned my back-side with his belt. I guess I must have been twelve."

"You do not mean—he *beat* you?" Her tender heart was appalled. "But...that is terrible!"

He paused to look down at her. Her heart jumped nervously, then began to beat with a quick and painful rhythm. "Hey, what can I say?" he said softly. "He was a drunk. I guess I never told you that, huh."

No, Leila thought, precarious and wondering. *Betsy did, but you didn't. And little else about yourself, either.* And she held her breath and prayed that he would not stop now.

He lifted his head to gaze beyond her. "Actually, he was a pretty decent guy when he wasn't drinking. Of course, he was drunk most of the time. Although to be honest, on that particular occasion—from his point of view, anyway—I probably deserved the licking."

"What did you do?" Her voice was hushed; she did not believe he could have done anything that would deserve a beating.

He gave a bark of laughter and his eyes came back to her. "Took my bike apart. Brand new—just got it for my birthday. Don't know what it cost, but it had to be expensive. I'd been begging for one for months, knowing my parents couldn't afford it." He shook his head; his eyes seemed to glow with remembering. "I couldn't believe it when I went out that morning and there it was." He paused, but Leila did not interrupt.

After a moment he drew a breath that seemed to hurt him, but inside, not where the cactus spines were. And when he tried to smile again, there was only the slightest flicker at the corners of his mouth. "Anyway, when my dad came home that evening, I had that bike in a million pieces. Had 'em all spread out on a blanket on the floor of the garage. I thought he was going to kill me. Darn near did. Then he rolled all those pieces into the blanket and threw 'em in the back of his truck and drove off. Last I ever saw of my bike." He drew the pain-filled breath again. "That hurt worse than the licking."

"But, why?" Leila dared to whisper. "Why did you do such a thing to this bike you wanted so much?"

He shrugged. "I just wanted to see how everything worked, find out how it all fit together. I was going to put it all back. It's just the way I am—the way I've always been." He frowned, looking past her again. "My mom understood that, but for some reason Dad…" After a moment he brought his eyes back to her, and the pain in them almost made her cry out in instinctive response. Because, as before, she knew this pain was not caused by the cactus spines, but by memories carried deep in his heart. "Anyway, my folks split up a couple months after that. For years I thought it was because of me. Silly, huh?" He gave his head a rueful scratch.

Then, in what even to Leila seemed an obvious attempt to escape these "unmanly" emotions, he gruffly muttered, "Where the hell's my hat?"

No, she thought, I do not think you are silly at all. I think you are a very strong and imposing man with a little boy inside you. A little boy who has been very much hurt. And I love that you have told me these things, even here in the middle of a cactus patch. I wish that you would not feel embarrassed that you have told me. And I wish that you would not stop.

But all she said out loud was, "There it is. Wait—I will get it." And she ran to scoop up his cowboy hat from the path. "Now it is my turn to rescue *your* hat," she said in a bumpy voice as she held it out to him, and as she did, touched his eyes with hers. And with that look, with all that was in her eyes, she was offering her compassionate woman's heart to the hurt little boy she had seen in his.

Offering her newfound strength to him as she might have given her hand to a child.

The look lasted for uncounted seconds, in a silence that seemed to shimmer with electricity, to rumble with tension like distant thunder.

Leila spoke at last, in a choked whisper. "We do not seem to have very good luck with hats, you and I."

And at that moment the rain came, rain such as Leila had never seen before. It fell with a great rushing sound, hard and heavy, straight down on their heads, as if someone had turned on a giant faucet in the sky. In seconds they were both drenched and gasping, and Leila's hat, which, unlike Cade's, was not meant to withstand all kinds of weather, had begun to wilt like a paper boat in a fountain.

"*You* sure don't," Cade shouted, and reached out to tip the sodden wreck of her hat backward and off of her head. "Look, why don't you go on—you know the way back to the ranch from here, don't you? Take the mare and go. I'll meet you back—"

"Are you *crazy?*" Leila shouted back through the curtain of rain, not even thinking that perhaps it was not the sort of thing a woman should say to her husband. "Do you think I would go away and leave you?"

"What, do you think I'm helpless?" Cade sputtered, looking very much like a stubborn donkey. "Go on—get in out of this!"

"Of course I do not think you are helpless. And I do not dissolve in water. This is only a little rain. So, we will walk home. It cannot be far."

Cade glared at her. The rain was already beginning to slacken at little, so he did not *really* have to shout at her the way he did. "Do you know that for a princess, you are awfully damn stubborn?"

"Yes," she said, flashing her dimples, "I suppose that I

am.'' And she was surprised, because it was the first time all day that she had even remembered that she was a princess.

"Damn," Cade said gloomily, "I should have known." He flicked the light switch up and down again, with the same result. The power was out again. Naturally.

"It is not so *very* dark," Leila said as she slipped past him. "We can see quite well. It will not be night for several hours. By that time perhaps the electricity will be back on."

Cade made an ambiguous sound as he closed the door behind him. Then he stood for a moment and regarded her warily in the dim, shadowy light. He wasn't quite sure what to make of this new Leila, couldn't even decide in exactly what ways she *was* new. Her cheerfulness in the face of all the various discomforts and inconveniences he'd put her through was unexpected, maybe, except when he stopped to realize that he never really had heard her complain. Ever. Then there was the way she'd stood by him, out there in the cactus and the rain, when she could have been nice and cozy in a dry house. And he hadn't forgotten what had happened between them up there on the hilltop. God, no. But this "newness" didn't have anything to do with those things.

No...if he had to put a name to it, he'd probably call it self-confidence, though that commodity wasn't exactly new to her, either. She'd sure had no lack of it when he'd first met her. But this...whatever it was...was nothing like the unabashed cheekiness that had made her seem so young— and which he'd found so alluring-in the fairy-tale atmosphere of Tamir. He couldn't quite put his finger on why, but he knew this was different. And that his awareness of it, and her, was a vibrating knot of energy in the core of his body, like a miniature dynamo pumping out electrical impulses along all his nerves, keeping his senses charged to full capacity and tuned to her precise wavelength.

Those humming nerves made him cranky and snappish. "Yeah, well, it's gonna be tough to see to pull out these damn cactus spines," he growled, hunching his shoulders and heading for the kitchen like a man walking on eggs.

She pivoted as he passed her, then followed him. "How are you going to do that?"

"What, pull out the spines?" He was rummaging in the drawer where he kept the flashlights and other essentials, and didn't look at her. Though he could have gauged his distance from her as accurately as if he'd been equipped with his own personal GPS. "Only thing I know of that'll do the job is a pair of needlenose pliers. Like these right here." Having located his in the drawer, he brandished them at her.

"No, I mean, how are *you* going to do it?" She was regarding him calmly, all shades of black and gray in the murky light. "The cactus is in your back, is it not?" He glared at her, unable to think of a thing to say. She came toward him, and his skin shivered with goose bumps. "I think that you will need help to pull out these spines." And she had taken the pliers from his hand before he could stop her.

When she would have taken the flashlight as well, though, he jerked it away from her like an obstinate child. "No," he croaked. "No way. I'll manage. I'll...I'll use a mirror."

"And who will hold the flashlight?" He was sure he could hear laughter in her voice. "Will you grow a third hand?" Cade made a growling sound in his throat and headed for the bathroom. In his wake he heard a patient little sigh. "Cade, please do not be stubborn. You know that you cannot possibly do this by yourself. You must let me help you."

She stood in the bathroom doorway and watched him struggle with it, watched him strain to find a reason why she must be wrong. She did not know why it was such a struggle for him. That was why she sighed.

Daringly, she said, "Is it so difficult for you, to let a woman tend you? Perhaps I do not understand. Is this not allowed in America—in Texas? Is it not—what is the word I have heard—*macho?*" She dimpled shamelessly at him; whether or not he could see them in the dimness, he would hear them in her voice.

He must have, because the sound he made was only a half-hearted snort. He did not growl at her as fiercely as before.

But then pain hissed between his teeth. He had unbuttoned his shirt and pulled it open, and was trying to shrug it away from his shoulders and back. The flashlight in his hand was an encumbrance to him now, and she thought it a minor victory that he did not object when she took it from him.

She switched the light on and trained it on his back.

"How bad is it?" He was straining to see over his shoulder.

She hastily turned off the light. "Not so terrible as I expected." She imagined the lie balanced on her tongue like a soap bubble. "I will have them out in no time. But first, we must have some antiseptic, I think. There is something here, surely? A medicine kit?"

Cade braced on the sink and glared at his hands, anchoring himself in the familiar shape of them, dark against the white porcelain as he felt his world, his life spin out of his reach. He felt an odd sense of fatalism, like an off balance skier heading down a treacherous slope. One way or another he was bound to get to the bottom.

"Yeah, in the plane," he muttered. "Somewhere around here, too, probably, but I'm damned if I know where."

"Never mind, I think I have seen something…" Her voice, somehow both breathless and tranquil, had retreated back into the kitchen. "Yes—here it is. This will do, I think…"

Curious to see what it was she'd found, afraid he already knew, he met her in the hallway. Sure enough. There was just enough light for him to see the bottle in her hands.

"Hey," he said, in a voice ragged with outrage, "that's good bourbon."

"Yes—it is alcohol, is it not?" He watched as she unscrewed the cap and took a sniff. His jaws cramped and his mouth began to water. "Mmm, and it smells good, too. Much nicer than the medicine kind. Come—" she waved the bottle imperiously "—it will be better, I think, if you lie down."

Cade meekly followed her into the bedroom she'd chosen—the one with her things in it. His heart was thumping and the energy dynamo inside him was whining away at fever pitch. And this rushing noise in his head—was that the sound of his life—events, fate—racing by, just beyond his reach?

She stood beside the bed and watched him come to her, the bottle of bourbon in one hand, the flashlight and needle-nose pliers in the other and her eyes full of mysteries. She drew a breath and when she spoke her voice was breathless still, but no longer the slightest bit tranquil. "First," she said—and he *knew* he could hear a tremor in it— "it will be necessary for you to remove your trousers."

And he felt a shivering, quivering, wholly unexpected desire to laugh when she abruptly turned her back and closed her eyes. He thought it was so like her. His virgin princess…

Oh, Leila thought, I really wish my voice had not trembled. She felt shaky all over, and she really could not allow that. It was not fear that made her tremble—she still felt that heady and wonderful sense of power, a kind of strength she somehow knew must be uniquely female. No—she shivered now with *excitement.* Something new…something she had never felt before. She shivered and shivered and could not seem to stop.

"I think," Cade said in a muffled voice, "that's about the best I can do. Hurts too much to bend over…"

She opened her eyes and turned, and her heart felt as though it had lodged in her throat. He was lying facedown across the bed, looking all gangly and ungraceful with his feet hanging over the edge. His trousers were bunched around the tops of his boots. Except for that, and a strip of white cloth across his buttocks, he was naked.

She placed the bottle of bourbon, the pliers and flashlight on the bed and gulped a breath of air. "Well," she said brightly, "I told you you would need my help."

She snatched another breath. Then she firmly grasped one booted foot and pulled. She felt his muscles tighten and pull against hers, and in another moment the boot slipped off and dropped onto the floor with a thump. Light-headed with that triumph, she went to the other foot and quickly did the same. Then she took hold of both legs of his blue jeans at the same time and pulled them off, then dropped them on top of the boots. By that time her legs were trembling so badly, it was a relief to sit down on the bed.

Except that when she did, she heard the gasp of Cade's indrawn breath. "What?" she whispered, afraid that she had hurt him. *Already!* She had not even begun to pull out the cactus!

"You're all wet," he mumbled. "You'll catch cold."

Yes, she was. Strange, but she had not thought about her wet clothes at all. Leila was quite certain she would not catch cold—she was never ill—but clearly she could not proceed with this delicate business dressed as she was.

There was only one thing to be done. One by one she pulled off her riding boots and dropped them on the floor beside Cade's. Then she stood up. "I will only be a moment," she whispered, and sternly added, when he raised himself on his elbows to try and see what she was doing, "No—you must lie still. And...close your eyes."

Then, as quickly as she could manage with nerveless, shaking fingers, she peeled off her blouse and jodhpurs and let them fall to the floor along with the rest of the wet clothing.

Her flesh cringed with goose bumps as she sat once more on the bed, taking care this time not to let her clammy skin touch Cade's. Her breasts felt hard as marble, and hurt where they brushed the inside of her bra. She drew yet another deep breath—why could she not seem to get enough air?

"I am ready," she whispered. Cade's only reply was a mutter she could not understand.

She picked up the flashlight and switched it on—caught her lower lip between her teeth and exhaled carefully through her nose. She had seen men's naked bodies before in pictures, of course, and in Rome and Paris, and in the British Museum there had been statues. But there was a great difference, she was discovering, between flat paintings and cold bronze or stone, and a warm, vital male body. What astonished her most was an almost overwhelming desire to *touch*. That little valley low on his back, just above the waistband of his underwear, dark with a furring of golden brown hair. The longing to bury her nose and mouth in that valley, to feel the softness of his hair on her face...it was so intense it made her head swim. Even as a small child Leila had liked to explore with her nose and mouth, lips and tongue, smelling and tasting as well as touching.

And she would—she silently promised herself that. But first there was the impediment of the cactus spines to deal with....

They did not look like much, really, just a scattering of

prickles not very different in color from his skin, and a few
drops of blood. Some of the prickles had already come
away with his clothing. There were a few on his shoulders
and elbows and thighs, more on his lower back, and quite
a few more, she was certain, imbedded in the white cotton
that covered his backside. Her hand shook as she picked
up the pliers. She set them back down on the bed and
picked up the bottle of bourbon instead.

"Well?" Cade's voice sounded muffled. "What's the
holdup? Let's get this over with."

"Be still," she said. Her voice sounded cracked and
strange. Balancing the flashlight across her lap, she unscrewed the top of the bottle. The flashlight teetered as she
pulled up one leg and turned herself toward him. Carefully,
she poured a tiny amount of the liquid in the bottle into
that golden nest of hair.

His muscles contracted and his spine arched. He muttered something she could not hear.

"What?" Breathless, she held the bottle poised…
motionless.

"I said, 'That's a helluva waste of good bourbon.'"

"Do you think so?" Leila tilted her head and regarded
the bottle thoughtfully. Then she sniffed it again. It did
smell good. Perhaps… She lifted the bottle to her lips and
took a very large swallow.

What the hell—? Cade pushed himself up on one elbow
to stare at Leila, who all of a sudden had begun to gasp
and choke and wheeze as if she were dying. It took him
about half a second to figure out that it wasn't lighter fluid
she'd swallowed, but only a pretty good slug of his bourbon. He snaked out a hand and rescued both the bottle and
the flashlight while he waited for her to get her breath back.

"But—it tastes *terrible,*" she croaked when she could
speak again, glaring at him accusingly, as if it were somehow Cade's fault. "How can you drink this?"

"It grows on you," he said, and automatically, because of his father, added, "Too much, if you let it." But his mind wasn't on bourbon, or the words coming out of his mouth.

Because he'd just realized what he was looking at, pinioned in the yellow circlet of the flashlight beam. Something that up to now he'd only dreamed about. Leila...wearing bikini panties and a lacy white bra and absolutely nothing else. It was a sight to fill a man's dreams...an athlete's thighs, smooth and sleek...womanly flare of hips... The waist he'd held in his hands up there on the hilltop seemed even more slender than he'd imagined, contrasted with the lush femininity above and below. And her breasts... It was all he could do to keep himself from reaching out, pulling those bra straps down over her shoulders.

Then, for an instant he wondered if she'd somehow guessed his thoughts, when she pressed a hand to her chest and her skin seemed to darken to a dusky rose. But he realized that she was stroking, not hiding, and making an odd little pleasure-sound, like a large cat purring.

"Mmm...oh," she murmured. "Yes, I see what you mean. It feels very nice, now. Nice and warm...all over inside me." She gave herself a shake and added with delightful primness, "Well—it is a pity that something that smells so nice and feels so good must taste so awful. But, perhaps it is just as well, since I do not believe it is very good for you." She plucked the bottle and the flashlight from his hands. "Now you must lie down and let me finish," she said, and gave him a severe look that had the opposite effect on him than she probably intended.

He obeyed her with a groan, somehow managing to quell the impulse he'd just had, which was to just say the hell with the cactus, and roll her under him and kiss her breathless.

He never knew how he got through the next hour, quite possibly the most intense pleasure and the most exquisite agony he could ever have imagined. And the cactus spines had very little to do with it.

Lying there on his belly with his mind full of the last image he'd had of her—lush, curving flesh and taunting strips of lacy white—first he'd feel a tiny *zzt* of pain, then the sweet burn of the bourbon, and then the far sweeter warmth of her mouth…gentle heat and drawing pressure…and sometimes, when she forgot to hold it back out of the way, the cool silky kiss of her hair. Between times, she sang to him in a sweet, soft voice, in a language he didn't know. And when she had cleared an area of spines large enough, she would pour more bourbon into her hands and rub him all over with it…stroking, massaging…kneading the sting and the ache away. That was the pleasure.

The agony was elsewhere. In his groin, of course, but in his belly, too, and the muscles of his arms and legs, his neck and jaws. Desire had taken over his body; it was a white-hot starburst in his brain. He was being consumed by desire. Sooner or later, he knew, he would have to do something about it, and when he did, he was desperately afraid he wouldn't be able to control the monster that was eating him alive.

And he knew the worst was yet to come. She'd worked her way down his back to the elastic waistband of his shorts. She'd plucked the last of the spines from the backs of his arms and legs. When he felt her fingers slip under that elastic he knew he'd endured all he could. He made a sound somewhere between a sob and a groan and tried to turn.

"No, no," she said softly, "you must let me finish." Gently but firmly she pushed him down. Even more gently she lifted his shorts away from his pricked backside, drew them over his legs and tossed them away.

And he found there was more he *could* endure, after all.

But just barely. He'd never felt so vulnerable. The cool air stirring over exposed skin, like a touch that never quite came, the cold wet tickle of alcohol between his legs and down his sides, and then—with all his strength he braced for it—*her mouth*. Yes, even there, laving, sucking…soothing away the sting. He could hear her quick, shallow breathing above the labored pounding of his own heart—for some reason, she'd stopped singing.

He knew when she'd pulled the last of the spines. He heard her take in a breath and let it out in a soft and oddly replete little sigh. He felt her weight shift as she set the bottle of bourbon on the nightstand. Then shift again. He felt the cushiony weight of her breasts as she bent over him. Relief and alarm slammed into him and his heart skidded and lurched out of rhythm. *No.*

Had he spoken? What did it matter? His body shuddered and shivered with adrenaline as he caught her around her waist. In an instant he'd pinned her, flat on her back, to the mattress.

The flashlight rolled away somewhere, but it spilled enough light across the bed that he could see her face staring up at him…the dark enigma of her eyes, utterly without fear, just tiny lines of puzzlement between them.

Her breasts heaved beneath his arm as she whispered, "You do not wish me to continue?"

"No." This time he knew he'd spoken, but it was in a voice he didn't recognize. "And it's not a matter of wishing. I can't let you."

"Why? I do not understand. Do you not like it?"

Looking up and away from her, he gave a soft, croaking laugh. Then he brought his eyes back to her, and was caught off guard by a treacherous, shimmering fog of overwhelming tenderness. Like that strange, protective tenderness he'd felt for her before, only this was much, much worse. He couldn't speak, but had to look away again, and take deep breaths and laugh a little the way men do when they dare not humiliate themselves with symptoms of emotion.

When he was able to look at her again, he lifted a hand to touch her face. Softly, with wondering fingers he traced the ink-black line of her eyebrow, the clean, pure sweep of her cheek and jaw.

"Don't you know?" He shrugged one shoulder and said it with aching simplicity. "You're a virgin."

Chapter 12

She didn't say anything for several seconds, while her heartbeat fluttered against the barricade of his arm like a captive bird struggling to free itself. Then she made a sound, a perplexed and impatient little sigh.

"In my culture," she whispered, and her frown deepened as she searched his face, "a man would consider a woman's virginity a treasure...a gift. I think that for you this is not true. I think...for you it is only a burden."

"Not so much a burden..." He considered, his voice gravelly and soft. "More like...a responsibility."

"But...why?" She gave a hopeless little sigh and said again, "I do not understand."

And again Cade had to gaze into the shadows beyond the light while he gathered his courage. She couldn't know, could she, how hard it was for him to talk about such intimate things? "I'm too full...too hard...right now. Too...aroused." He took a breath, but the words wouldn't come, and finally he whispered it brokenly, "I don't think I could stand it if I hurt you."

"Oh," she cried, "is that all?" Her eager innocence nearly shattered him. Her fingers closed around his wrist. She turned her lips into his palm like a bird snuggling into its nest, and he could feel them form a smile against his skin. She closed her eyes, and something glimmered like tiny diamonds in her lashes. She whispered, "I thought…it was because you did not want me."

He was too precarious; he dared not laugh. With a soft groan he lowered his forehead until it touched hers. "Not want you? No, no, it's that I want you too much."

Her fingers left his wrist and wove themselves into his hair. Her face tilted and her lips touched searchingly here and there on his face…his chin, the edges of his jaws, the corners of his mouth. Between touches, in breathless little puffs he heard words. "But I am…your wife. How…is it possible…to want…your wife…too much?"

Your wife. He replayed the words in his head and his heart shuddered as if from a violent collision. In a sense it was—a collision between heart and head…between reason and emotion. If you do this, his head reminded him, it can't be undone.

To which his heart responded, *I don't care!*

In slow, sighing surrender he brought his mouth into alignment with hers…barely touching…brushing her breath with his. He felt her go motionless with wonder. Her lips opened in a blissful, waiting smile. She moved her head slowly back and forth, caressing his lips with hers, mercilessly teasing nerve-endings already honed to needle points. He felt the caress in his temples and breastbone, in the soles of his feet and the backs of his knees, in the pit of his stomach…and with a deep, burning ache in his groin.

If I kiss her now, he thought—he absolutely knew—*I won't be able to stop.*

"It is all right," she murmured, as if she'd heard his

thought, her words tickling his lips. "I have been told it is normal for there to be pain the first time. I do not mind."

With a quick, violent motion he caught her wrist and held it pressed against the bedspread while he drew back to look at her. Her breasts rose and fell in uneven rhythm, brushing against his arm. He frowned down at them and muttered groggily, "Who told you that?" Whoever it had been, in his heart he was vowing there and then to make that person a liar.

"Salma. When I was very small she was my nanny. Now she is my very dear friend. And she gave me something to help soothe the pain...a special recipe of herbs and oils. She said it is from her grandmother."

Herbs and oils? He was beginning to get *The Arabian Nights* feeling again. That sense of unreality grew more encompassing as he listened to the muffled thump of his heart...heard his own voice as if through layers of wool. Carefully, trying not to smile, he said, "And you...brought this magic stuff with you?"

"Yes, of course—I have it right here, in my bag." And lithe as an otter she twisted under him, rolling onto her stomach as she stretched an arm to reach for her overnighter.

He barely knew when she opened it and began to rummage through its contents. Raised on one elbow, he gazed at her body...the pale, curving shape of it against the darker bedspread...and paler still the narrow stripe across her back...the triangle that barely succeeded in covering the rounded mounds of her bottom. He was thinking about himself in just that position, the treatment she'd put him through...his terrifying vulnerability, the exquisite sensations...his overwhelming arousal.

She gave a soft "Hah!" of triumph and held up a bottle, graceful in shape and iridescent in color. But before she could roll back to him, he growled, "Not so fast," and with a hand on the small of her back, pinned her there on her belly. In a moment he was kneeling astride her thighs, bending over to whisper in her ear, "Now it's my turn...."

Though the pain of desire, the pressure of his arousal as merciless as before, now his mind, at least, was clear. He felt in control again, of himself and of circumstances. Confidence surged like a drug through his veins. He felt light-headed with his power over her, and at the same time he quivered inside with tenderness.

Oh, so gently, because he knew from firsthand experience how helpless and vulnerable she must be feeling, he drew the silken skein of her hair away from her face and neck, pausing to trace, with a delicacy he'd never known he possessed, the outline of her ear. He heard her exhale as he brushed her cheek with the backs of his fingers, and felt the tickle of her lashes as she closed her eyes.

He straightened, then, and deftly unhooked the fastening of her bra, and with his fingers fanned outward like a moth's wings drew his thumbs downward along her spine, acquainting her with his touch. Her skin felt hot and smooth, as if she had a fever.

He eased the bottle from her curled fingers and opened it, then held the bottle to his nose. The fragrance was exotic...mysterious...intoxicating...all the things he associated with *her*. It filled his head with images...impressions... memories...of sun-drenched gardens heavy with the scent of roses, of laughing fountains and brightly colored birds, and of a black-haired princess with a winsome, dimpled smile.

Setting aside the cap, he poured a small pool of oil into the valley between her shoulderblades. He began to spread it over her body, working like a master sculptor, kneading and molding, sometimes with his fingers, sometimes with his whole hands, utterly engrossed in the artistry of her body, the utter perfection of her muscles, the way they arranged themselves so beautifully over her bones. The clever symmetry of her spine…

She wasn't as relaxed as she seemed. She stirred when he eased himself backward, fingers reaching under the lacy top of her underpants.

"Fair's fair," he whispered as very slowly he peeled them over the rise of her bottom, and forgot to breathe as he watched with a schoolboy's fascination this final unveiling of her nakedness. He moved to her side at last in order to shuck her panties the rest of the way off, and felt her spine contract when he leaned over to kiss, like one bestowing a benediction, the matched set of indentations just where the firm resilience of muscle began.

With upmost care, and marshaling all the self-control he had left, he poured oil into the gentle valley at her waist. Then began to spread it downward…down her sides, over the smooth mounds of her buttocks to the backs of her thighs. He poured more oil and with it slipped his fingers into the cleft between her buttocks, gauging minutely her response to this first invasion of her body's most private places.

Her breathing grew quick and distressed. She stirred again, and it was instinct, perhaps, that made her move her legs a little apart. He lay beside her, then, stretching his body all along hers and raising himself on one elbow so he could murmur assurances to her as he caressed her. She tried to turn her face toward him, searching…seeking…but he pressed his face against the side of hers to keep her still and kissed her ear, and then her neck. She gasped and squirmed closer to him, but didn't try again to turn.

And then he soothed her with kisses and wordless sounds while he slipped his oiled fingers between her thighs and penetrated for the first time her virgin softness.

She was tight…so tight…breathing in little pants and whimpers, but not, he knew, with pain. Gently, he withdrew, then penetrated once again, then again, easing farther into her body each time. The oil and her own moisture made it easy. Her skin was hot where it lay along his, her hair damp with sweat and musky with her own unique, exotic scent. His heart pounded wildly, giddily, as he brought his open mouth to her nape and immersed himself in the heat and smell of her...as he pushed deeper, and yet deeper into her body. And when he had penetrated her as far as he could in that way, he heard her give a sharp little cry—more surprised than frightened—and felt her flesh contract and pulse around his finger. He held her so gently, housing her safely in his hand, soaking himself in her heat, and his own body was shot through with ripples and shudders—of pleasure, and other emotions even more bewildering.

Presently, when her body had quieted, she turned her face again—not toward him, this time, but downward, as if she wanted to hide from him. With her arms drawn in under her she spoke in a muffled voice to the bedspread. "Cade, I am sorry. I did not mean for that to happen...I do not know why—I could not help it. Such a thing has never happened to me before."

Please, oh please, he thought, just let me do this right.

With careful gravity, he said, "No, probably not. What you felt, Princess, was an orgasm." He paused. Then, letting a smile leak into his voice, he added, "A small one."

She lifted her head to stare at him, half her face veiled behind the midnight fall of her hair. "Really? Is this true? I did not know it would feel like that. I have read about this in books, but—"

"Books?" It was such a relief to laugh. "Where in the world did you get hold of a sex book?" There were obviously unplumbed depths to this princess of his.

"In boarding school, one of the girls had one. I think she was French. We used to look at it at night under the blankets with a flashlight.'' She looked down, catching her lip and dimpling at remembered mischief. Then she brought her eyes back to him and in that feeble light he caught the tiny movements of her swallow, the quivering of her mouth. ''But it is impossible to know from reading a book how something will *feel*.''

He lifted his hand, slipped it under her hair and gently cupped her cheek. ''I don't know, either, how it feels for you,'' he said softly. ''I only know how it feels for me.''

She tipped her head, resting it in the cradle of his hand as her eyes clung to his face. ''It must feel very, very good for you, then.''

''Oh, yeah...'' The words vibrated under his sternum like a tiger's purr.

Her lips quivered again, this time with a smile that flickered out before it could reach her dimples, then vanished when she turned her lips into his palm. ''I want you to have this feeling,'' she said huskily as her eyes drifted closed.

''Oh, I will, don't worry about that.'' Again, the laughter felt good to him.

''And...you must not be afraid of hurting me.''

For a moment he was silent, struggling with emotions new to him and words he didn't know how to say. He'd been enjoying the interlude; it was new to him, this quiet intimacy wrapped in a cocoon of almost-darkness, with his mind at least temporarily at peace and his body like a pressure cooker on slow simmer. He'd been in no hurry to have it end, using those moments to marshal his strength and shore up his sagging self-control. Because he knew, as she didn't, that she was nowhere near ready for him, not if he was going to have a prayer of keeping the promise he made to her then, in a fierce and determined growl, ''I'm not going to hurt you, Princess.''

She gave a patient, acquiescing sigh. He allowed her to

turn onto her back then, and his eyes to feast on the banquet of feminine beauty he'd only seen, before tonight, camouflaged in the modestly elegant clothes she always wore. Camouflaged now by the darkness, allowing him veiled hints of creamy mounds and dusky hollows, of purple-rose areolas and an ink-black triangle, kitten-soft above the juncture of her thighs. Hungry for more, he was reaching for the flashlight when she spoke, raising herself up on her elbows.

"I would like to see you," she said.

And he kissed her instead, and murmured against her mouth, "You will...but not now."

"But why?"

So he kissed her again, and more and more deeply until, overwhelmed, she sank back onto the bedspread and reached hungrily for him, already panting and gasping and arching her body toward him as she drove her fingers into his hair. He drew back, then, and stared down into her dazed, midnight eyes. "You have to trust me," he said.

Trust me... What choice did she have?

She was lost in a world she could not have imagined, a world of senses and sensations, some so exquisite and lovely she wanted to reach for them, hold them in her hands like a child grasping at soap bubbles. Some so overwhelming she was in awe of them, frightened by their power, like one standing on the edge of a waterfall. She was lost, and yes, she was frightened, too. But there was a delicious, shivery excitement to her fear. Because there was Cade.

Yes...she trusted him. There it was...as simple and glorious and mystifying as that. She trusted him with all her heart and soul. Her body was no longer hers to command—she was his, now, completely, only clay in the potter's hands.

A potter? No. Though she had no scale by which to judge such things, to her it seemed he must be an artist...a master.

His hands…his mouth…they commanded and consumed her…controlled and demanded, molded, manipulated and presumed. But never, never did they cause her pain. Only the most exquisite joy and unimagined pleasure. Twice more she felt the strange and wonderful sensations as her body first seemed to grow hot and huge and intense as the sun, then come suddenly apart into a cascade of a thousand pulsing infant stars, once when he had drawn apart her thighs with his hands and kissed her…kissed her the way he kissed her mouth, deeply, with his tongue…just *there,* where she was already so hot and swollen and sensitive to the slightest touch. The feeling then…it was so intense she cried out and arched and trembled in his hands, not knowing whether she struggled away from, or toward the terrifying sensations, only certain she could stand no more than this—more than this, and she would surely die.

Then…and now it seemed too quickly…he was holding her tightly and she was rocketing over a precipice and falling, falling, breath forced from her lungs in pants and cries, and her body throbbing inside and burning, tingling all over, in every part of her, and she understood finally what Cade had meant when he had said, ''A small one.''

She trusted him. Completely. And when at last he drew her legs wide apart and knelt so carefully between them…when he had taken Salma's bottle of soothing oil and poured some in his hand, then stroked it gently between her legs and deep, deep inside her…when he leaned over, bracing himself on his hands, and looked a question and a promise deep into her eyes…she gazed back at him from under half-closed lids that had somehow grown too heavy to lift…and smiled.

She trusted him. But she gasped when she felt him fit himself to her softness; she couldn't seem to help it. She gasped again when she felt the first intense, steadily building pressure. And instantly he was there, taking her face between his hands and stroking her cheeks, her eyelids, her temples with his thumbs. Taking over her consciousness, whispering urgently into her mouth, *"Stay with me…relax, sweetheart…don't tense up on me now…"*

She nodded, let her breath out and opened herself to him.

By slow and careful degrees she let him come into her body, and she accepted the mounting pressure with something akin to triumph. *Was* this pain? She did not know, and anyway, if it had been she would not have let *him* know. She simply did not care, for this was her husband…from this moment he would forever be a part of her. She could never have imagined such a fierce and all-consuming joy.

Oh, but now, as the pressure in her body was increasing almost beyond her ability to endure it, so was another kind of pressure altogether. She could feel it coming, feel it filling her throat, making her chest jump and quiver…making her breath whimper and her eyes sting. She tried to stop it, but it came anyway, like that other tumult her body could not control.

"I am sorry," she gasped, and her chest was heaving, her voice high and broken with panic. "I do not mean to cry—I do not want—it does not mean—please do not think you are hurting me. I do not know why—I cannot seem to stop it—"

She had trusted him in all else, she should have trusted him to understand this, as well.

For he only whispered, "Shh…it's okay," and she could hear a smile in his voice as he kissed her and stroked her puddled eyelids. "It's just emotions…go ahead and cry if you want to."

Then, strangely, she began to laugh instead. But it was a different kind of laughter than any she had ever known…laughter mixed with tears, gentle, wondering laughter. Miraculously, he seemed to understand that, too, kissing her tears, then her lips, again and again, mixing his laughter with hers.

"You do not have to stop," she murmured, awed and sated by the feel of him inside her.

"Yeah, actually, I do," he said with an odd, breathless little chuckle. He lowered his head to touch a tiny kiss to the end of her nose. "That would be…about as far as I can go—in more ways than one." He kissed her again, her mouth this time. She could feel tension vibrating in his arms, could hear it in his voice, as if his jaws were clenched. "I'm afraid…I've had about all I can take. It just feels…too good inside you, sweetheart. I think…you're going to have to let me have that feeling, now…"

Before she could even really understand or prepare, she felt him gather himself…felt him pull back and his muscles bunch and harden…felt him surge into her with a force that drove the breath from her lungs. Dazed and a little frightened, she was simply caught up and swept away by the strength and power of his maleness…and for the first time understood the extent of his control, the depth of his restraint, the price of his gentleness.

This was Cade—*her husband*—imposing and magnificent and powerful.

Yes, but vulnerable, too. Along with her understanding of her husband's maleness, for the first time she understood her own femininity as well. Understood that this man she had married might be bigger and harder and physically stronger than she was, but that *she* was powerful, too. Because, all his wonderful strength and vitality he must pour finally into *her. She* had the power to make this strong man tremble…to make *him* vulnerable.

That realization came to her in a great wave of that strange protective tenderness she'd felt for him, out there in the rain. Only now she knew what it was.

But…this can only be love, she thought in wonderment. *Yes, it must be. It is true. I love him.*

Another wave of emotion swept over her, this one cold and terrible, full of longing, and it made her hold on to him with a kind of fierce desperation as his big body surged and emptied into hers.

Cade, I love you! Her heart cried it, but she could not say it out loud. She loved him. She knew it, now. And that made it all the more terrible that he did not love her.

The evening had long since eased into night and the flashlight had burned itself out hours ago. Leila's breathing was soft and even in a darkness thick as wool when Cade slipped out of bed and made his way—with a confidence born of regular practice—to the bathroom. With the door closed he felt for the matches on top of the toilet tank and lit the candle he'd left there…oh, hours ago, now…stuck in a coffee mug with its own melted wax. How Leila had loved that.

He closed his eyes and gripped the edges of the sink with both hands as images swamped him…memories so recent, so sharp and clear he could actually see her now, right there, lowering herself into the bathtub, wincing a little when her soft feminine parts touched the barely warm bubbles. He'd felt such anguish, and had thought of bruised fruit and crushed flower petals, but then she had looked up at him and smiled that irresistible dimpled smile of hers, and a moment later he'd slipped into the tub behind her and what was meant to be the aftermath of something incredible had become instead the beginning of something even more.

Even now, exhausted and drained beyond all endurance, just remembering the feel of her soap-slippery bottom fitting itself between his legs, and himself sliding between hers…yes, somehow, both at the same time…her body arching and his hands filling with the sweet, hot weight of her breasts…even now, remembering that, his groin ached and his head swam with desire. How could it not?

He lifted his head and stared at himself in the medicine cabinet mirror. The candlelight made his face gaunt, his eyes shadowed and bleak. What the hell was the matter with him? A bridegroom after a night like this—he should be considering himself the luckiest, the happiest man in the world. Either that, or, considering his circumstances, he ought to be kicking himself all the way to kingdom come and back. In actual fact, he wasn't feeling either one of those things. Truth was, he didn't have any idea what he was feeling.

So, he'd made love to his wife. He'd consummated his marriage, even knowing what it would mean to both of them—so much for his willpower. And it had been about the most mind-blowing, intense pleasure of his life. And, except for the fact that it pretty much committed him to this marriage whether he wanted it or not, what had it changed? The woman sleeping in there in his bed was still, in almost all the ways that counted, a stranger to him. The woman he'd committed to share the rest of his life with came from a culture so different from his, she might as well have been from another planet. The woman he'd held in his arms, immersed himself so totally in he couldn't have told where he left off and she began…the woman into whom—God help him—he'd poured his genes…was still Leila Kamal, princess of Tamir. Wasn't she?

So why did his arms feel empty now without her? Why did his body still ache with wanting her? And most mystifying of all, what was this terrible ache of tenderness he felt for her in his heart?

Having no answers for himself, he went into the bedroom where he'd stowed his overnighter, took out a clean pair of shorts and put them on. Then he went out onto the porch and sat on the steps and watched the dawn come.

At least he knew what he was feeling, now. Blitzed, shell-shocked, bewildered. And scared half to death.

Leila woke up with a delicious stiffness in every muscle and joint, the kind that felt so *good* when she stretched, long and luxuriously, like a great, lazy cat. There was also a mysterious swollen ache between her legs that registered her pulse in little pleasure taps, tiny echoes of what had happened there not so long ago. Under the blankets, she hugged her nakedness against a shiver of…what? Fear? Happiness? Perhaps, Leila thought, what I am is fearfully happy.

She was not surprised to find herself alone in the bed she had shared with Cade, but she was disappointed. When, she wondered, would she finally know what it was like to wake up in the morning beside her husband?

But she would never say anything of the kind to Cade. She must not presume too much. After all, just because he was her husband, just because he had *made* love to her, did not mean he *loved* her. She was not so naïve as to think those two were the same. And just then she was far too vulnerable to want to know the truth about how Cade felt about her.

Last night he had seemed so tender. She had even allowed herself to believe he *must* love her, in his own way, perhaps in some buried part of him. But this morning, he was gone from her bed, and no…she would not allow herself to presume. Never again. The risk was far too great. She would guard herself, as she had been doing ever since that terrible moment in Cade's bedchamber in the palace, when she had realized how disastrously she had misunderstood him.

Her body was now and would always be Cade's. So was

her heart. But that was *her* secret, and for now she must bury it in the innermost keep of her soul.

She rose and dressed quickly in slacks and a long-sleeved blouse—and she really must, she told herself, buy some blue jeans, which seemed to be all people in Texas ever wore. After a brief stop in the bathroom, she went looking for her husband. He wasn't in the house, and for the tiniest moment she felt twinges of unreasoning panic—ridiculous, of course, did she think he would leave her here? But then through the living room window she caught a glimpse of him, on the front porch. Before going to join him, she paused and with her forehead pressed against the door, said a prayer. *Please, God, let my face be serene. Please...let it not show him how hard my heart is beating.*

He was leaning against a post and looking out over the railing, smoking one of his thin, brown cigars and holding a heavy crockery mug with symbols on it that Cade had told her were brands for cattle. Though he did not look much like a cowboy this morning, wearing blue jeans, yes, but with a white short-sleeved polo shirt and sunglasses. He looked fresh and clean as rain, lean and relaxed...and utterly unapproachable.

He turned when she came onto the porch. His face was composed as he lifted his mug to her and said, "Good morning."

"Good morning," she said back to him. She wished she could see his eyes. She wished he would smile at her, just once with that lifting, unfettered joy she'd seen that morning in the palace courtyard. *Just once.* Then I would know, she thought.

"Want some coffee? There's still plenty..."

She glanced over her shoulder toward the house, then shrugged and said, "Yes, thank you. I will get some in a minute." She hesitated, then asked, "Have you been up long?" Making it light, casual, not presuming too much.

He took a sip of coffee, then the cheroot. "Awhile," he said, blowing away the smoke. Then, softly, "How 'bout you? Sleep well?"

Her heart gave a bump, and to keep it from her voice, she took a deep breath. "Yes, I did, thank you. Very well." We are like two strangers, she thought bleakly. How she wished she could go to him and slip her arms around his waist with the perfect faith that should be natural between husband and wife, lay her face against his chest and tell him joyfully and without reservation what was in her heart, that this morning was beautiful beyond words because he was in it.

Instead, she walked to the railing a little distance from him, and, leaning on her hands, looked out upon a morning that was fast becoming less beautiful. "It smells fresh, after the rain," she said, filling her lungs with air that felt heavy and smells that were alien. "Will it be a nice day, do you think?"

"Hard to say." Cade shifted restlessly and tossed away his cheroot. "This is thunderstorm weather. You never know where they'll pop up."

"Will we ride again today?"

Cade threw her a look of surprise. After last night, how could she even suggest such a thing? Either she wasn't thinking clearly, or he'd done a better job of taking care of her than he'd thought. He smiled crookedly. Memories made his voice husky. "I don't think so. My backside's still a little bit sore. Besides—" he drank coffee and tossed away the dregs "—I think we'd better tidy up the place and then head on back."

"So soon?" She looked at him and then quickly away, but not before he saw the look of disappointment that flashed across that all-revealing face of hers.

"I think we better. If we wait till this afternoon we're liable to run into thunderstorms, and I don't know about you, but I wouldn't care to fly through something like what we had yesterday.'' His voice was rough with gravel, and he kept his face turned away from her so she wouldn't see the tension in it. Even with sunglasses on he didn't trust his own eyes.

And hell, why was it he couldn't just tell her how he felt, which was that he'd love nothing better than to stay here indefinitely with her in this old broken-down ranch house, live like a couple of bohemians, stay naked most of the time and make love whenever either of them felt like it? He didn't know why, except that even thinking about saying such a thing to her made him feel too vulnerable. He wasn't ready, yet, to hang his heart out in the open like that. Maybe he never would be.

''Besides,'' he said, more abruptly than he meant to, ''I have a whole hell of a lot of work to do to get ready for the week. Got a schedule coming up that won't quit.'' He lifted his coffee mug, saw it was empty and grimaced at it instead. Dammit, he'd done it on purpose, too, that was the hell of it. Scheduled himself to the brink of oblivion just to give himself an excuse not to go home to his wife. Well, *hell.* How was he supposed to know things were going to change on him so fast, and that he'd be *wanting* to spend time with her? ''I doubt I'm gonna be home much,'' he said bitterly, ''at least for the rest of the week.''

''Of course…I understand,'' she murmured. ''Then…I will go and get ready. Let me know when you would like to leave.'' And she turned and walked into the house, tall, elegant and regal. Even with her hair a tumbled reminder of a night of passion and unrestrained sex, she was every inch a princess.

As Cade watched her walk away from him he tried to think of her that way, naked and moist, panting in his arms. But though he could call the memories to his mind, he couldn't quite seem to make them touch his senses, not in the gut-wrenching, groin-tightening way they had come to him first thing this morning. Already, it seemed, his mind was protecting him, drawing an insulating veil around the night just passed.

In a little while, if he was lucky, maybe last night would begin to seem like those days and nights in Tamir...like something that had happened to someone else, long ago, in a fairy tale.

Chapter 13

On Friday, Cade phoned to say that he would be home early, perhaps even in time to have dinner with his wife.

When Leila heard this she felt first a great surge of joy. That was followed almost immediately by an equally powerful wave of anger. She had been experiencing this same roller coaster of emotions all week long, while her husband had been hundreds of miles away in a place called Odessa. She was, in fact, a cauldron of emotions, bewildering emotions. Loneliness and longing, frustration and fury were only the few she could name.

Over and over she thought, How could he do this to me? How can he be so cruel? To have opened the doors of Paradise to her, to have shown her such happiness, all that her heart had ever desired—and in the next moment to have snatched it away from her, slammed the door shut and trapped her once more in her lonely cage.

Yes…that was what it felt like. She was locked up in a cage. *No! A coop,* she thought, remembering what Cade

had told her that night on the terrace. For the truth was she
felt more "cooped up" here in Texas, with all its wide
open spaces, than she ever had in the royal palace in Tamir.

Tamir. When she thought of the palace, with its clean
white lines, with its gardens and courtyards and clifftop
terraces overlooking the sea, and of her sisters, her mother,
Salma and Nargis...and Papa, with his great comforting
girth and snowy white beard, and eyes that always held a
sparkle of affection for her...she was almost overcome with
homesickness. And that was followed inevitably by anger.

I will not take this treatment much longer, she told herself, fortifying her faltering reserves of self-confidence with
something she had always had in great abundance. *Pride.*
After all, she reminded herself, I am a princess!

But then she remembered the feeling of power that had
come to her there on the ranch, in the cactus patch and in
Cade's arms. And an even more exhilarating, ennobling
thought came to her: *I am a woman. I deserve better. I
deserve to be loved.*

And she would tell Cade that, she had decided. This
evening, after they had shared the dinner Betsy had prepared.

But for some reason, to Leila's dismay, Betsy decided
on this particular Friday that she must leave work early.
She had things to do, she and Rueben, and they must make
a trip into town. Leila was not to worry, dinner was all
prepared, all she would need to do was heat it up in the
microwave. Betsy showed Leila the platter of beef ka-
bobs—cubes of marinated beef skewered on sticks with
chunks of onion and peppers and tomatoes, already grilled
and arranged on a bed of fluffy rice that had been seasoned
with broth and sweet red peppers. It was one of Cade's
favorite dishes, Betsy said, guaranteed to put him in a good
mood for the evening. And she had given Leila a wink.
Then she had caught her up in a hug and had whispered,

"Don't give up on him, honey. You just need to be patient."

Patient? Well, it was true that patience had never been one of Leila's greatest virtues. And as the time approached for Cade to arrive, she became more and more impatient and nervous. She paced in the kitchen, looking again and again at the digital clock on the stove. Was it time yet? Should she take out the food now? She had never prepared and served a meal for her husband before. Many times she went over the checklist in her mind—she had already arranged the dishes and silverware on the table in the dining room, just the way Betsy had taught her, and had even cut some roses from the bushes in the yard and arranged them in a crystal vase. There was iced tea chilling in a glass pitcher in the refrigerator, and Cade's favorite bourbon on a silver tray on the sideboard.

Everything was ready. But where was Cade?

He had told Betsy he would be home early, in time for dinner—but what did that mean? Six o'clock? Seven? And now it seemed to Leila that it was growing dark very rapidly. What if something had happened to him? An automobile accident, perhaps, driving home on those freeways with so many cars.

She paced and paced, growing more and more nervous. Finally, she could stand it no longer. She would at least get out the food. Put it in the microwave oven, so it would be ready at a moment's notice, the minute he came home...

Thunder rumbled in the deepening dusk outside as she opened the refrigerator and oh, so carefully slid the heavy, plastic-wrapped platter toward her. She picked it up in both hands and turned to bump the door closed with her hip.

From out of nowhere, it seemed, came a great boom of thunder. With all her concentration on the platter in her hands and her nerves honed to knife-points, Leila reacted to the sound as if she had been shot. She gave a startled cry and the platter dropped from her hands.

Her heart seemed to stop. Her world went silent. Encased in a bubble of shock, she stared down at the swath of rice and juices, chunks of meat and brightly colored vegetables scattered across the tile floor amidst sparkling icicle shards of glass.

No! her mind shrieked, refusing to believe what was before her own eyes. Refusing to believe such a disaster could have happened, and that *she* was responsible. *No!* This could not be her fault. She had never done such a thing before in her life.

This would not have happened if she had not been so nervous, so worried and upset. About Cade. *Cade! Yes!* This was all *his* fault.

With a howl of unprincesslike fury, Leila hurled herself across the kitchen, snatched open the door and plunged outside into the rain that had just that moment begun to fall.

Cade couldn't remember when he'd ever been so glad to be home. He couldn't believe, either, how much he was looking forward to seeing his wife. The nice buzz of anticipation he'd been nursing all day had intensified during the time he'd spent sitting in rain—and accident-snarled traffic on Houston's outbound freeways until now it was a throbbing weight in his belly and a smoldering fire in his groin.

He hadn't been able to get her out of his mind all week. Images, bits and pieces of the day and night they'd spent at the ranch, kept invading his conscious and unconscious thoughts, making a joke of his concentration during the day and total chaos of his nights.

The truth was, he'd done quite a lot of thinking about Leila and his marriage during those lonely nights in a barren motel room out there in the vast Texas midlands. And the conclusion he'd come to was that, since it looked like he was stuck in this marriage for the duration, he'd better find a way to make it work. He'd come back to Houston full of new vows and determination—to spend more time with his wife, for one thing. He thought—he hoped—if they did things together, if he got to know her better, maybe he'd find they had something in common after all. Maybe he'd even learn how to talk to her.

One thing for certain: he was tired of fighting his desire for her. Literally. Worn out. It was sapping his strength, physically, mentally and emotionally, and if he didn't do something about it, sooner or later it was going to start affecting his ability to run a business. Not to mention what it was doing to his disposition.

By the time Cade got home rain was coming down in buckets, so he parked his car right beside the back gate, the better to make a run for it. Conveniently for him, the gate was wide open. Surprising, too, since it was a poolyard gate and therefore supposed to be self-closing. The way it looked, the gate must have been thrown back with some pretty good force, so that the latch had caught on the fence, holding it open. Which was unusual, but not unheard of, and probably explainable because of the rain—somebody running for cover in a big hurry. He didn't begin to feel alarmed until he saw that the kitchen door was wide open, too.

Calling Leila's name, he went into the kitchen. His heart was already beginning to pound. He was so intent on looking for her that he almost stepped in the mess on the floor before he saw it. "What the hell—?" he muttered. Quickly skirting the disaster, he stuck his head into the hallway, calling more urgently now. And he was halfway up the stairs when the significance of the open door and thrown-back gate finally penetrated the alarm-clamor in his brain. Then he knew exactly where he'd find her.

Leila was in the center aisle of the stable. She was brushing the foal, Sari, while Suki, her mother, watched with anxiously pricked ears from a nearby stall. Leila was singing in Arabic as she usually did when she worked with horses, not in her usual soothing croon but in short, breathless whimpers that were not soothing to anyone. Least of all Leila.

When she heard the scrape of footsteps on concrete, she did not want to look. She wanted to go on calmly brushing Sari as though she had not a care in the world, but how could she, when every beat of her heart felt like a blow that rocked her whole body, when her hands could not hold the brush steady, but instead jerked and shook as if she had a violent chill.

Then, of course, she *must* turn to look. And she did not even think how melodramatic it looked—Cade, drenched and wild-eyed with his hair all on end, framed in the stable entrance while lightning flickered and flashed behind him like a scene from a horror movie. She was utterly lost in the storm of her own emotions. And what a bewildering mix of emotions! Relief, and longing...overwhelming love and unreasoning fury.

"Leila?" He came rapidly toward her, and his voice was hoarse with concern. "Hey, are you okay? What are you doing out here?"

"Your dinner is ruined." It seemed to Leila that her voice came from somewhere outside her own head. Half-forgotten in her nerveless hand, the brush traced an erratic zigzag across the foal's mottled charcoal back. "There was thunder...I dropped it on the floor."

"Yeah, I saw." He touched her arm gently, a tentative turning pressure. "Hey, look—it's okay. It doesn't mat—"

She whirled on him like a dervish. *"Where...were... you?"* Her fists thumped against his chest, her eyes spurted fire and tears together. "You said...you would be home early. And I waited and waited…and then it got dark…'' The pressure of pent-up emotions had finally blown, and she could not have stopped herself if she'd tried. "And I thought…I did not know where you were!" She wasn't aware, nor did she care what she looked or sounded like, or whether she was acting like the classic shrewish wife. "And I thought…I thought…that you were…''

"I'm sorry—the traffic was…the rain…there were accidents." Cade mumbled, dazed. His brain was reeling. All he could think was that this felt a lot to him like the moment out there in the live oak grove when his horse had abruptly gone one way and he another. His emotions and desires were all of a sudden galloping off in unexpected directions, beyond his ability to control.

After a brief struggle he gave up trying. He got his arms around Leila's quaking body and caught her hard against him. Wrapped his hand in the humid tangle of her hair to hold her still, and kissed her.

What came next was a conflagration. It exploded upon them so unexpectedly and burned so voraciously it gave him no time to think at all.

When he first kissed her, Leila gasped in surprised outrage, then struggled against him—for all of two seconds— and the next thing he knew they were panting and whimpering and tearing off each other's clothes. He dimly remembered backing her into an empty stall…the deep cushioning straw coming up to meet him and his body already half-entwined with hers.

With almost a week's worth of pent-up desire clawing at his insides and fogging his brain, it didn't even occur to Cade that he might have pushed into her too abruptly, or too soon. Nor to Leila, either, not then. She gave a sharp cry, but it was of passion, not pain, and her body arched against him, not away. Her body was hot…so hot, feverish in his arms, and she wrapped herself around him like that all-over glove he remembered. And it felt good…so *good* to be inside her…as if, after a long and perilous journey, he'd finally found his way home.

A fierce, exultant joy invaded him as she met his thrusts with tiny passion-cries…when she gasped out his name as he released the flood of his passion into her. When she writhed and clung to him as he kept thrusting, until only moments later he felt her come apart…her body go light, limp and pulsing in his arms.

Exhilarated, happier than he could ever remember being in his life, quaking with it, wanting to share his shaky, wondering laughter with Leila's, Cade slipped sideways enough so he could touch her face. His joy turned to despair. Laughter hardened inside him and became instead a throbbing lump in his belly.

She was crying. Not the half sobbing, half laughing overflow of emotions that had bewildered and dismayed her so when he'd made love to her the first time—*that* he'd understood. This was different. This was *misery*. Grief-stricken, heartbroken despair.

"Sweetheart, what is it?" His voice was rasping and raw. "Did I hurt you? I'm sorry—"

She shook her head wildly, and because there was no one else from whom to seek comfort, turned her face to his chest.

But what could he say to comfort her, when he didn't begin to understand the reason for her tears? So he said nothing at all, while his mind battered helplessly against the bars of his ignorance. Until, with a glimmering of hope, he thought of something that might, just possibly, make her feel better.

"Hey," he murmured to her still-quaking silence, gazing down through a fog of mystified tenderness at the damp tendrils of hair draped across her ear. "I didn't have a chance to tell you. Guess who called today?" After only the briefest of pauses he gave her the answer. "Elena. And Hassan. They're back from their honeymoon. Just got back a couple days ago."

She pulled away from him just enough so she could look at him. "Really?" She sniffed. One long hand came, furtive and embarrassed, to wipe at her tears. "They are here? In Texas?"

Cade nodded. "Yep. They're going to be at Elena's ranch this weekend. How'd you like to pay 'em a visit?" His throat ached as he smiled.

She gave a little gasp and sat up, both her tears and her nakedness forgotten. "A visit? Elena has a ranch? I did not know. Is it very far? Will we fly?"

"A little one…and not far at all, just outside of Evangeline. An hour's drive from here. How's tomorrow sound?"

"Tomorrow? Oh, yes—oh, Cade…" She kissed him, and her face, still wet with tears and alight with happiness, was like the sun coming out after a rainstorm.

Cade's heart was in dark despair. Just as when she'd kissed him after he'd given her the foal for her bride gift, his thoughts now were bleak. *It's gratitude. She's only happy because I've given her something she wants. And it's not me.*

Elena came out to greet them, waving from the wide front porch of a house that, although it was made of white painted wood rather than brownish stone, reminded Leila of Cade's ranch house where she had been so briefly and blissfully happy. Reminded her of it so much, she had to swallow hard and blink away tears.

Cade had barely parked the SUV before Leila was out of the car and running up the graveled path. She met Elena on the steps. "Oh, I am so glad to see you," she breathed impulsively as she returned the other woman's hug. And now she *did* lose control of a few tears. Elena seemed very like a sister to her now, which made her miss her own sisters all the more.

She drew back, though, when she saw Hassan's tall form, standing just behind Elena. She did not know how to greet this relaxed and smiling man who seemed so different from her so-arrogant older brother, who had always lorded it over her and tried to intimidate her with his piercing black eyes. "Hello, Hassan," she said formally, and was even more bemused when he stepped forward and caught her up in a hug as warm as his wife's had been, and laughed and called her "Little sister." In *Arabic*. Hassan almost *never* spoke in Arabic!

Then Elena was hooking an arm around hers and saying in a happy rush, in her Texas way, "We're just so glad you guys came—we're barely unpacked ourselves, but we just decided to say the heck with it and come out here for a few days. We'll have some lunch in a little bit, but right now, I just can't wait to show you around."

"But…shouldn't we—" Leila looked toward the men, who had shaken hands and now were deep in conversation and drifting off across the porch in the direction of what looked like stables.

Elena waved them away with a smile. "Ah, let 'em go— they'll just want to talk horses and oil. What I'm dying to hear about is *you* guys. I still can't believe it—talk about sudden! I wish Hassan and I could have stayed for the wedding. So…tell me all about it. How was the wedding? Did you have a honeymoon?" She paused to consider her own question. "Probably not, if I know Cade. Well—we're going to have to do something about that."

"Cade has been very busy with his work," Leila said carefully, and Elena gave her a piercing look that made her glad she had decided to wear sunglasses to hide the tear-shadows around her eyes.

Leila summoned a smile as she tried to divert Elena's attention. "It seems as though you and Hassan are very happy."

Elena closed her eyes and smiled in a way that made Leila's heart ache with envy. "Oh, yeah. I can't tell you. Actually, if you want to know the truth, it's even kind of surprised me." She threw Leila a bemused look. "Not that I had any doubts that we loved each other—finally—but I thought it was going to be a lot harder to make it work."

"Work?" Frowning behind the sunglasses, Leila paused to look at her.

Elena gave a rueful laugh. "Oh, yeah—marriage takes work, don't ever kid yourself about that." Her laughter grew light again. "Especially when you have two people as different and bullheaded as Hassan and I are."

"At least...you know your husband loves you." Leila hardly knew she had spoken it out loud. They had been walking as they talked, past the stables and up a gentle slope covered with grass and the same little yellow flowers that grew in Cade's pasture. Now, standing on a hilltop overlooking still more hills that rolled away to banks of trees and a huge hazy sky beyond, she thought of her dreamed-of spaces and was almost overwhelmed with misery. She hardly even knew Elena had put her arm around her shoulders until she spoke.

"Oh, honey, of course Cade loves you!"

"No," said Leila with a proud lift of her chin, "he does not."

"Look," said Elena flatly, "I know him. He wouldn't have married you if he didn't love you."

Leila firmly shook her head. "He only married me to save me from disgrace."

Elena gave a hoot of laughter, which she quickly stifled when she saw the tears leaking out from under the edges of Leila's sunglasses. She gave her another hug and said with an exasperated sigh, "Okay, hon, tell me why you think that husband of yours doesn't love you."

"He does not act as though he does." Leila's voice was choked and angry. "And he certainly has not ever *said* so." She was startled and a little hurt when Elena made a very rude noise in reply.

The older woman shook back her short, dark hair and looked up at the sky for a moment as if in hopes of divine guidance. Then she put her arm around Leila's shoulders again. "Let me tell you something about your husband," she said quietly, as she began to walk with her back down the hill. "Cade Gallagher is just about the sweetest, most good-hearted man alive, and the best friend a woman could ever have. But the truth is, when it comes to emotional issues, he's pretty closed up. That's why he's never gotten married, I think—he never could find a woman he trusted enough to open himself up to. He wasn't always that way, I don't think. I think it happened when his mother died— he told you about that, I guess? It was a car accident—a hit-and-run driver ran her car off the road into the river, and she drowned."

Leila tried in vain to stifle a horrified cry, and Elena glanced at her in sympathy. "Yeah, I know…terrible, isn't it? They never did find the one who did it.…" Her voice trailed off, and Leila saw a grim and bleak look settle briefly over her features. Then she went on, in a voice that was harder and more clipped than before.

"It happened about a year after his mom got involved with my father. He'd have been…fifteen, I think—I know I was only about eight when I first met him. But I remember he had this wonderful, absolutely spectacular smile—it would light up his eyes, I swear, brighter than the lone star of Texas."

And Leila caught her breath and looked intently at her.

Yes, she thought, her heart quicking. *I have seen it too, that smile! Just once...*

"Anyway, after his mom died," Elena continued softly, "I never saw that smile again." Her lips curved, but not with a smile. "And I don't think it helped that a few years later he found out my father, the man who'd adopted him after his mom died and treated him like his own son, had actually cheated him out of his inheritance."

Leila gave another horrified gasp. "Oh, yeah, it's true," said Elena. "I only found out myself recently—Cade told me just before I married Hassan." She took a breath. "It was a shock, believe me. His mom had left a will naming Yusuf Rahman as Cade's guardian, as well as trustee of her estate, which at that time was what was left of her daddy's oil company after Cade's dad had pissed away most of it. When Cade turned twenty-one, he found out my father had worked it so there wasn't anything left of his mother's holdings at all. Everything had been absorbed into Rahman Oil."

She stopped walking to look back at Leila, who was standing still with her fingers pressed against her mouth. "So you can see," she said gently, "why the man might be a *little* bit slow to trust anybody with his heart, even after all this time."

"But," Leila whispered through trembling lips, "what can I do? I do not know how to make him open himself up to me." The task seemed too hard, the obstacles enormous...insurmountable. She felt overwhelmed, defeated before she had even begun.

"For starters, have you tried telling him how you feel about *him?*" Elena's voice was dry, as if she already knew the answer.

"Of course not," said Leila, drawing herself up stiffly. 'And I will not—not until I know for certain that he has the same feelings for me." She was a princess. She had her pride!

Elena made an exasperated sound. "You Kamals! You're all alike—the most bullheaded, proud bunch of people I ever met." They walked on down the hill in silence. Until...

"I think...I have an idea."

Leila looked at Elena in hope, and was surprised to find that she was smiling...smiling and gazing down the hill toward the stables, where Cade and Hassan could be seen leaning against the corral fence, still deep in conversation. She turned back to Leila, and her eyes were once again serene. "Hon, what you need to do is take a little trip. How'd you feel about a nice visit to Tamir? You know— go home and see your folks?"

"Leave...Cade?" Leila's heart gave a leap, and she felt a cold wash of panic. "But—I don't understand. How—"

"Hey," said Elena with a placid shrug, "it worked for me."

"You mean, *you* left—"

She shook her head, and her smile was a little crooked, now. "Uh-uh. Hassan left *me*. I'd refused to marry him— I guess I was afraid I didn't love him enough...*then*. So off he went, back to Tamir. It took me...oh, maybe a day to figure out I'd made the biggest mistake of my life. So I went after him. The rest," she added with a sound like a cat's purr, "is history."

"But," Leila mumbled, "what if I go to Tamir, and Cade does not come for me?" Her heart was hammering. If Cade did *not* come for her, she knew she could not possibly come back here, not to live as she had been living for these past weeks. And yet, the thought of never seeing Cade again...never feeling his arms around her...frightened her so she could scarcely breathe.

"Oh, he'll come," said Elena. "Trust me."

"But...I cannot possibly ask him—"

"Hey—don't worry about it. You just leave this to me."

Cade leaned against the corral fence and watched them come toward him...two women, one he'd known nearly all his life, as familiar as the grass around him, the other as alien and exotic as an orchid blooming in the desert. Both beautiful, but for one he felt nothing but the deep, abiding affection of a brother for his sister, while the other made his pulses thunder like a buffalo stampede. Why did it have to be the wrong one? He felt betrayed, somehow. Double-crossed by his own heart.

"Hey, guys," Elena called out when they were near enough. And Cade watched with a pang of envy as she came with the ease of certainty to kiss her husband, while his own wife hesitated and hung back, unsure what she should do. "Catching up on the latest gossip?" Elena teased, an arm around her husband's waist.

Cade squinted at her and shook his head, while Hassan said loftily, "Men do not gossip."

"Right." Elena laughed. "No, I mean, from Tamir. Hey, what did you guys think about Nadia?"

"Nadia?" Leila was alert and tense. "What about my sister? I spoke to her only last week. Is she all right?"

"She's getting married," said Elena. "Can you believe it? The fourth wedding in the Kamal family this year." She nudged Hassan. "I guess that just leaves Samira, huh?" Then she looked with concern at Leila, who had her fingertips pressed to her mouth and a stricken look on her face. "What, aren't you happy about it?"

Leila cleared her throat and said faintly, "Then...she will marry Butrus after all?" Elena nodded, and Hassan said gruffly, "With our father's blessing."

"But," said Leila, "she does not love him. She told me so." Her cheeks were pink, and Cade could see that, at her sides, her hands were clenched into fists. "She cannot do this—she must not. Oh, if only I could talk to her!" Her voice was tight with distress.

"Why don't you?" Elena asked, as if it were the simplest thing in the world.

"I have. But on the phone it is not—"

"No, I mean, go to Tamir." Elena looked at Cade.

A great stillness seemed to fold itself around him. Leila seemed not to be breathing. He looked at her and she averted her face quickly, but not quickly enough. Even with her sunglasses she couldn't hide the light of hope, a flash of joy so keen and pure, he was sure he'd felt it pierce his heart.

"Sure, why not?" Elena went on, enthusiastic...oblivious. "Go for a visit. It's not like you can't afford to send her, Cade. Leila *should* be with her sister at a time like this."

Cade cleared his throat. His heart lay in his stomach like a dead weight—and how well he remembered *that* feeling. "What about it?" he asked Leila, keeping his voice carefully neutral. "Would you like to go to Tamir? Visit your folks?"

She lifted her head and looked at him a long, suspenseful time, while he stared at his own reflection in her glasses and wished with all his heart that he could see her eyes. Except for the briefest tremble in her mouth, then a tightening, her face was utterly still. For the first time in his memory, he couldn't read her emotions there.

Then she drew a lifting breath and smiled. "Yes—oh, yes," she said softly. "I would like it very much."

"Well, there you go," said Elena with a shrug. And she and Hassan exchanged a secret look.

"Well, okay," Cade said, squinting as he met the radiance of his wife's smile, "I guess you're going to Tamir. How soon do you want to leave?"

"Is...tomorrow too soon?" Oddly she sounded as if she was one good breath away from bursting into tears.

"Tomorrow it is." And on a hot and sunny May day in Texas, Cade felt cold clear through.

That evening, Cade went into the bedroom where Leila was packing her suitcases. "All set," he said on an exhalation. "Plane leaves here at two. You're gonna have a little bit of a stopover in Atlanta, but not too bad. You're nonstop to Athens...arrive there Monday morning, local time. Then it's just a short hop from there to Tamir."

"Thank you." Her voice sounded muffled as she watched her hands...watched them methodically smoothing filmy cloth. Her hair had fallen over her shoulder, hiding her face from him. He resisted the urge to pull it out of the way.

"Need any help?"

"Thank you, but no. I am nearly finished." She straightened and tossed her hair back over her shoulder, though she still didn't look at him. A frown pleated her forehead. "I do not think I will need to take much with me...so many of my clothes are still in Tamir."

Maybe he should have found reassurance in that. Instead, he felt a sudden surge of anger that was mysteriously mixed with grief. Childishly, he wanted to shout at her. *What kind of a woman are you? How can you go away and leave me like this?* Selfishly, he wanted to plead with her. *Please don't go. Forget your sister—I need you!*

What he couldn't understand was *why*. It had been his idea to send her back to Tamir from the first. So why this gnawing fear that, once she was there with her own family, she wasn't ever going to come back to Texas?

She was trying to fold over the top of the suitcase to zip it closed. "Here—let me get that," he said roughly, needing some activity, an outlet for his emotions. And reaching heedlessly across her, brushed her breast with his arm.

He went absolutely, deathly still. Except for the lifting of each breath, so did she. Then, slowly, slowly, he turned toward her. She turned, too, and tipped back her head to look at him. It went on so long, that look, and in such tension and stillness…it reminded him of something.

Then it came to him—that evening on the terrace. And the memory was so vivid, so immediate, it seemed to him he could hear the pounding of the surf on the rocks below the cliff…until he realized it was only the beating of his own heart. He remembered the way she'd looked at him so intently, and what she'd said to him next.…

"Do you want to kiss me?"

He didn't know he'd said it aloud until he saw the flash of recognition in her eyes, and heard her say in a small, tentative voice, in a much more delightful French accent than his had ever been, "Kees you? Oh, *oui, Monsieur*…"

He didn't even realize, then, the significance of that moment, that mutual, instant understanding, the acknowledgment of a history of shared intimacy, the first of countless moments like it that would form a bond to last a lifetime. He only knew that he was terrified. My God, he thought as he slowly lowered his mouth to hers, I can't let her go! *I love her.*

How can I leave him? Leila thought as she opened herself to her husband's embrace. *I love him so*… If only, she thought, he would ask me to stay…tell me not to go. Then I would know he loves me…

But he didn't say anything at all, though his kiss was so deep and poignant it made her ache in every part of her being, and it would have been easy to believe he meant it as love. Leila was not so naïve.

No, Elena was right. She must go to Tamir. If her husband loved her, he would come for her and bring her home.

And if he does not? Her heart trembled, then plummeted inside her, and she clung to him in desperate, unreasoning fear. *He must come for me. He must.*

But how to ensure that, and yet preserve her pride? Trying without words to let him know the love and longing that was inside her, she gave him her body with a kind of desperate tenderness, worshipped his with such unreserved devotion…and hoped that he would somehow hear and know what was in her heart.

Dazed by the intensity of her lovemaking, shaken by the intensity of his feelings for her, Cade buried his face in the fragrant fall of his wife's hair. *For the last time?* He held her closer and shuddered with fear.

On Monday afternoon, Cade called Elena from his office in Houston. "Well," he said, "I hope you're satisfied."

She responded with a little trill of laughter. "What in the world are you talking about?"

"Leila's gone," he said morosely. "She called a little while ago to tell me she made it home okay. Sounded happy to be back with her folks." He paused, took a deep breath and tried to make it sound as if he didn't care. "I don't think she wants to come back…anytime soon." He added the last part only to keep from sounding too melodramatic.

"Well, don't say I didn't warn you, Cade." She made an exasperated sound. And after a pause, "What do you intend to do about it?"

He snorted right back at her. "What *can* I do? I sure as hell can't seem to make her happy here."

"Oh, for—that is just *so* like a man!" There was a pause, and then, bluntly, "Cade, do you love her?" And before he could answer, "Don't you know, it doesn't take any more than that to make a woman happy? If she loves you…"

"Well," said Cade with gravel in his throat, "that's the question, isn't it?"

There was another, longer pause, while he swallowed hard a couple of times. Then Elena's voice came softly. "You can't stay closed off from your emotions forever, Cade."

He righted his chair with an angry thump. "What the hell do you mean by *that?*"

"Come on—you've been shut down ever since your mom died—and...what my father did to you."

"That's ridiculous. I have emotions."

"I'll bet you do. But you sure don't like to show 'em."

"How does that make me different from almost any other man you know?"

"It doesn't," she admitted, "but most men trust *somebody* enough to let their feelings show. I know Hassan trusts me. Do you think because of what happened with your mom and my father, that you're afraid—"

"Cut the crap, Elena. That's just psychobabble bull—"

"Cade, can I ask you something?" Her voice was different, now. Hesitant...almost fearful. He waited, half-resentful, saying nothing, and after a moment she came out with it. "Do you think...has it ever crossed your mind, since all this has come out about my father...Rahman... about him killing my mother, and...all that...that he might have been the one responsible for your mom's accident?"

He couldn't answer, just stared at the Houston haze through his office window. His pulse tapped nervously at his belt buckle.

"It must have occurred to you, Cade. You were supposed to be in that car, too, remember? If you hadn't talked your mom into dropping you at your friend David's house on the way home..."

"What do you want me to say," he said harshly.

"What's the point? The man's dead. Can't very well kill him twice."

"No," said Elena quietly, "but you can sure as hell kill your marriage if you don't find a way to come to terms with this. You have to find a way to trust, Cade. Trust yourself to love. Trust somebody to love you and not let you down."

"Psychobabble crap," Cade muttered.

"Maybe it is." He heard tears in her voice. "Maybe I just want everybody to be as happy as I am." And damned if she didn't hang up on him.

That evening, Cade was in the stable checking out a new foal with Rueben when Betsy came down with the bottle she'd prepared. She handed it to her husband, then stood back, planted her hands on her hips and glared at Cade.

"Okay," she said, "when are you leaving?"

"What?" He had his arms full of a balky colt just then, and couldn't look at her. "Leaving for where?"

"Tamir—whatever the name of that place is. When are you gonna go get Leila and bring her back?"

Cade snorted. After his conversation with Elena, he was feeling about as cooperative as that foal. "I guess she'll come back when she's ready."

"Uh-uh," said Betsy, "you got to go get her." She glared at him and folded her arms across the shelf of her bosom. "How else is she gonna know you want her to come back? You ever tell her?" She gave a snort of monumental exasperation. "I bet you never even told her you love her, did you?"

He let go of the foal, who was finally beginning to get the idea there was something good for him in that rubber nipple. "She never told *me* that."

Betsy threw up her arms. "She's a *woman.* You expect her to tell you *first?*" Cade didn't say anything. He looked over at the foal, who was nursing greedily, now. "I packed your suitcase already," Betsy said.

Cade looked at Rueben, who lifted one shoulder in a shrug. "I think you better go get your wife," was all he said.

Alima was having breakfast with Leila on the east terrace, though she had eaten only a few bits of fruit and some tea. It was difficult to swallow when her throat was aching so...when her mother's heart was breaking for her youngest child.

"I do not understand why she will not listen," Leila was saying stormily. "Nadia thinks she knows so much, because she is older, but she does *not*. She does not know what it is like to be in a marriage without love. She does not know what she is doing!"

"But," Alima gently reminded her, "that must be Nadia's decision, must it not? Your sister must make her own choice." She paused, then placed her hand over Leila's, which was restlessly tearing an orange peel into tiny pieces. "My dearest one, why does it trouble you so much? What is really bothering you? Are you...so very unhappy in America?"

Leila's hands jerked, then went still. Then, all in a rush, she raised them to cover her face...and a sob. "Oh, Mummy, I do not know what I should do. I believe Cade is a good man—I do. And I want to be a good wife to him. But I have been so lonely—and I do not understand him at all." Her voice dropped to a whisper. "I do not even know whether or not he loves me."

"Leila," her mother began, fighting anger against the man who had made her precious one so unhappy, "you must not give up on your marriage...." A movement caught her eye, drew it across the tiled terrace to where a tall figure stood framed in the arched portal that led to the gardens.

A little breeze blew in through the portal, bringing with it the scent of roses.

Alima took in a breath of it…and smiled. "My daughter," she said softly, without taking her eyes from that tall figure, "if you truly love your husband, you must never give up on him. Tell me the truth…*do* you love this man, Cade Gallagher?"

Cade stopped breathing while he waited for her answer. It seemed an age…an eternity before Leila slowly drew her hands away from her face, revealing its radiance…and desolation.

"Oh, yes…I do. I love him. I did not believe it was possible to love someone so much. So much…sometimes…it hurts…inside." She placed her fist over her heart, and he felt himself moving toward her, though he had no sense of his feet touching the ground. "And then I am so frightened…and I do not know how I will survive it if I am never to see him—"

Leila felt a hand touch her shoulder, a hand that shook.

"Why would you think you'd never see me again?" said a voice—a voice as ragged and torn as the bits of orange peel on the table in front of her.

She stared at the bits of orange, not moving…not breathing. Her mother smiled at her, lifted her eyes and murmured an Arabic blessing, then rose from her chair and quietly left her.

I am a princess…I am a princess… Shaking like a blossom in the rain and clinging to the shards of her pride, Leila drew herself together. "What," she demanded breathlessly, lifting her head but without turning around, "are you doing here?"

Cade's heart gave an odd little quiver…of laughter, of tenderness and pride. Well, hell, she's a princess, he reminded himself. He tightened his hand on her shoulder, and felt his voice grow deeper and even more gruff. "Thought you might have forgotten where you live. Or that there's a lonesome little filly who needs you. Thought I'd better come and bring you home.''

"Why?" she asked, hurling her question at him in defiance, like an obstinate child.

Bravely, Leila lifted her chin still higher and looked into his face. *Did he hear me?* she wondered, quaking inside. *Oh, he must have heard me say I love him.* She had never felt so vulnerable, not even lying naked in his arms. *Oh, please, let him say it to me now. If he does not, I do not know what—*

"What do you mean, *why?*" Fear made Cade's voice harsh. He'd never felt more vulnerable in his life, not even when his mother died. How could he expose himself so? He hadn't the courage....

She's a woman. You expect her to tell you first? And all at once he felt himself relax. His heart grew warm...and light filled all his insides.

"Why do you think?" Cade's voice had lost its roughness. It was tender...tender as a caress. "Because...I love you, Princess." She caught her breath, but he wasn't finished. "I love you!" he said. And again: "I *love* you!"

Then she saw it. At last, the smile she had carried so long in her memory...the smile she had longed for...the smile that lit his face and eyes with purest joy.

And she knew that it was true.

Epilogue

Sheik Ahmed Kamal sat at the head table in the Great Courtyard of the Royal Palace of Tamir and beamed upon the assembly that had gathered to celebrate the *Walima* of his youngest daughter and her husband, Cade Gallagher. Sated with good food and good wine, he felt humble, and richly blessed.

Had any monarch ever had more reason to sing the praises of Allah? First his sons and now a daughter well and happily wed, and soon there would be yet another wedding, this one as satisfactory as he would have wished. His oldest daughter was to marry his closest advisor—what could be more desirable?

Relations with his neighbors the Montebellans were on solid footing at last, and with the addition of oil-rich Texans to the family, Tamir's economic future had never been brighter. And next spring, if things went as he hoped, perhaps there would be more grandchildren to keep Alima happy…and, he must be honest, himself, as well.

Yes…life is indeed good, thought the old sheik.

* * * * *

Next month, look for ROYAL SPY
by Valerie Parv
(IM#1154) when
ROMANCING THE CROWN
continues, only from Intimate Moments!
Turn the page for a sneak preview…

Chapter 1

Gage Weston could think of worse ways to spend an afternoon than watching a princess get undressed. What other job in the world would let him do so, where he wouldn't be considered some kind of Peeping Tom? Fortunately, he only peeped by invitation or in the line of duty, as he was doing now.

He was determined to find out what the princess was up to. Certainly not legitimate royal business, or she would have left her father's palace dressed for her task, instead of waiting until she was out of sight to furtively exchange clothes with her maid.

Princess Nadia Kamal was the eldest daughter of Sheik Ahmed Kamal, ruler of Tamir, who was famous for his old-fashioned morality. Nadia was equally well known for pushing the boundaries of convention, but Gage would bet her father knew nothing about this little caper.

Not that Gage planned to tell him. He wasn't working for the sheik, but for his opposite number, King Marcus of

Montebello. Marcus needed to know who in Sheik Ahmed's circle had ties with the terrorist group known as the Brothers of Darkness before they could derail the fledgling peace process between Tamir and Montebello.

Gage had another reason for spying on the princess. The traitor was also involved in the murder of his best friend, Conrad Drake. Though Gage's first duty was to the king of Montebello, this mission had a lot at stake for him personally.

With luck, he could trap the traitor and Conrad's murderer in the one assignment.

He tightened his grip on the binoculars, a sense of loss sweeping over him as he thought of Conrad, who should have been at his side at this moment.

Now Conrad was gone, gunned down while on a top secret fact-finding mission for King Marcus whose son and heir, Prince Lucas, had been taken hostage by the Brothers of Darkness after his plane crashed in the United States.

Thanks to the information sent back by Conrad, and hard work by members of Marcus's family in Montebello and the States, Lucas was now safely home in Montebello, slowly picking up the pieces of his royal life.

Gage sighed. Conrad hadn't been that lucky. Anger gripped Gage as he thought of his friend ending his life lying beside a back road in Texas, a bullet through his head.

Gage was determined to find the person responsible.

Could he be looking at her now?

He trained the high-powered glasses on the princess again. She was the most beautiful sight he'd had in the crosshairs in a long time. Her short, raven colored hair was feathered around her face, making her look a lot different from the other women in her family. With her tall, athletic figure, Gage might have taken her for an American from a distance. Close up, her exotic features and high cheekbones belonged to the heroine of an Arabian Nights tale.

It wasn't hard to picture her reclining on a bank of embroidered cushions, clad in brightly colored silks. It would be a pity to veil such a tempting mouth. No veil then, but keep the cushions and the silks. The same untamed imagination insisted on painting himself into the scene, resting on more cushions while she popped succulent dates into his mouth. His heart picked up speed at the notion.

Since when did you become so capricious, Weston? he asked himself on a swell of annoyance. Her behavior was downright suspicious. He couldn't afford to be distracted by her looks, nor by the dazzling smile he saw her exchange with her maid. The reminder didn't stop him imagining how he would feel if she smiled at him like that.

Princess Nadia was talking to the maid, both of them shielded from any eyes but Gage's by a thick screen of bushes, but she didn't stop moving, swiftly shedding her culottes and white silk shirt until she was clad only in a lacy camisole and panties that left her legs bare.

They had to be the longest legs in the sheikdom, Gage thought. Movements like hers, so graceful and unconsciously seductive, while she was clad in so little, should be outlawed in Tamir. Come to think of it, they probably were.

Pleasure shafted through him as inappropriate as it was unexpected. Instead of acting furtive, as befitted a potential traitor, her movements and ready smile made her look young and carefree, as if she had shed her cares with her clothes.

He frowned as the maid slid out of the traditional Tamir long dress called a *galabiya* she'd worn to accompany the princess from the palace. Then she took the culottes and shirt, and put them on, while the princess pulled the galabiya over her head and settled the folds around her slender body. The two women were of a similar size, so everything fit. And the movements were so slick that Gage guessed this was a regular routine.

Within minutes, the maid was the image of her mistress except for the long hair that she tucked away under a wide-brimmed straw hat. The princess draped the maid's floaty silk scarf over her cropped tresses and shoulders. Both women popped dark glasses over their eyes. Voilà. Instant transformation.

Gage panned the glasses around in a wide arc. Where the devil was the princess's bodyguard while all this was taking place? Or was the man in league with his mistress? Seconds later he had his answer. On the other side of the bushes, the bodyguard was unloading a heap of equipment from the back of the princess's car. As Gage watched, the man carried the load back to the two women. They kept their faces averted, pretending to talk, so the man didn't notice anything amiss.

The equipment turned out to be painting gear, Gage saw as the man set up an easel, stool and other artist's paraphernalia. Immediately the maid, in the princess's clothes, settled herself on the stool and began to sketch. The princess gave a low bow to her supposed mistress, then hurried away.

Nicely done, Gage thought, with a twinge of professional jealousy. As far as the bodyguard knew, he was still keeping an eye on his princess while her ''maid'' was sent off on some errand. Gage decided to find out what the errand was.

She had aroused more than his curiosity, he accepted, not convinced that his interest was as professional as he wished.

He gave himself a few seconds to see which direction her car was headed in, then retrieved his hire car from where he'd secreted it in a grove of trees after following them from the palace.

Though Gage still didn't know whether Princess Nadia Kamal had any connection with Conrad's death or with the Brothers of Darkness, he knew she was definitely up to something. Unmasking her was going to be a pleasure....

INTIMATE MOMENTS™

presents:

Romancing the Crown

With the help of their powerful allies, the royal family of Montebello is determined to find their missing heir. But the search for the beloved prince is not without danger—or passion!

Available in June 2002:
ROYAL SPY
by Valerie Parv (IM #1154)

Gage Weston's mission: to uncover a traitor in the royal family. But once he set his sights on pretty Princess Nadia, he discovered his own desire might betray *him*. Now he was determined to discover the truth about the woman who had grabbed hold of his heart....

This exciting series continues throughout the year with these fabulous titles:

Available only from Silhouette Intimate Moments at your favorite retail outlet.

Where love comes alive™

Visit Silhouette at www.eHarlequin.com

SIMRC6

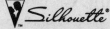

*Silhouette presents an exciting
new continuity series:*

**When a royal family rolls out the red carpet
for love, power and deception, will their
lives change forever?**

The saga begins in April 2002 with:

The Princess Is Pregnant!

by Laurie Paige (SE #1459)

**May: THE PRINCESS AND THE DUKE by Allison Leigh
(SE #1465)**

**June: ROYAL PROTOCOL by Christine Flynn
(SE #1471)**

Be sure to catch all nine Crown and Glory stories: the first three appear in
Silhouette Special Edition, the next three continue in Silhouette Romance
and the saga concludes with three books in Silhouette Desire.

───────────────────

And be sure not to miss more royal stories,
from Silhouette Intimate Moments'

Romancing
the Crown,

running January through December.

In June 2002